SENTINELS

of the

NIGHT

SENTINELS
of the
NIGHT

A Tracker Novel

Anita Dickason

Mystic Circle Books

Publisher: Mystic Circle Books
Cover Design: Mystic Circle Designs
Cover image courtesy of Pixabay

ISBN: 978-0-9968385-0-4 (Paperback)
ISBN: 978-0-9968385-1-1 (Hardback)
ISBN: 978-0-996835-2-8 (eBook)

Library of Congress Control Number: 2017915451

To my daughters,

Julie and Christy

Thank you

for your loving support and endless patience.

To the members of the

Waxahachie Write-On Group

Thank you

for your helpful comments and suggestions.

The night season is mine. I wake when others
sleep.

I can see in the darkness and discern coming
danger.

I have power to help the people to be watchful
against enemies while darkness is on the earth.

I have power...

I ride the night wind
Evil does not escape my vigilance

One

The black-clad woman melded into the shadows cast by a line of idle railroad cars and diesel engines. Even the barrel of the pistol gripped tight in one hand failed to reflect the faint illumination from the light poles scattered in the deserted railroad yard.

"Got him. Two rows from the control tower. He's headed toward the fence. Where are you?" she whispered into her mic.

A voice softly echoed through her earpiece. "I'm on the row to your right."

Focused on the man striding ahead of her, FBI Special Agent Cat Morgan eased her way over the gravel surface as she glided from car to car. Certain this was the man dubbed by the media as the Rail Killer, her grim determination pushed back the discomfort of the sweat-soaked shirt under her vest and the rancid odor of oil and diesel that hung in the humid air. Over the last four months, she'd chased the killer who rode the rails in empty boxcars. He'd find a house near the tracks and brutally murder the occupants for money and supplies, then hop another train.

After plotting locations, dates, times, and railroad schedules, she discovered a pattern in his movements. While Cat had predicted the killer's next move, it wasn't in time to prevent the murder of an elderly couple.

This time, they were ready. At dusk, teams of agents moved into position along several miles of track around Beaumont. Cat and her partner, Ben Kennedy, had drawn the short straw for the railroad yard and set up surveillance in the control tower. Near midnight, they spotted a man jump from a boxcar of a passing train. Climbing down from the tower, they lost sight of him and had split up, working their way along the rows of cars.

Cat picked up the pace and needed only a few more yards to close the gap. Then, her foot slipped on the edge of a pothole. At the loud rattle of rocks, the man glanced over his shoulder. His gaze locked onto her before he leaped between two cars.

"Damn, he spotted me. He crossed the track." Cat jumped the rail, climbed over a coupler, and paused to scrutinize the deep shadows cast by the cars on the next row. *Where the hell did you go?*

"I'm behind you," Ben said.

When rocks clattered again, along with a grunt and a couple of cuss words, she figured Ben must have stepped in the same hole.

A flash of movement at the far end of the cars sent her racing along the tracks. Ben's footsteps pounded behind her.

Danger! The word exploded in her mind. A piercing screech resounded, and two large owls, their powerful talons outstretched to strike, swooped toward her head.

Cat shouted, "Take cover!" and dropped to the ground. Then did what the yard supervisor told them not to do—she rolled over the track and under a car as a shot ricocheted off the metal rail. Lungs heaved, and her heart pounded from the surge of adrenaline as she stared at the undercarriage. What just happened? It certainly wasn't the time to figure it out.

At her warning, Ben had jumped between two cars and was on the other side. "Cat, where are you? Are you okay?"

"Yeah," she said as she crawled from under the car and readjusted her headset that had come loose.

Winded, Ben sucked in several deep breaths. Pushing fifty, the last couple of years he'd added weight, most of which had settled around his waist. "I'm getting too damn old for this. Where the hell is he?"

"On the roof of a tank car opposite this one. We can pick him off if we box him in between us. You go left."

Slipping around the end car, Cat leaned forward until she could see the tanker. Even lying flat, he would be visible on top of the cylindrical-shaped body. "He's on the ground. I've lost him." Another sprint and she reached the tanker.

"I'll head to the other end," Ben said.

He had to be hidden somewhere in this row of cars. With a ten-foot, chain-link fence on the other side, the killer had run out of room. Her back against the metal, she slid down until she could peek underneath. Moving to the next car, she stopped, ducked to check under it before going to the next.

"FBI! Stop!" Ben shouted.

A shot, then a second. In front of her, a man burst across the tracks.

"Drop the gun!"

He pivoted to face her. The hand with the gun swung upward.

Cat double-tapped two rounds to his chest. Falling backward, he struggled to lift the pistol as she rushed toward him. A quick kick sent it flying across the gravel.

Her voice sharp with fear, she cried out, "Ben?" Had he been hit?

"Here," he said as he came around the end of the boxcar.

Relieved, she holstered her weapon and shifted her attention to the man on the ground. Blood spurted and pooled around him.

With a look of loathing, he stared up at her. In a faint and raspy voice, he said, "You should be dead." The eyes changed as if a light had blinked out.

When Ben stopped beside her, she glanced at his red, sweat-drenched face. "What happened?"

Disgusted, he shoved his gun in the holster. "He took a potshot at me when I stepped out from between two cars. Damn! I can't believe I missed the bastard." Crouched beside the body, he pushed his fingers against the side of the man's neck.

"He's dead. I wonder if he's got any identification on him?" His hand patted pockets not covered in blood. "Nothing. We'll have to wait to find out who he is. Hey, check out the watch. Doesn't it look like the one stolen in that last homicide?"

Cat dropped to one knee as Ben pushed back the coat sleeve. The expensive timepiece didn't fit with the unkempt appearance. Dressed in dirty jeans, t-shirt, and frayed jacket, he was unshaven, and strands of greasy hair fell over the sightless eyes. Surprisingly, he appeared to be younger than the profile had predicted.

"I think you're right. If it is, there is an engraving on the back."

Ben tugged it over the man's hand and turned it over. He read, "To James, my beloved husband."

At the words, a pang of grief hit as Cat remembered the elderly couple who had been murdered. "I'm certain this is the Rail Killer."

Ben stood. "I'll call it in, then grab an evidence bag from the car. Do you want anything?"

"Yeah ... a bottle of water."

With a phone to his ear, Cat watched Ben walk away, then turned to stare at the body stretched across the rail. A sense of relief flowed through her. He wouldn't kill again.

Overhead, a deep hoot echoed, followed by the flap of wings. Two owls settled on top of the railroad car. Perched side-by-side, the formidable talons that could crush the spine of their quarry in an instant clung to the edge. Tufts of feathers on top of their heads that looked like horns and the glow of huge golden eyes gave the birds a fearsome appearance.

Motionless, she eyed the large raptors while she pondered the bewildering deviation from their normal behavior.

"Hmm ... that was a rather ... dramatic entrance, even for you."

They blinked, and their bills clacked as if in protest.

"Not that I am complaining, of course."

Heads swiveled in unison when their intense gaze shifted to the body on the ground. A few seconds later, they refocused on Cat. She felt the odd twitch tug in her mind, and a strange sense of approval mixed with fear flowed into her thoughts. *Jeez, this is getting even weirder.*

"I'm wondering, though, how do I explain this one to Ben? He couldn't miss seeing you, and he's already suspicious."

Another blink before their wings spread, and they lifted off. No help there, not that Cat expected any.

Her gaze returned to the body. Without their warning—well, she didn't want to think about what might have happened. As for Ben, she'd come up with some excuse to fob off his questions. She always did.

Two hours later, the corpse had been loaded into the Medical Examiner's van and was headed to the morgue. The other agents who had arrived—not that they had anything to contribute, just being nosey—had left. Cat, Ben, and their supervisor, Casey Horner, stood by Ben's car.

"How'd you know he was on top of the tanker?" Ben asked.

A bottle of water in her hand, she leaned against the side of the SUV. "Hmm ... oh, I saw him when I looked up at the birds."

"What was going on with that? It looked like they attacked you." He glanced at Casey and said, "Just before he took a shot at us, two owls dived at her head."

"We might have spooked them," she said, before taking a sip of water to stop the grin that threatened to erupt.

Ben frowned at her. "Still, it was damn strange. This isn't the first investigation where owls appeared. Casey, do you remember when Cat found the missing doctor buried in the woods? Two owls perched in a tree the entire time we dug. Never moved, just sat there with that eerie gaze fixated on us. And ... that was another one of your deals you never fully explained how you knew."

Cat couldn't stop the grin this time. "Just a damn good hunch."

"I didn't know about the owls, but I remember the incident, plus a few others," Casey said. "Do you know you've been dubbed the 'witchy woman?' Most of the agents believe you have a divining rod that finds dead victims."

Laughter bubbled. "Oh, my, god! Witchy woman, a divining rod. No, hadn't heard those." Her hand brushed the moisture from her eyes.

Casey chuckled, then said, "Other than your report, Cat, you're done here. When do you plan to leave? We're going to miss you."

She had accepted a position as a Tracker in a new unit and should already have been in Washington D. C. At her request, the transfer had been delayed until she finished the railroad killer investigation.

"I'll grab a few hours' sleep and then head out. The last two weeks, I've been staying at a hotel." She motioned toward the two men with the bottle. "I'll miss you guys as well. I hope I'll be back. Right now, the offices in D.C. are temporary. Maybe my new boss, Scott Fleming, will move the team to Texas."

Casey said, "Hmm …" A look of uncertainty crossed his face. "There are still a lot of rumblings about your new unit. Agents are wondering what the hell Fleming is up too. If it doesn't work out, you've still got a place on my team."

"Thanks, Casey. I'll keep that in mind."

He glanced at his watch. "I've got to get back to Houston. My boss wants a briefing before he meets with the media. Glad we got this one wrapped up." With a nod toward his two agents, he walked away.

"You okay with what happened tonight?" Ben asked. While they had been in some tough incidents in their years as partners, Cat had never used deadly force.

"Yeah, I am."

When a questioning look crossed his face, she sighed. "Yes, Ben. I really am. I'm not spoofing you. He didn't give me a choice. What's important is that we stopped a killer. I wonder how many lives we saved?"

He shrugged. "Wish we had nailed him sooner."

"Yeah ... so do I." A final hug and Cat headed to her car.

"Hey," he said.

When she glanced back, Ben grinned and said, "One of these days, I'll find out the truth about those damned birds. Ever since I started to work with you, I've known you've been hiding something."

Chuckling, Cat waved her hand at him and slid behind the wheel. Coping with her unique talents had always been difficult; concealing them from her fellow officers, especially Ben, had become an increasing challenge. *Witchy woman, if only they knew,* since she wasn't exactly sure herself what had happened today.

Two

Though Cat planned to sleep late, her room was still dark when moons dripping with blood filtered into her dreams and brought her awake. The lingering remnants that floated in her mind left her uneasy and unable to go back to sleep. Instead of a leisurely, mid-morning departure, the sun had barely peeked over the horizon as she stared at the Houston skyline in her rearview mirror.

Once she reached the interstate, she hit the cruise control and settled in the seat. A sense of disquiet left her edgy. What was it—the fragments of the crazy dream, the owls? Cat still hadn't solved the riddle of their intervention. They always appeared after someone died, never before. But yesterday, they'd done more than just show up. They reacted to the danger she faced, a disturbing change she didn't understand.

Then, there was the peculiar warning from Casey. How odd was that? Sure, the Bureau's grapevine had rumbled for weeks over the new squad. Agents were interviewed, but none of the highly qualified individuals received a transfer order, and no one understood why. Of course, the rumor mill went crazy. She chuckled at the recollection of agents clustered around the coffeepot in deep discussion over Fleming's intentions. What was he up too? No one came up with a conspiracy theory faster than a bunch of cops.

Taking a sip from the cup of coffee she had grabbed at the hotel, she remembered her surprise when she received the memo scheduling an interview. Since she liked Texas and didn't want to move, she'd viewed the meeting with trepidation. Once she met Fleming, his relaxed manner and straightforward description of the position reassured her. No one could dispute the fact many criminals managed to evade detection by traditional law enforcement methods. Nothing mysterious about a specialized squad set up to track them down. Intrigued by the concept, she accepted his offer to become a Tracker.

Obviously, whatever caused her uneasiness wasn't going to be solved anytime soon. Maybe, it was just a lack of sleep and took another sip of coffee.

It was dusk when she entered the outskirts of Clinton, Mississippi. Her comfort level had dropped over the last several miles, and she shifted in the seat to ease her distress as she scanned the service road for a pit stop. Startled by an unexpected tug that pulled at her thoughts, her eyes darted upward. Ahead, owls circled and then drifted off the freeway. She groaned. *Cripes, how do I tell two birds this wasn't a good time to go off on a trek somewhere?*

Taking the next exit, she spotted them perched on a hotel sign. As she parked under the canopy, she breathed a sigh of relief. At least it wasn't a hotel with the promise of bed bugs or worse. In the past, she'd been led to some rather unsavory places.

When Cat stepped into the lobby, the desk clerk asked, "May I help you?"

"Yes, I'd like a room, but first, where is the restroom?"

The young woman smiled and pointed. "They're by the elevator."

Her immediate needs taken care of, Cat checked in and lugged her suitcase to her room before moving her car. Since the front lot was full, she drove to the rear of the building to find an empty spot.

A young girl, eighteen or nineteen, paced along the sidewalk. Dressed in jeans and a T-shirt, her long, reddish-blond hair fell over her shoulders. She nervously rubbed her crossed arms as her gaze darted across the parking lot.

Cat studied her as she backed into a parking space. She knew the girl's agitation wasn't due to the cool temperatures or lack of a jacket. When she approached, the woman abruptly stepped back, then started to turn away.

"Please stop," Cat said.

The girl's voice was a whisper. "You can see me?"

"Yes, I can. What happened to you?"

"Uh … I don't know. I was at the mall, and …" her hands fluttered, "then I was here. I tried to talk to people, but they didn't answer. Can you help me?" Her body dimmed.

"Yes. What is your name?"

Her voice floated in the night air. "Janet Lewis."

Cat studied the parking lot. A low concrete wall separated it from an adjacent strip shopping center. A driveway connected the back of the property to an alley. Other than a few parked cars and a dumpster in the back corner, it was empty.

A sound, the screech of owls, grew in intensity. They landed on the edge of the dumpster. She stared at them for a couple of minutes, hoping they would move. They didn't. Damn! Resigned, she grabbed a flashlight and rubber gloves from her car.

As she approached the container, she glanced up at the birds who stared back. Motionless, they looked like twin statues. "God, I hate searching through garbage. And why … is it always a commercial bin, one that holds oodles of waste?" she grumbled.

They blinked in unison, followed by the strange clacking sound.

"Yeah, I know—don't kill the messenger. You didn't put her in here."

Her steps slow and cautious, she circled the receptacle, examining the ground for evidence. Finding nothing, she stuck the flashlight in her back pocket, pulled on the gloves, and climbed the side of the bin. Their gaze never wavered as the birds scrutinized her every move.

With her feet braced on a strip of metal riveted to the side, she leaned over the edge. Thank god for small favors. It wasn't full. She should be able to shift the bags to see what they covered. Otherwise, she could imagine the discussion with the police.

"Yes, officer, I am aware it's not normal to toss the trash out of the dumpster, but you don't understand. These owls told me there's a body inside, and I'm trying to find it. Oh, … you want to know who it is. Uh, her name is Janet Lewis. How do I know? Hmm … I talked to her. When? A few minutes ago, she was standing on the sidewalk. Yes, I work for the FBI. No, they don't think I'm nuts."

While the imaginary conversation ran in her head, she inspected the stinking mess for any clue and nearly missed it. When the light from her flashlight crossed a stack of bags in the corner, an object glinted. She made a second pass with the beam, and it appeared to be a piece of metal, too far away to reach. She dropped to the ground. Heads swiveled as the birds tracked her movement and watched her climb the other side.

From the new position, she could push the rubbish aside that obscured the object. It was a ring on a hand nestled in the garbage.

Cat's voice was a soft whisper. "There you are." She lightly stroked the back of the hand with her fingertips. A familiar rush of anger and grief flooded her mind. *This never gets any easier. I always hope I won't find another one.*

She looked at the owls and nodded her head. They blinked, then unfolded their broad wings and rose as one to disappear into the night. How do they do that? Their perfectly synchronized movements were something else she'd never figured out.

Back on the ground, she stripped off the gloves and stuffed them in her pocket. She couldn't toss them in the dumpster for the crime scene personnel to find. She already had enough to explain. *So, what am I going to do?* With so little of the body visible, it wouldn't be easy. Which story should she use, animals, or accidentally tossing her car keys along with a bag of trash? Both had worked on other occasions. Since she didn't have anything to throw in the dumpster as a backup to her story, it would have to be animals.

Her first call was to 911, the second to her new supervisor, Scott Fleming. Although she hated to disturb him at home, there wasn't a choice.

"Fleming."

"Scott, it's Cat. I have a bit of a problem. I'm at a hotel in Clinton, Mississippi, and found a body."

"Holy hell, Cat! How'd you do that?"

"Oh … uh. I'd parked my car and thought I heard odd noises as I walked past a dumpster. When I looked inside, I spotted the body."

"You checked a dumpster just because you believed you heard a sound. Did I get that right?"

"Yep."

"What caused the sounds?"

"Um … an animal, maybe a raccoon rooting through the garbage."

"A raccoon. Was there one? No, don't answer. I don't want to know. Where are you now?"

"At the hotel. I'm waiting for the police to arrive."

"Call me after you've talked to them." His voice faded, "Raccoons … my ass!" and the call disconnected.

Great! Just great. That certainly wasn't the best start to her new job, sliding the phone into her jacket pocket.

The wail of a siren died, and overheads flicked off as a Clinton PD police car pulled into the parking lot. The man who emerged scanned the area before he strode towards her. "Did you call about a body?"

She motioned with her head. "Over there, a young woman is in the dumpster."

Not bothering to hide his skepticism, he asked, "What's your name? Have you been drinking?"

Cat had told the dispatcher she was an agent. Either the officer didn't know or decided it wasn't true. She pulled her badge case from a pocket, flipped it open, and handed it to him. Glancing at his name tag, she said, "Officer Harris, I'm Special Agent Caitlin Morgan, and no … I haven't been drinking."

Since her appearance wasn't typical for a federal agent, she wasn't surprised that he studied the credentials with a couple of glances at her face. Handing the case back, he said, "You're sure you saw a body?"

Irritated by his disbelief, her tone was emphatic as she said, "I'm certain. She's in that container," and pointed to the far side of the trash bin. "Climb the side next to the wall. Her hand is visible between the garbage bags."

The officer hesitated as if he still wanted to argue, then spun, stomped to the receptacle, and crawled up the side. After gazing inside for several seconds, he jumped to the ground and keyed the radio mike hooked to the shoulder of his uniform.

Cat moved to the sidewalk and watched the controlled mayhem build. When the wail of sirens announced the arrival of several squad cars, an unhappy hotel clerk ran out. Officer Harris's attempts to calm the agitated woman and get her back inside failed. Finally, he grabbed her arm and marched her into the building.

Officers stretched yellow crime scene tape around the parking lot. Two men in plain clothes, probably detectives, disembarked from an unmarked car. The county medical examiner's van arrived, followed by Clinton PD's crime scene unit. Cases pulled from the vehicle were spread on the ground. One man hung a camera around his neck, and flashes of light soon lit up the lot. A fire truck was next, and a fireman propped a ladder against the container. That was smart, she thought. The detectives and crime scene techs took turns to peer over the side.

Frustrated, she paced. Unless asked, she couldn't get involved, and it annoyed the hell out of her.

Officer Harris returned and joined the group near the container, where an intense conversation ensued. From the hand gestures and number of times heads turned in her direction, she was a major topic of the discussion.

Finally, one of the detectives headed towards her.

"I'm Detective Roger Mueller. I understand you're an FBI agent and found the body."

"Cat Morgan," she said as they shook hands.

"How'd that happen?"

Cat described the events and watched the doubt build on his face while he took notes.

Mueller stared at the small notepad, then glanced at her. "And … you just found the body by accident?" he asked, unable to keep the disbelief out of his voice.

"Yes."

"I'd appreciate it if you stuck around." With a sharp flip, he closed the notepad and stuck it in his shirt pocket. "There could be more questions."

"I'll wait here."

Thanking her, he walked back to the cluster of personnel. A second ladder now leaned against the side, and two officers were removing the trash bags that covered the body.

Just when she thought everyone had arrived, another squad car pulled behind the crime scene van. A man in jeans and a lightweight jacket exited and surveyed the parking lot. Eyes flicked over her, then swung to stare at her again, his scrutiny intense and authoritative. Refusing to allow the arrogant look to intimidate her, she lifted her chin and stared back.

He broke the standoff of their 'eye lock' and approached Detective Mueller. After a short conversation, the newcomer glanced at her again before signaling to an officer to climb down. He scaled the ladder and gazed inside. When he lifted his head, he glared in her direction, his face rigid and grim under the parking lot lights. Back on the ground, with long strides, he crossed the lot and headed toward her.

Dark and forbidding, he moved with the fluid confidence of a predator stalking its prey. Tall, well over six-foot, with broad shoulders and narrow hips, he'd hit at least two-ten on a scale. Black hair, long for a cop, brushed his collar and framed a thin face. Eyebrows cut a black slash across deep-set eyes. His face bristled with disapproval.

Despite the heartbreak of a young girl lying dead a few feet away, Cat felt a shiver of awareness.

He stopped in front of her, hands on his hips. A cold, hard gaze raked her from head to toe. "You're Agent Morgan?" he asked, his deep voice contemptuous.

Even with the extra inches from her boots, he towered over her. Instinctively, she lifted her chin and glared. "Yes, and you are?"

"Police Chief Kevin Hunter. Why are you in Clinton?" He didn't offer to shake hands.

"Just passing through and stopped for the night."

"Explain to me just how you found the body."

"No offense here, Chief Hunter, but I did provide a statement to one of your detectives."

"Agent Morgan … I want to hear it from you. Unless there is a reason, you don't want to repeat it!" The words erupted with the precision of a rifle shot.

Let's not piss off the natives. Be agreeable.

Cat smiled and then replied, "I'll help any way I can." Once again, she went through the series of events.

Like Detective Mueller, the police chief's incredulity was unmistakable and far less tactful. He looked over his shoulder at the dumpster, then turned to her. "You want me to believe … that you crawled up the side of a dumpster and snooped through stinking trash—all because *you* heard noises?"

"That's right," Cat said. *Oh, boy. Here comes the same question Scott asked.*

"What were these sounds?"

"Hmm … I'm not sure. It may have been raccoons."

"Raccoons! You saw raccoons?"

"No. I actually didn't. I probably scared them away."

For a few seconds, the only sounds were from the officers clustered around the bin. Hunter stared at her, the cold stare replaced by a blaze of anger.

"How did you know it was a woman?"

"What!"

"You told Officer Harris and Detective Mueller it was a woman. To be more precise, a young woman. How did you know when the body was buried in the trash?"

Stunned, Cat realized she'd made a huge mistake. She shouldn't have known. *Jeez, how do I get out of this one? The hand!*

"Her hand and the ring."

"What the hell are you talking about?"

"I saw a woman's hand with a ring. It's the style a young girl would wear."

"Dammit, Agent Morgan, just stop with the bullshit. A young woman has been murdered, and if you know anything, I expect you to tell me. This is my city ... my investigation ... and no one, including a federal agent, is going to get away with concealing information. And ... I don't appreciate a preposterous tale that involves raccoons."

If you don't want to believe my raccoon story, you sure as hell won't like owls and a ghost. "Chief Hunter, I can't tell you anything else. I checked into the hotel for one night and didn't expect to find a body." *Hmm ... a small stretch of the truth, but why muddy up the waters anymore at this point?*

"Before you leave, I want a statement. You are leaving town?"

"Yes, unless there's a reason I need to stay."

"Agent Morgan—absolutely none!"

"I'll stop at your office on my way out of town." She turned and walked into the hotel. Her neck muscles twitched when she envisioned the hole his stare bored into her back.

Kevin watched her walk away, and a jolt of lust hit a second time. His first view from across the parking lot had stopped him in his tracks. Tight jeans and leather coat did little to conceal a slim, curvaceous form. Short, curly hair framed an incredible heart-shaped face. The haughty lift of her chin added to the allure. He had a firm rule not to become involved with women he met on the job. Yet, here he was, gaping like a fifteen-year-old dumbass kid. He couldn't take his eyes off her as she strolled toward the hotel entrance. Just his luck she was a fed, then add in a corpse, and that ludicrous story about raccoons—hell, all good reasons to avoid Agent Cat Morgan.

Three

Disquieting fragments, fleeting images held a sense of terror that hovered just beyond her conscious mind as Cat tossed the covers aside. This was two nights in a row. Was this an aftermath of the shooting in Beaumont? Perched on the edge of the bed, she tried to recall the images, but they were gone. Somehow, it didn't feel right that whatever caused the dreams were connected to Beaumont.

Whatever it is, there is nothing I can do but wait. In the meantime, the known instead of the unknown demanded her attention. At the top of the list was the death of a young woman.

Wrapped in a towel, she contemplated the folded jeans and T-shirt on the dresser. *No. I can't stroll into his office, looking like a teenager.* Convinced the switch was necessary to project a professional demeanor, and not because thoughts of the sexy police chief sparked a tingle of anticipation, she rummaged through the suitcase for another outfit. Spinning in front of the mirror, she viewed the black pants paired with a dark red top and her black leather jacket. *Oh yeah, this works.*

Before leaving, she checked in with her new boss.

"I hope this call is not to tell me you found another body."

"No, update only. The police chief requested a written statement before I left town. While I'm there, I hope to find out more about the homicide."

"Don't get involved unless they ask and call me when you leave."

She chuckled. "Don't worry. I won't. Considering the police chief's attitude, I'm certain the man won't request my help. Still, I want to know more about the case."

As Cat walked out of the hotel, she scanned the parking lot. Though a few cars remained, there was no one around, living or dead. Her suitcase loaded into the trunk, Cat turned and gazed at the ugly, dirty hunk of metal designed to hold garbage. A light breeze scattered the remaining pieces of the yellow crime scene tape and was the only reminder of the grim discovery. The memory of the young woman's death sent a surge of anger rippling through her, along with an intense compulsion to take down whoever killed her.

Finding a parking space took longer than the drive to the police department. With the backpack that substituted for a purse slung over her shoulder, Cat headed to the front door. At the reception desk, she was directed to Hunter's office.

She pushed open the door engraved with Clinton Chief of Police and entered a waiting room with a couple of tables and several chairs. A desk was positioned next to a door to an inner office.

An older woman, fiftyish, her salt and pepper hair pulled back in an old-style ponytail, was busy on the computer. At the sound of the closing door, she looked at Cat with a sharp glance that scanned her from head to toe.

Keeper of the gate, I bet. "I'm Special Agent Cat Morgan. The receptionist at the front desk said Chief Hunter was expecting me."

The woman's face lit up with a broad smile. In a robust, southern accent, she said, "I'm Jessie Barnes, his administrative assistant. He told me to send you in as soon as you got here. So, you just go on in there."

She probably bullies him too. The thought put a smile on her face.

She tapped on the door and then opened it. Hunter held the phone to his ear with one hand and a pen in the other. He pointed the pen at a chair in front of his desk. Cat sat and in seconds, was avidly listening to Hunter's side of the conversation. He was discussing the Lewis murder, and she assumed the medical examiner was on the other end of the call.

Watching Hunter scribble notes, she realized he'd pulled an all-nighter. The shirt he'd worn the night before was wrinkled, and he needed a shave though the dark stubble added to his rugged good looks. His face was drawn and tired until he glanced at her. The alert gaze antagonized and challenged at the same time.

Ignoring the warm quiver that rushed through her, and determined to smooth over troubled waters, Cat relaxed her body, crossed her legs, and smiled back. To convey her lack of concern at his hostility, she shifted her gaze to study the inside of his office.

The absence of clutter surprised her. A computer and keyboard sat on the short section of an L-shaped desk. A leather pad covered the middle, along with several neatly stacked folders and phone. A coffee cup with a tiger emblazoned on the side was centered in a coaster. *Just a little too tidy, I bet he's a bit anal.*

File cabinets lined one wall of the room. On the other side, bookshelves held legal and reference manuals. Scattered among the books were several framed pictures and sports memorabilia, including an autographed football. Diplomas and commendations hung on the wall on each side of the large window behind his desk. One caught her attention. It was from the FBI Academy in Quantico.

While Kevin jotted notes and talked to Doc Morris, he watched Cat scope out his office. A faint, tantalizing scent of rain on a spring day drifted across the room. Damn! The woman looked even more alluring in the daylight. The impact of her heart-shaped face, high cheekbones, catlike green eyes, the small, elegant nose covered with a dusting of freckles, all framed by short curly red hair, had not been clearly visible in the semi-darkness of the parking lot. The enticing glimpse of red under a leather jacket was compelling, even sensual, and ratcheted the pounding of his heart. Heat spiraled downward.

Ignoring the surge of sexual attraction became easier when he reminded himself that she was a federal agent. Kevin never hid his dislike of the feds. A couple of years ago, the FBI and DEA had rolled into town and taken over a drug investigation. The memory of their contempt for his officers still festered.

When Hunter said goodbye, Cat shifted in the chair to face him. "Was that a report from the M.E. on last night's victim?"

"Yeah. Janet Lewis. She was only eighteen."

"A local girl?"

"No, she lived in Vicksburg. Two days ago, she disappeared from a mall."

"Did the M.E. provide a cause of death?"

"She bled out from cuts on her arms and wrists." He reached for his phone. "Jessie, I need you to record a statement." Kevin turned to Cat. "This won't take long."

Not exactly forthcoming, are you? Hmm ... I wonder if the word cooperation is even in your vocabulary.

The door opened. "Agent Morgan, this is Jessie Barnes, my administrative assistant."

"We met when I arrived."

Over the next few minutes, Cat reiterated the details of the events leading to the discovery of Janet Lewis. In the quiet office, the story sounded worse. Even Jessie raised her eyebrows while she listened. Once Cat finished, Jessie picked up the tape recorder and left to transcribe her statement.

Kevin stood. "I have to leave. It will only take a few minutes to type your report. There is a break room across the hall. Help yourself to the coffee."

"Before you rush me out of your office, here's my card with my supervisor's name and number on the back. If you decide you want any assistance, give him a call," she said and dropped it on his desk.

Ignoring the card, Hunter moved to the door and waited for her to leave. Closing the door behind him, he nodded to Jessie and left.

Well, so much for interagency collaboration. Nothing like being kicked out of a police chief's office.

It didn't take Jessie long to finish and hand the document to Cat to sign. When she walked out the front door, Kevin stood in the parking lot talking to an officer. He glanced her way, then turned his back to her.

Tossing her backpack on the front seat, she slid behind the wheel. With the phone cradled between her shoulder and ear, she waited for her boss to answer and studied the provocative view of Hunter's backside. Tight jeans over an impressive butt was a hard sight to ignore. Scott's voice interrupted her musings, and she reluctantly pulled her thoughts back to the reason for the call—the results of her meeting.

"Any problems with the local police?" he asked.

She laughed before saying, "Nope."

Pulling out of the parking lot, she took one last glance at the man who believed he'd seen the last of her.

Four

Cat's first glimpse of the gray walls and muddy-brown carpet in the unit's office was less than favorable. At least, the desks were modern, not the archaic, metal ones still in use in many government offices. The only cheerful note was the mid-morning sunlight that streamed through the window.

Scott and another man stood in front of a desk. She had liked Scott from the first moment she met him. He was on the high side of thirty, around six-foot with a solid build. His face was rough-hewn, his eyes dark, with a gleam of keen intelligence. A small scar split an eyebrow, and another curved over his cheekbone.

When he spotted her, he broke off the conversation. "Cat, I didn't expect to see you this soon," he said as he strode toward her.

She shook his hand. "I spent the night with my parents in Bristol, Tennessee, but decided to cut short my vacation. I wanted to follow up on the homicide in Clinton."

"I'm glad you're here and appreciate your foresight. We need to discuss Clinton. Cat Morgan, meet Ryan Barr."

She greeted the agent while Scott turned to introduce the two individuals seated at their desks.

"This is Nicole Allison and Adrian Dillard. Since Cat is here, I want a meeting with everyone in the conference room."

Dropping her backpack and briefcase on an empty desk, she pondered Scott's comment about Clinton. A whisper of anxiety floated in her mind. Had something else happened? The unanswered question had to wait. She grabbed a notepad and pen from a nearby stack of office supplies and followed the rest of the team members.

While everyone took their seats around a large oval table, Scott organized a stack of file folders. In Cat's interview, he came across a no-nonsense style team leader. Early in her career, she worked for an individual who played mind games with his subordinates. It hadn't been a pleasant experience and prompted a search of Scott's background before she accepted the position. She wondered if the other agents were aware of his impressive credentials. He'd been responsible for the investigation of several cases dealing with multiple homicides. One received considerable publicity when he solved the murders of twenty-six women, killed over two years in seven states.

Seated, Scott sipped his coffee, his gaze shifting to each agent. If he had to choose one word to describe this team, it would be extraordinary. One of his unique abilities was analyzing patterns in human behavior and what they meant. A handy advantage when applied to a criminal's actions that had culminated in a high number of arrests. While his superiors may not have understood his methods, they recognized his results and was the reason he'd been tagged to head the new unit.

He'd applied the same process to the selection of the team members. He'd spent months evaluating agent profiles, their case closure rate, and conducting interviews.

Once everyone settled, Scott said, "Let's begin with a brief introduction. I'll start with myself. Before joining the Bureau, I was a homicide detective with the Boston Police Department. I've worked in the Chicago and Atlanta field offices. Over the last few months, I've been involved in developing a new software program, TRACE, that will allow us to identify and correlate unsolved homicides."

Since Cat was the closest to him, he started with her. "Cat, tell us your background and experience."

While she talked, his mind drifted to the information in her personnel file next to his elbow. She proved to be a formidable investigator and his first choice. Cat had a built-in homing device when it came to locating bodies. She also an uncanny knack for finding key details that led to an arrest. Case in point was the takedown of the railroad killer. Predicting his movements had been brilliant. Fellow agents referred to her as 'the witchy woman.'

Nicole, she preferred Nicki, was next. She excelled in logistics and research. Her brain seemed to be hard-wired to a computer. In several investigations, it was her research that led to the apprehension of the criminals. Her skills would be invaluable to the TRACE program.

The profiler was Ryan. After the grapevine had started to buzz over the new unit, Scott received a call from a friend in the San Francisco office. He recommended Ryan for the profiler position even though he didn't have an official profiler designation. Scott had evaluated the results of Barr's investigations and agreed. If Nicki's brain was hard-wired to a computer, Ryan's was on a direct link to a criminal's mind.

Adrian had a singular talent for reading a crime scene and connecting the dots along with an uncanny sense when someone was lying. It had proved to be a useful ability during many suspect interviews.

Adrian finished his short introduction, and all eyes turned toward Scott.

"There are still two positions open. I hope one will be filled by the end of the week. Since the Tracker Unit is a new concept, we have no established guidelines or procedures. We'll set them up as we go. Our primary focus will be criminals who operate under law enforcement's radar. Many unsolved homicides are viewed by local agencies as a random, isolated murder. With no link between the victim and killer, the investigation ends up in the cold case file."

He glanced at Cat. "Too often, the victim simply vanishes. TRACE will allow local agencies to input the details of unsolved cases and identify any similarities. Now that Nicki is here to help, I expect it will be online within the next few months."

He smiled at the surprise on her face. This was a development he hadn't discussed with her. He picked up his pen and lightly tapped the table while he contemplated his next topic.

The agents believed the only reason they received an offer to join the Tracker Unit was their previous accomplishments. *What I didn't tell them is that I had another list of qualifications. When I examined the case files, I looked for anomalies, the irregularities in the investigation that could only be explained by an underlying, hidden ability. Everyone at this table has a secret, including me. It will be interesting to see their reaction to my next comments.*

"This squad is unique. You were selected because of the inexplicable skills you demonstrated in the field. But … if you're going to function as a team, you must be willing to be honest with each other about your special gifts. I expect it'll be disconcerting and even uncomfortable."

Startled, eyes darted around the table, and Scott knew he had struck a nerve. It would take time to earn their trust. He was a patient man.

"I received a request this morning that requires Nicki and Ryan's expertise and leads to our first guideline. The squad will review each new case. Let's take a break. Cat, I have the paperwork on my desk for your vehicle along with the keys. I had it delivered last week, and it's in the parking garage."

Holy hell! What was that all about, Cat wondered as she followed him into his office. What did he mean—a unique squad, inexplicable skills, and this business of being open with each other? The man couldn't possibly know her secrets, no one did. She'd eyed the other agents, and they were all doing the same. Casey's vague warning popped into her mind. Was there something to the rumors after all? Wow—didn't see this one coming. Uneasy, she wondered if she'd made a mistake joining this unit.

When everyone had reassembled in the conference room, Scott said, "Before I discuss the specifics of the case, I'd like Cat to review the details of the homicide in Clinton."

Taken aback, it took a few seconds to gather her thoughts. When Scott said they'd talk, she assumed it would be the two of them.

Cat quickly recapped the events that occurred. When she skipped the bit about the raccoons, she caught the surprised expression on Scott's face. She expected he'd question the omission; surprisingly, it came from Ryan.

"Any idea what caused the noise?"

Scott cleared his throat. Cat glanced at him. His lips curved with an amused smirk.

"Umm … no, I don't. Once I spotted the body, whatever the source of the sounds became a moot point," she said, hoping to end any further discussion of the raccoons.

Scott cleared his throat again before asking, "What's your opinion of Chief Hunter?"

Relieved to be back on safe ground, Cat turned her thoughts to an assessment of the police chief. "He doesn't like federal agents. Other than that, he is intense and committed. He could have turned the Lewis homicide over to one of his detectives. It was obvious when I met him the next morning he hadn't been to bed. For a police chief, that's dedication."

"What's your take on the homicide? Is this an isolated case?" Scott asked.

Cat hesitated. What should she say? Since the discovery of the body, she'd wrestled with her instincts over the possibility. She believed there were more victims. Still, no details, no facts, nothing to support her suspicions. *I sure can't say I had a premonition.* She glanced around the table. Everyone waited for her answer.

"I can't say for certain, but I believe there is a high probability whoever killed Janet Lewis has killed before, and there are other victims. He will strike again. This is just an opinion since I don't have any facts to support it." *Damn! Talk about putting yourself out on a limb and handing someone the saw.*

Instead of disbelief, Scott had a thoughtful air when he flipped open a file in front of him and reviewed the typed pages. He closed the folder, slid it in front of Cat, and pushed a similar one to each of the other agents.

"The folder contains a written request from Chief Hunter for research and forensic support, along with copies of his investigation notes and the medical examiner's autopsy report. In his opinion, Janet Lewis is not the only victim. He's also concerned there could be more homicides. Cat, did you discuss any of your suppositions with Hunter?"

"No. I could barely get him to tell me about the cause of death. He was extremely uncooperative."

"Interesting. Both of you came to the same conclusion, and you had less information than Hunter did." He paused while the agents scanned the documents.

Cat pulled the autopsy pictures from the file. The body was nude. Blood from cuts on the forehead matted in her long red-gold hair and dried streaks covered her face. Deep incisions were in both arms and wrists. For a moment, the image of the young woman at the hotel superimposed the face in the photo. Anger stirred deep inside her at the sight of the mutilation, and a young life so brutally cut short.

A pricking sensation touched her neck. She glanced up. Scott's gaze was fixed on her face. A strange awareness filtered into her mind. *He knows the dead girl spoke to me! No, that can't be, it's impossible.* When he slightly tipped his head as if to acknowledge her thoughts, the uneasiness she'd felt earlier intensified.

Scott turned to Nicki. "See if you can identify a pattern in the cuts on the forehead. In the meantime, broadcast an alert to law enforcement agencies and medical examiners for homicides that match the Lewis case. Ryan, work up a preliminary profile. I know there's not much there to work with, just give us what you can. Cat and Adrian, run a search for similar homicides through agency databases. I'll call Hunter and tell him the steps we've taken. Any questions?"

No one answered. Scott picked up the remaining folders and stood, hesitated, then said, "For now, we'll provide assistance from here. However, I want to be prepared to escalate our response. Cat, you'll take the lead on the investigation. Be ready to head back to Clinton. Nicki, Ryan, you'll go with her, so get packed."

Stunned, Cat left the conference room. The lead investigator and no one seemed to think her comments were peculiar. It was a first. Then the thought of Hunter's reaction to the FBI camped on his doorstep, instead of several hundred miles away struck her. She chuckled. *Oh, he will hate it.*

Five

Stained fingers caressed the amulet as JD searched the murky landscape. Nothing, other than the reflection of a narrow face framed by long, dark hair. He pushed back the strands that clung to his damp forehead. Heavy throbs of pain in his head had slowly intensified, then shifted to sharp stabs, a signal the drugs had worn off.

Turning from the window, he stumbled to the table and pawed through the clutter of used needles, marijuana butts, and empty crack bags on the broken and dirty surface until he found the foil-wrapped object, a joint laced with angel dust.

Fingers trembled as he lit the discolored, homemade cigarette and sucked the smoke deep into his lungs. Leaning against the counter, JD closed his eyes, savoring the ecstasy of the rush. He took another hit, this one held for several seconds to get the full effect of the drugs that ignited all his senses.

The pungent smoke mixed with a sickening, metallic odor. Turning his head, he gazed down at the source of the stench, smiled, and took another drag.

A glance at the window and the joint, forgotten, fell to the floor. The wait was over. It was time to finish it.

Picking up a large knife, JD dropped to his knees. Outstretched arms held it over his head as he chanted, "I call to you, the Old One. You are my Master. I worship at your altar. Bring forth your power and make it mine. Accept this sacrifice from your servant and seal your power within me. Master, heed my call."

Squatting in the tall grass, Kevin assessed the large object wrapped in trash bags taped together. A section of the thick plastic was torn, and an arm with deep incisions protruded. While he couldn't see the face, he'd bet next year's pay the forehead would be crisscrossed with cuts.

A pair of large boots stopped beside him. Lifting his head, he squinted against the glare of the bright sunlight. The man who towered over him was the Medical Examiner, Emmitt Morris.

"We've got another one, Doc. I figure it's going to be the same as the Lewis homicide," Kevin said as he stood and backed away to give the man room to get to the body.

"From the cuts on that arm, I'd say you're right," Morris said.

Excited chatter caused him to look over his shoulder. Three boys, fourteen to fifteen, sat astride their dirt bikes. The field where Kevin stood was a favorite place for dirt bike riders. The boys had spotted the odd-looking bag dumped behind a trash pile near the road. Of course, they compromised his crime scene when one of them puked out his guts. Kevin was certain the kid would be the brunt of many jokes from his buddies.

The crackling of plastic brought his attention back to Morris, who had slit the bag and peeled back the sides to expose the nude body of a woman covered with dried blood. Multiple incisions had been carved into the forehead.

His gloved hand pushed and prodded the cold flesh. After a few minutes, he said, "Right now, I'd say she's been dead ten to sixteen hours. Once I get her on the table, I'll be able to narrow it down. She hasn't been here long enough for the animals to get to her."

Kevin glanced at his watch. That would put it between midnight and six.

Morris stripped off the gloves and turned toward Kevin. "If you're ready to release the body, I'll get it loaded."

Kevin motioned to an officer who waited with a camera. "All I have left are the pictures." Kevin hesitated, then said, "Doc, I'd like for you to measure those cuts, same as you did with the Lewis girl."

"I figured you'd ask. I've been the medical examiner for close to thirty years and never seen anything like this. In my opinion, you've got someone who has decided to use our city for his hunting ground."

"I can't disagree. I suspected as much after I got your report on the other victim."

The doctor nodded and walked to his van, where his attendants waited. As he watched them bring the stretcher up, Kevin's thoughts turned to his actions after Cat Morgan left town.

When he received the Lewis autopsy report, he'd sat at his desk for several hours, studying every detail. He'd tried to convince himself it was a random crime; someone had gone off the deep end. It didn't work. His instincts said he had a serial killer in town.

He had to accept his department didn't have the resources to deal with a killer who had likely left a string of bodies behind him. Those cases might have evidence to help him find the man before he killed again. He couldn't locate them, but the FBI could.

The day Cat Morgan left his office, he'd tossed her business card in the trash. Then for some inexplicable reason, he retrieved it and dropped it in a drawer. Setting the autopsy report aside, he'd shuffled through the papers in the drawer until he found it. On the back was the number for Scott Fleming. Despite his aversion, all that mattered was the apprehension of a killer. Besides, a request for computer and forensic assistance shouldn't bring the feds to his doorstep. His decision made, he'd reached for the phone.

Now, as he watched two attendants pick up another body, the premonition that had persisted since the discovery of the Lewis girl had become a reality. The killer had struck again. He'd notify Fleming to expect reports on a new victim and wondered how long it would take before Agent Morgan was front and center in his office. He ignored the twinge of anticipation.

❧

Hunched over the keyboard, Cat's eyes locked onto the computer screen as she clicked through images on a website, the last one on her list. Nothing. Frustrated, she leaned back in her chair and stretched to work out the kinks in her body. As her fingers massaged the tense muscles in her neck, she glanced around the room at the other agents, each absorbed in their own research. Their personalities and work habits would take time to learn.

Scott had informed them not to be concerned about the dress code. As she studied each agent, she wondered how soon everyone would ditch the standard FBI attire.

Nicki's petite body was muscular and compact. Cat suspected she hit the gym on a regular basis. The heavy coil of coal-black hair against her neck would probably reach her waist. Her high cheekbones and dark, deep-set eyes bespoke her native American heritage. When they knew each other better, Cat hoped to compare notes over their common ancestry.

Her gaze shifted to Adrian. Exchange the dark suit that molded his lean, whipcord body with ragged jeans and t-shirt, let the hair grow, and he'd be a typical street thug looking for trouble. Dark eyes seemed to reflect the auburn gleam of his hair, a wary and cautious glint that hinted of enigmatic secrets. Hmm … odd, Nicki's eyes had the same inscrutability.

Ryan was just the opposite. With his head bent as he jotted down notes, strands of blond hair with a slight curl fell over his forehead. His good looks could easily grace the cover of a magazine. When Cat was first introduced to him, she had felt a strange sense of forewarning. As her gaze rested on him, his head shot up as if aware of her scrutiny. The hard look in the brilliant blue eyes vanished as a smile crossed his face. Maybe she imagined it. Uneasy, she shifted in her chair.

33

Adrian glanced at her and asked, "Anything?"

"Nope. You?"

"Nothing," he said.

"Since Adrian and I have hit a dry well, what about you, Nicki?" Cat asked.

Nicki was a computer addict and had a wide variety of devices that included two large monitors on her desk. When Cat asked why two, Nicki went into a long explanation of the reason the two were linked, and why she needed to convince Scott to get her a third. Since she didn't understand half of Nicki's technical jargon, Cat had just grinned.

While Nicki studied one of the screens, she said, "I'm still working on the cuts on the forehead. Based on the medical examiner's report, there are two sets. Several occurred before death; the rest are post-mortem. Evidently, the killer tried to destroy the original design. Hunter's report didn't include all the autopsy photos. I called the M.E. and asked for the rest. One might provide a close-up that'll let me isolate the original cuts and identify a pattern. I have a list of the salient points from the autopsy report. Give me a minute to pull it up."

She typed for a few seconds and then continued, "No DNA from the killer and no sexual assault. There were bits of candle wax on the skin. The toxicology report identified a high level of ketamine."

"Ketamine is an unusual choice of drugs," Cat interjected.

"I thought so. I'll come back to it once I finish this list. Based on the amount of the drug, the M.E. believes she was unconscious until she died. Personally, I hope to hell it's true. Death was due to a loss of blood from the cuts on her arms and wrists. She bled out. The nude body was wrapped in a sheet, then several trash bags and secured with duct tape."

She glanced at Cat. "When the body was tossed in the dumpster, the bag split, which is why you saw her hand. Cat, if you hadn't found her, there is a possibility she might never have been discovered. Once that dumpster was full, it's doubtful the trash personnel would have even noticed her bagged body."

Nicki paused and switched to the other computer. "Like Cat said, ketamine is an unusual choice. The primary use is an anesthetic for animals and comes in powdered or liquid form. As a street drug, it can be injected, snorted, or added to marijuana or cigarettes. The street version is highly dangerous because it is usually mixed with other drugs. Here's what is significant in the toxicology report on Lewis. No other drugs were found, which indicates the killer used pure ketamine. That's all I have. Okay, Ryan, you're up."

He stood, flipped open a folder, and removed several documents. "This is a summary of what I learned from the autopsy report. So far, I don't have a lot of information, though several elements do point to a ritualistic incident," he said, and dropped a stapled set on each of the agent's desks.

"Candles are an essential part of many religious ceremonies. From the location of the wax, they circled the body. Lividity established the body lay face-up with her hands crossed on top of the stomach. This position also points to a sacrificial offering. The cuts tell me it was a blood-driven event, and that connects to the theory of a ritual. It's likely the carving on the forehead is a symbol and is tied to the reason for the ceremony. I found the attempt to eradicate it strangely curious."

He stopped and sorted through the documents on the desk. Picking one up, he quickly scanned it. "The abduction indicates a disorganized style killer. He finds his victims by chance rather than premeditated stalking. Even though a mall is a high-risk location, as a hunting ground it provides an ample supply of possible victims. If we follow the pattern for this type, he's a white male between twenty-five and forty years of age. Lower than average IQ, low self-esteem, and it will show in his style of dress and probably even in his hygiene. He'll be anti-social and typically lives with a single parent or alone. He could have a history of drug abuse, or been exposed to drugs through the medical system, possibly a mental hospital."

He hesitated, laid the paper on the desk as a look of uncertainty crossed his face. He glanced at each of the agents before he continued. "I believe there is enough evidence to hypothesize the killer's state of mind."

Cat felt a sudden empathy for Ryan as she remembered her dilemma when Scott asked her opinion on whether Lewis was an isolated case.

Ryan said, "I agree with the medical examiner's opinion. The victim was kept sedated as there are no marks from the use of restraints. Her fear was not a button that turned him on. The body was nude, but since he didn't sexually assault her, it indicates her only purpose was her role in the ritual."

Hands braced on each side, he leaned against the desk. "He's not interested in her as a woman. Dumping the body in a trash bin conveys his opinion of the victim. Once the girl had fulfilled her role in whatever sick ritual the killer performed, Janet Lewis became waste. It also tracks with the secondary mutilation to the forehead. I don't believe the purpose was to hide it, rather it suggests the vessel is no longer worthy of wearing it. In this case, the vessel is the victim. I'll enhance this once we progress deeper into the investigation," and dropped into his chair.

After a moment of silence, Cat said, "Geez, Ryan. Damn impressive. What can we expect when you do have a lot of information?" The chuckle from the group caused his cheeks to turn red. *My god, the man is blushing.*

Ready to quit for the day, Cat gathered up her files. Scott strode into the room and said, "Everyone, sit back down. There's another victim."

Even though Cat had expected another woman would be killed, a cold knot still formed in her gut.

"I just received a call from Chief Hunter. A woman's body was dumped on the outskirts of Clinton. From what he shared with me on the phone, she was killed by the same person that murdered Lewis.

Cat, how soon can you leave?"

"I'm already packed. I can be on my way within the hour. How'd Hunter respond to my return?"

"He doesn't know. I'll let you handle the issue once you're there."

His comment surprised her. She expected he would have obtained Hunter's agreement. "Hmm ... that could be difficult. He's asked for help with forensics, which is a lot different than my walking into his office. Hunter wasn't receptive to my presence the first time and came close to physically shoving me out the door."

"I have a feeling you'll be able to convince him to include you in the investigation. If you can't, I'll call the Attorney General. I hate to go over his head, but I want you in Clinton. Nicki, Ryan, hold off on leaving until we receive the new reports from Hunter. I want them analyzed before you leave town. Cat, when do expect to arrive in Clinton?"

"I'll be there tomorrow," she answered.

"I want a conference call with you and Hunter as soon as possible."

Cat gathered up her files and laptop. Within minutes, she was on her way to her apartment to pick up her suitcases.

Once she cleared the city limits, she engaged the cruise control. The drive would allow time to figure out a way to reverse Hunter's animosity.

Intrigued by the contrast of an FBI diploma on his office wall and his negative attitude toward federal agents, she'd run a background check, hoping to find the reason for Hunter's antagonism. Instead, his personnel file dealt with the basics of his career.

Kevin was thirty-three and had graduated from LSU with a degree in criminal justice and computer science. He'd come up through the ranks in the Clinton Police Department. Promoted to police chief two years ago, he was the youngest to hold the position. He'd received several awards and commendations. Cat had read each one. Kevin's impressive record confirmed her opinion—tough, honest, and committed.

That's it, there's my answer! Although he might not like the FBI in his investigation, the man would make a deal with the devil if it would save lives. She laughed at the idea. *Since he probably does classify the feds as devils, I just have to convince him to make the deal.*

Satisfied, she relaxed in her seat. She'd ignore the one piece of information that caused a ripple of anticipation. Hunter had never been married. However, it did occur to her his attitude might not be her main problem. It could be her reaction to a very, sexy police chief.

Six

After spending the night at her parent's house in Tennessee, it was mid-morning when she reached Clinton. Since she'd made a reservation at a downtown hotel before leaving D.C., there was no reason to delay the confrontation and headed to the police station.

The receptionist recognized her and motioned toward the hallway when Cat mentioned Chief Hunter. Jessie wasn't at her desk, and Hunter's door was open. Angry mutters emanated from his office.

She stopped in the doorway. Engrossed in typing, Kevin was unaware of her presence. Cat leaned against the doorjamb to enjoy his obvious annoyance while he poked at the keyboard. As he paused to study the screen, his fingers combed the hair back from his forehead.

No wonder the man looked like he'd just crawled out of bed. A momentary vision of his nude body rising from rumpled sheets sent a frisson of tingles down her back. Vexed by the unwanted image, she straightened and shook her head.

Her movement alerted him. His head jerked up and swiveled toward her. The compelling gaze latched onto her.

"What the hell! What are you doing here?"

She grinned, then replied, "Hello, and it's nice to see you again, Chief Hunter. My boss sent me."

He glared at her for a few seconds before saying, "I didn't ask for your help. Call Fleming and tell him you're headed back to Washington."

"Now … I'm sure you know I can't," she said. A frown crossed his face when she sat in the chair in front of his desk.

"You do realize you can't participate in my investigation without my permission?" he said and settled back with a smirk on his face.

"Humph," she snorted. The man's an idiot if he thinks that'll convince her to leave. She stood, put her hands on his desk, and leaned forward.

Her voice almost a growl, she said, "Chief Hunter, I get it. You don't like the FBI, or maybe it's me. Whatever … it doesn't matter. This is your investigation, but you have two homicides with the same pattern. These are not random or isolated crimes. A killer is targeting women in your town. Since we believe there are more victims, my team is already searching for other homicides. This is not federal agents taking over an investigation. This is about officers working together to find whoever brutally murdered two women and stop him from killing again."

She straightened as she glared at him. "I will be involved in this investigation, with or without your permission, though it would certainly be easier to have your cooperation — Chief Hunter."

As Kevin listened, he thought, she's a feisty one when she gets riled. Of course, what she didn't know was he already agreed with her. When he saw Cat in the doorway, he couldn't resist yanking her chain to see what type of reaction he could provoke.

Her stance rigid and fisted hands on her hips, she scowled at him while she waited for him to say something.

He couldn't stop the grin that spread across his face. With an exaggerated drawl, "Well, ma'am, I guess this means we'll be working together on this investigation."

Stunned, Cat dropped into the chair, gazed at him in amazement, then with suspicion. "Damn! That was all *just* an act, wasn't it?"

"Hmm … no. I wouldn't say that since I still don't trust any federal agent. But I do have two dead girls and would take help from the devil himself if it meant I got the bastard who killed them."

Cat couldn't stop it. Laughter rolled out so hard her stomach hurt, and tears threatened to trickle down her face.

"Is there a joke I missed?"

"No, not really, some private thoughts. I don't think anyone has ever compared me to the devil." She took a deep breath and wiped the moisture from her eyes.

He eyed her in disbelief before he said, "Welcome to Clinton, Agent Morgan, and call me Kevin."

"It's Cat, and do you have a copy of the file for the latest victim?"

"I knew you'd be pushy the moment I met you." He picked up a folder from a stack on the corner of the desk and handed it to her. "The girl's name is Susan Benson. There's a copy of everything I have along with the M.E.'s pictures. I'm still waiting for the autopsy report."

"What were you planning on doing with this file if I hadn't appeared in your doorway?"

"Oh, I figured you'd show up. It was just a matter of how long it would take."

She grinned. "Do you have an office I can use along with two other agents who will arrive later this week? One is Ryan Barr, our profiler. The other is Nicki Allison, who handles computer research. I can rent a room at the hotel. However, I'd much rather be located here."

Kevin led her to a conference room at the end of the hallway. "Will this work?"

"Absolutely," she said as she viewed the room with a large square table in the center.

"Do you need a computer?"

"No, my laptop's in my car. I'll get it. I do need access to a printer, so I can scan the reports and send them to Scott."

"Jessie already has them on her computer. I'll have her send the file to your boss."

After retrieving her laptop and briefcase, Cat booted the laptop before pulling out the Lewis file. She arranged the reports on the table, then did the same with the Benson documents.

Kevin walked in. "The file's been sent. I'll have a printer in here tomorrow. I'm sure we will need it."

"Thanks. I'll call Scott once I have this organized. We need to compile a list of the main points of each homicide. It'll make it easy to spot similarities. If I miss a detail, tell me." She slid a notepad from her briefcase.

Cat started with the Lewis reports. "She was last seen at a shopping mall in Vicksburg. Her friends left her at a table in the food court while they went into a store. When they came out, she was gone. They searched the mall and called her cell phone several times. When they couldn't locate her, they called her mother, who called the police. Until I discovered her body in the hotel dumpster, no sign of her had been found."

She shuffled the reports and then asked, "Okay, where's the report on the interview of the friends?"

"The notes should be ..." Kevin answered as he sorted through the documents in front of him. "Here it is. There were two girls. Basically, the same information, though the detective did add a note that he showed a picture of Lewis to the employees working in the food court and surrounding stores. No one remembered seeing her."

Cat opened the folder labeled Susan Benson. "Local girl who was a student at Mississippi College. She disappeared from the Burger Grill. Hmm ... another place to eat."

Kevin interrupted. "The Burger Grill is on the west side of town near the freeway."

Cat made a note of the location. "How'd you connect her to the restaurant?"

"That's in Detective Mueller's report. An employee called and wanted a car towed from their parking lot. The dispatcher ran the plate and realized it was registered to our victim. The car was locked, and my crime scene techs didn't find any evidence."

Cat studied the rest of the report. "A trash dump in a dirt field. Three boys found her. How'd that happen?"

"It's used by the dirt bike riders. The bag split, similar to Lewis, and they saw her arm." He couldn't resist the dig. "Except—there weren't any raccoons," he said, then smirked.

She glanced at him and sniffed. "I'm not going to dignify that with a comment."

"Didn't think you would," he muttered.

"Are you one of those people who always has to have the last word?" she asked.

His lips curved in another smirk. "Maybe."

Deciding it was best to ignore him, Cat pushed the reports aside and spread the Benson photos in front of them. "We'll need a large corkboard to post these."

He nodded his head as he inspected each one.

Cat pulled several photos of Janet Lewis from another pile and laid them on the table. When she finished, she had two rows of pictures of each girl. "Oh, my god, look at the similarity in the cuts on the forehead, arms, and wrists."

Kevin said, "The image of those cuts has kept me awake at night. Have you ever watched a butcher carve a piece of meat? Every stroke of the knife is precise, same depth, even pressure, no ragged edges. It's because he has made the same cut, over and over."

He selected a picture of each victim and handed them to Cat. They were close-ups of the arms and wrists.

"Take a close look at those cuts. The position of each incision is the same on both victims, and the same length, and depth. I had Doc Morris measure them."

He pushed away from the table, leaned back in his chair, and stared at the pictures scattered in front of him. "Whoever did this is experienced in handling a knife and has made those cuts many times."

For a few minutes, there was silence in the room. Cat finally asked the question rolling in her head.

"The M.E. measured the cuts on Janet Lewis?"

"Yeah, I had him measure the cuts on both girls."

"I understand Benson, because of the similarity. But … you weren't aware of that fact when Lewis was killed. So, why, Lewis?"

"Doc Morris was also surprised by the request. It's not something he normally does. The cuts bothered me. It took a while to figure out why they were so disturbing. Then it hit me—too precise, too exact."

"Still, why measure them?"

Kevin realized she was not going to let it go. He shrugged. "Intuition, a gut feeling. I felt it could be significant."

"You were right." She pulled her cell phone from her backpack and hit the speed dial. "It's Cat. I'm at the police department, along with Chief Hunter. I've got you on the speakerphone."

Once Scott and Kevin had greeted each other, Cat asked, "Did you receive the Benson reports?"

"Yes, and I forwarded a copy to Ryan and Nicki. Anything I should know?"

"Tell them to examine the cuts. Kevin has evidence that Benson and Lewis were killed by the same person. I'll let him explain."

Cat glanced at him and caught the surprised expression on his face as he leaned toward the phone to discuss his findings with Scott. *Did he think I would take the credit?*

When Kevin finished his explanation, Scott said, "I have to agree. This certainly supports our conclusions. Cat, anything else?"

"No, that's it for now. Has Nicki come up with anything yet?"

"Last I saw, her fingers were flying over a keyboard. I have no doubt she will have something soon."

"Scott, I want to set up a conference call with Ryan and Nicki in the morning," Cat said.

"I'll tell them to expect a call."

Cat disconnected and considered the documents on the table. "Is it possible to talk to the Benson family tomorrow?" she asked and picked up the folders she wanted to take to the hotel to review.

"Shouldn't be a problem. I'll call in the morning and make the arrangements. It's getting late, do you want to grab a bite to eat?" Kevin asked.

Despite her odd flashes of heat that seemed to surge at the most unexpected times as they discussed the homicides, Kevin was trouble in capital letters. She dated, and there had been a couple of short relationships. Still, it wasn't something she actively pursued or even wanted at this stage of her life.

"I'll pass, but thanks for the offer. I need to get checked into my hotel and unpack."

"Can you be here at eight for a meeting with two of my detectives?"

"Okay." She slung her backpack over her shoulder and picked up her briefcase and computer. "I'll see you in the morning."

Watching her walk out the door, he thought, why did I ask her to go out to dinner? *Dumb move, Kevin.* He didn't need any unnecessary entanglements. But it had been a long time since he had experienced such an intense reaction to a woman. Of course, the last one ended in a disaster, a fact he couldn't forget.

Confused and disoriented, he stared at the shadows on the ceiling. It must be getting dark. JD pushed up with one arm to glance at the alarm clock on the dresser. The movement sent excruciating jabs of pain rippling in his head.

When he eased back, sharp needles pricked his neck. What the hell? He rolled his head to the side. Crusty, dried blood covered the pillow. Another nosebleed. It happened every time he snorted cocaine.

What day was it? JD remembered dumping the body in a field. He had failed even though he had prepared the sacrifice in the same way as before. Disgruntled, he bought several bags of cocaine from the dopehead who lived across from him. After that, his memory was a blur of bizarre images.

It must have been one hell of a trip as he swung his legs onto the floor. Dizzy, he sat on the edge of the bed, arms braced on each side. With a deep breath, he pushed himself up and stumbled toward the kitchen.

The air reeked with the stink of marijuana. Blackened matches, remains of joints, empty plastic bags, and beer cans littered the kitchen table and floor. JD poked at the burnt stubs, looking for one large enough to light. What was left crumbled to ashes. *Damn, the weed's gone.*

At least, he still had several cans of beer. Grabbing one from the refrigerator, he cracked the lid and gulped down several deep swigs. Even though the icy liquid eased the raspy pain in his throat, he needed something stronger than beer.

Old prescription bottles filled the drawer in the bathroom cabinet. JD shoved the containers around until he spotted one labeled Vicodin. There were still a couple left. His hand trembled as he shook one out and popped it into his mouth. Head tilted back to swallow, his eyes drifted to the mirror over the sink.

The sight caused him to gag, and the pill caught in the back of his throat. Another face overshadowed his image. The gleam of eyes, dark with hatred, stared at him. A tremor of panic made him look over his shoulder. No one was there. JD leaned toward the mirror. The swish of a bat, then a scream echoed in his head. Images flickered in his mind—the knife, a face, blood splatters flying in the air, and a voice laughed. Terrified, the can slipped from his hand. It hit the sink with a clank and rolled around the edge.

JD rubbed his hand across the mirror, trying to wipe away the image as he shouted, "No, no, you can't be here. You're dead!"

Seven

fter another restless night, Cat was at the PD just as the sun started to rise. Expecting to be the first to arrive, she was surprised to see Jessie in the hallway.

The woman must have noticed the look on her face as she grinned, then said, "No, I don't typically come to work at this hour of the morning. With what's going on, though, the Chief needs extra help. He's already here and down the hall. Sometimes, I wonder when the man sleeps."

In the conference room, Cat spotted several additions. Two tables were positioned along a side wall, one with a printer. Kevin and two men stood in front of a large corkboard on wheels set against the back wall. When Cat's backpack hit the desk, they turned.

"Good morning. You're early," Kevin said.

When he smiled, she had a momentary flashback to her musings before she had fallen asleep. Several had involved a nude police chief. The memory sent a prickle of heat through her, and she hoped her cheeks didn't have a telltale flush.

"I thought I'd be the first one here," she said, and smiled at the two men. One she recognized as the detective who had interviewed her at the hotel.

Flipping his hand toward them, Kevin said, "You've already met Detective Roger Mueller. The other is Ed Butler."

The detectives were in their forties, stocky and overweight. Their eyes conveyed an impression of resignation as if they expected pain and death. Something she had observed in many of the older officers she encountered.

She shook hands with each. "Please call me Cat, and I do remember Detective Mueller." When he shook her hand, a broad grin crossed his face. *I bet he remembers the raccoon story.*

"I told them about the two other agents," Kevin said.

Ed asked, "When will they arrive?"

"I'm not sure." Stepping to the corkboard, she said, "I arranged for a conference call this morning."

She studied the pictures and documents tacked to what would now be their murder board. Her phone chimed. "Morgan."

"Where are you?" Scott asked.

"At the PD. Chief Hunter and two of his detectives, Roger Mueller and Ed Butler, are here."

"Nicki is in my office and has a report."

Cat clicked the button to activate her speakerphone. "This is Scott Fleming and Nicki Allison," she said for the benefit of the men in the room.

Nicki said, "I sent an alert to medical examiners and police departments. Two M.E.'s, one in Canton, Texas, and the other in Minden, Louisiana responded. Each has a case matching the Clinton homicides. I should receive all the files in a couple of hours. Four victims, and we believe it's a PTC."

"Nicki, any indication from the two agencies why the homicides weren't linked to the same killer?" Cat asked.

"No. If I had to hazard a guess, it would be the typical problem with this type of crime. No way to connect the victims. If TRACE were up and running, this guy would have already popped up on the radar."

"Send me whatever you have," Cat responded.

"I just emailed the preliminary reports."

"Does Ryan have an update yet?" Cat asked.

"He's working on it. Chief Hunter, the prompt action you took on the incisions was invaluable," Nicki said.

Cat noticed the look of surprise that appeared on the faces of the two detectives as they glanced at their boss. She surmised he had not shared his conclusions with them.

Scott took over the conversation. "Since we have identified multiple homicides that cross state lines, I'm setting up a task force. It will be based in Clinton since it is the location of the most recent crimes. Chief Hunter, would you be willing to head the investigation along with Agent Morgan?"

As Kevin had listened to Nicki's report, distrust tied his gut in a knot. Despite Cat's reassurance, it was happening again. The FBI would take over, and his people would be left on the outside. He glanced at his detectives, knowing they would remember the debacle from their last interaction with the FBI. When Fleming made his request, their faces reflected the shock he felt. "Uh … yes," he said.

"Excellent! Nicki and Ryan will leave tomorrow. Cat, they're booked into your hotel. Call me if you need anything else, day or night."

When she disconnected the call, Kevin asked, "PTC?"

"A PTC is a peripatetic killer, a migrant. Stays for a short period then picks up and moves to new hunting grounds. They're hard to identify because local agencies usually view the homicide as an isolated case. The dots never get connected. They are one of the reasons the Tracker Unit was formed."

Roger asked, "What is TRACE?"

Cat explained the concept as she booted her computer.

"When will we have access to the profile?" Kevin asked.

Several new emails with attachments had arrived from Nicki and Ryan. "As soon as I am connected to the printer."

While they waited, Ed said, "Boss, what was the deal with the incisions?"

Kevin explained he had asked Doc Morris to measure them and his theory about the killer. A sheepish look crossed Kevin's face when he added, "I probably should have said something when I examined Janet Lewis's body. But it seemed to be one of those odd shots in the dark. It wasn't until the second victim turned up, I learned it wasn't so wild after all."

"I hope you get a few more flashes of inspiration. I think we'll need them if we're going to catch this guy," Ed said.

Within a few minutes, page after page shot out of the printer. Ed took the stack and told the group he'd make copies for everyone.

"Cat, I suggest we change the agenda for today. Instead of interviewing the Benson family, these files need to be organized. There might be additional facts for our list from last night," Kevin said.

Since she disliked searching through a stack of papers to find one crucial piece of evidence, she immediately agreed. While they waited for Nicki to send the case files on the new victims, numerous folders were set up for the different reports.

A lengthy discussion occurred between Kevin and his detectives over Ryan's profile and the use of ketamine. Although Kevin and Ed had heard of the drug, they weren't familiar with its applications.

Roger said, "I worked part-time at a veterinary clinic when I was in college. The vet routinely used the drug for surgeries."

When Cat added the details of the street use, Kevin picked up the toxicology reports for Lewis and Benson and quickly scanned them. "No other drugs, only ketamine, so what he's using must be uncut. Where's he getting it?"

"If I wanted to procure a quantity of pure ketamine, I'd get it from a clinic," Roger answered.

Kevin said, "Damn! You're right. We need to contact all the vet clinics in the county. Find out if anyone had a recent theft of the drug. We also need to broadcast a statewide alert to law enforcement agencies to notify us of any theft of ketamine or burglaries of vet clinics."

"Ed, I'll set up a list of the clinics to contact if you'll send out the alert," Roger said.

Listening to the two men talk, it was obvious they shared a rapport that came from working together over an extended period. It reminded Cat of her years with Ben as her partner.

Her computer beeped. Nicki's email with the two new case files had arrived. She downloaded and printed the reports. Roger said he'd make the copies this time.

While Kevin tacked the new pictures on the board, Cat studied each photo. The images portrayed a gruesome sight of four young women with near-identical knife wounds.

"The same person killed these women," Cat said. Her emotionless tone belied the grim look on her face.

Kevin turned to the table, picked up the two new autopsy reports, and quickly thumbed through them. "Ketamine again, and blood loss as the cause of death." Next, he examined the police reports saying, "One was abducted from a mall, the other from a restaurant."

Roger said, "How the hell is he getting to them. Your profiler indicated they were high-risk locations? Why didn't anyone notice him, especially if Barr's description is accurate? This guy should stand out like the proverbial sore thumb. Yet, according to these reports, not a single witness saw the abduction. That doesn't make sense." Frustrated, he tossed the report he had been reading on the table.

"I'm not finding any connection between the victims other than the similarity in locations," Ed added.

"I suggest we contact the Canton and Minden Police Departments and request the investigations be reopened. The fact we now have four murders committed by the same person might bring to light new details," Kevin said.

Roger told him, "I'll send out the request."

The next several hours were spent cross-checking the reports, identifying the county vet clinics along with several calls to the detectives who handled the investigations at Canton and Minden.

Cat glanced out the window. "It's getting dark. I don't know what else we can do today."

"Not much. We'll start in the morning," Kevin said.

Both detectives headed out the door. Kevin waited while Cat shut down her computer and packed the files in her briefcase.

As they walked to her car, she hoped he wouldn't suggest another late-night supper. Cat planned to make a stop on her way to the hotel and didn't want Kevin bird-dogging her steps. When he said he'd see her the next morning, her sense of relief mingled with disappointment. *Since I don't need to be involved with him on any level except work, this contradiction of feelings is just plain nuts.*

Clicking the remote on her key chain, she unlocked the door to her car. She reached for the handle at the same time as Kevin. The touch of his hand on top of hers sent a jolt of excitement racing through her. Looking up, the gleam in his eyes caused her breath to catch in the back of her throat. Was there any woman who could mistake the desire in a man's eyes? She quickly pulled her hand from underneath his.

"Uh … I really need to head to the hotel. I want to study these files again." Her voice sounded uncertain, even to her.

Even though he sensed there was something special about Cat Morgan, he knew asking her to go to dinner again was not a good idea and, somehow, kept the words from shooting out of his mouth. Despite the overwhelming yearning to learn what made the sexy agent tick, he stepped back and opened the door.

Cat glanced in her rearview mirror as she drove away. He stood in the parking lot—watching—until she lost sight of him.

Instead of heading to her hotel, she detoured to the one where she had found Janet Lewis's body. She wanted to examine the crime scene one more time. Cat parked in front and walked to the back of the building. The dumpster still sat in the same place.

She stopped in the middle of the parking lot and slowly turned to scan the area. According to Mueller's interview with the desk clerk, the hotel had been full due to a sales convention. The clerk said many of the guests returned late and continued to party most of the night. The two detectives had acquired a list of the guests and contacted each one. No one had observed any peculiar goings-on in the parking lot. So, how did he dump the body? And, why did no one notice him?

Okay, how would I do it? A two-foot-high concrete barrier separated the two parking lots. Climbing over it, she surveyed the bin from the other side. A vehicle could have backed up to the wall. However, it was too high to just step over, especially carrying a body. He'd have to toss it on the other side, then climb over the wall. Nope, far too risky.

Scrambling back over the wall, she dusted the dirt from her hands and pants, then strode toward the driveway at the back of the lot that led to the alley. Yes, this was his best option, a straight shot to the side of the dumpster.

She turned to look at the container. How did he haul a body, possibly still stiff from rigor mortis up the side? Someone could have driven onto the lot or even walked around the side of the building and spotted him before he could get rid of it.

While she played the different scenarios in her head, a breeze on her neck caused a shiver of chills to run down her back. Her jacket covered the pistol on her belt. She slid her hand until she reached the butt of the gun and turned.

Two girls faced her, Janet Lewis and Susan Benson. Startled by Cat's quick movement, they began to fade.

Her hand reached toward them, and in a quiet tone, said, "Please, don't go. You don't need to be afraid."

Janet said, "I saw you before. Who are you?"

"Cat Morgan and I'm an FBI agent."

Her gaze shifted to the other young woman. "Hello, Susan," she said as she studied the young woman. Dressed in jeans and a t-shirt, her short hair curled around her face.

Alarmed, Susan stepped back. "How do you know my name?" she whispered.

"I'm trying to find out what happened to both of you and need your help. Janet, what is the last memory you have?"

Her brow wrinkled as she struggled to remember. "I …uh …I was at the mall with my friends."

"What did you do?"

"Just shopped. I tried on clothes and some shoes."

"Did you get separated from your friends?"

"The only time was at the food court. They finished eating before I did and left to look at shoes in a store across the walkway."

"What happened after they left? Did you go somewhere?"

"Just to the counter for some napkins, then I went back to the table to finish my drink."

"Did you take your drink with you?"

"No. I left it on the table."

"When you went back, was anyone near your table?"

"It was really crowded. A lot of people were walking around."

"Did anyone seem unusual?"

Her form faded.

"Janet, stay with me if you can."

Cat could see the concentration on her face. "There was a man. He turned and left before I reached the table. I remember thinking he didn't seem to be the type of person who would shop at a mall."

Oh, my god, did she see the killer? "What made him stand out in your mind?"

"Bib overalls and his coat was dirty. He just seemed out of place."

"Anything else about the coat, color?"

"Uh ... tan, and I think it might have been canvas. I didn't pay that much attention to him."

"How about his face—a beard, mustache?"

"I didn't get a good look at his face. But he did have a beard, sort of straggly."

"Do you remember his hair color?"

"Dark and tied in a ponytail. He had on a ball cap."

"Height or weight?"

"I'm not sure."

"How tall is your dad, and what does he weigh?"

Janet looked surprised at the question. "He's six-foot and over two-hundred pounds. He's always complaining he needs to lose weight. Oh, god," she cried, her arms hugged her body as she rocked with grief. "I'll never see him again!"

The rage and despair of another life cruelly cut short rolled over Cat, and she instinctively reached out her hand though there was nothing she could touch. "Janet, I know how hard this must be for you. But I need your help to find whoever killed you—and Susan." Her gaze flicked to the other girl.

Janet lifted her head and stared at Cat, then nodded.

"Compare the man's size to your dad—shorter, taller, heavier?"

Janet's voice trembled as she said, "Shorter, maybe a couple of inches. The overalls were baggy, so I'm not sure about the weight. I don't think he was fat."

"When you went back to the table, did you take another drink from your cup?"

"Uh, huh. I finished what was left."

"What happened then?"

"I'm not sure. I started to feel sick, but I don't remember anything after that.

Susan said, "I saw someone who looked like the person she described."

Cat shifted her attention to the other girl. "Do you remember where?"

"At the Burger Grill, in a booth behind me."

"Did you leave your food or drink on the table?"

The young girl nodded her head. "I left my tray and went to the bathroom. When I came out, he was in the next booth."

"Can you describe him?"

"Like she said." Her hand motioned toward Janet. "A dirty brown coat and ball cap."

"Did you see his face or any features, beard, mustache?"

"No, his head was bent over. When I sat down, my back was to him."

"What's your last memory?"

"I was eating, and I got sick, dizzy. That's all I remember. How did I get here?"

Cat said, "Sometimes, victims can connect with each other. I think it's how you found Janet. What happened to her happened to you. Susan, when you drove into the parking lot, do you remember any of the vehicles parked there?"

She stared at the ground, seemingly lost in thought. Her eyes flicked up. "A yellow Volkswagen bug. I parked next to it. It's the only one I remember."

Believing she had all the information the two girls could provide, she said, "Both of you have done all you can by staying. You have helped, but now—it's time to go."

They looked at her and nodded. Janet took Susan's hand as they turned and walked away, their images fading. Cat heard a soft "thank you." A light flashed, and they vanished.

She stood motionless, held in place by her thoughts, and the information she had gained. The thud of footsteps caused her to pivot. Her hand instinctively reached for her gun. *Oh, hell, how will I explain this?*

Eight

Uneasy over a feeling he might have missed something, Kevin decided to re-examine the two crime scenes. The hotel where the Lewis girl had been found was the closest. When he drove into the parking lot, he saw a familiar black vehicle parked in front. *Yeah, right, so much for heading to your hotel to go over the files.*

He parked next to her car and walked around the corner of the building. Cat stood near the dumpster, her back to him. Hands fluttered in the air, gesturing as if talking to someone, but she was alone. *What the hell is she doing now? Is she carrying on a one-sided conversation with herself?*

He paused to watch for a few minutes. The longer he was around her, the more fascinated he became. He could hear her voice, though not what she was saying. His curiosity finally got the better of him, and he called her name as he strode towards her.

She spun, hand on her gun.

At the sight of him, her hand dropped away, but she exclaimed, "Hunter, don't ever sneak up on me!"

"First of all—I wasn't sneaking, and second—if you hadn't been so engrossed in whatever you were doing, you would have heard me. I called out. By the way, what are you doing? You said you were going to your hotel."

"After I left the PD, it occurred to me, it might be helpful to look at the crime scene again. I was debating different scenarios."

"It sure sounded like one hell of a discussion."

Was it possible he heard what she said? If he did, she didn't have a clue how she could explain a discussion with two ghosts. "Uh ... what did you hear?"

"Your voice, though I couldn't distinguish the words. Do you do that often?"

Her heart jumped with instant relief. "As a matter of fact, yes. I've found it helps to put my ideas into a proper perspective." Her voice sounded prim, even to her, as if she recited something she'd memorized.

"Proper perspective. Does that go along the same lines as ... raccoons making noises?" His lips twitched as a snarky grin appeared.

Cat glared at him.

"In your proper ... prospective, did you come to any rational conclusions?"

"It's probably better if I don't share them since I don't want to boost your skepticism," she retorted.

"Don't let my doubts stop you. I learned a long time ago to consider any and all information, no matter how outrageous it sounds. It's like the old adage—a blind squirrel finds a nut now and then."

"Chief Hunter, first you compared me to the devil, now it's a blind squirrel. You really need to work on your people skills."

He laughed. "Hey, calling it as I see it. Let's go eat and talk about what you know, and I don't."

Kevin suggested a Mexican restaurant a few blocks away. Since they had skipped lunch, she was starved. The misgivings over spending more time with him were rationalized as a need to discuss the investigation.

At the restaurant, Kevin ordered a beer. At his suggestion, she elected to try the house specialty, a margarita.

Kevin waited until the drink orders arrived before asking, "Okay, tell me what was going on back at the hotel?"

Stalling, she took a sip of the tangy mixture. She'd uncovered new leads, especially the description of the killer. Answering questions about how she got them would be worse than sounds in a trash bin. She sure couldn't say two ghosts told her. She had to figure out a way to get it into the investigation, but now was not the time.

"You're right, this is delicious," she said, setting the glass on the table. "I was just playing around with different possibilities. I don't have any more facts than you do, contrary to what you may believe." *Now, that's not really a lie, since information from a ghost wouldn't be considered a fact by most people, even if they believed the story.*

A frown of disbelief appeared on Kevin's face as she continued, "I was trying to figure out how the PTC tossed a body in the dumpster. My take is he parked next to it, and I had reached the point of how he maneuvered the body into the bin when you arrived."

"Huh! You want me to believe you stood there talking to yourself about how he parked his car?"

"Yep. What I call connecting the dots. You never know where they will lead. Consider this. The hotel was full the night the killer tossed Lewis's body. Lots of people partying, milling around. Cars probably coming and going. So, how did he get her in that bin without someone noticing him?"

"You're right, good question. According to the M.E.'s report, the body might still have been stiff. It would be difficult. Plus, where'd he put her, in the back seat, trunk?"

They looked at each other, and within a split second, both said, "Truck!"

"That's it, Kevin, a truck, and the body was probably in the bed. If he pulled next to the bin, he could climb into the back, wait until there was no one around and toss it over the side. We'll add a pickup to our profile."

"Okay, I'll give you this one. However, you were up to something else in that parking lot."

Cat grinned and took another sip of the margarita, then stared at the glass. "I think the killer is drugging their drinks," she said, lifting the glass for emphasis. "Every abduction so far has taken place where food and beverages are served. It is the only common denominator for the kidnapping locations."

There was silence while Kevin pondered the possibility. He finally nodded his head. "It's the only option that makes sense. An article I read today indicated ketamine is one of the date rape drugs—fast-acting, within seconds. They would go with him, not realizing what they were doing and might account for why no one noticed them."

Delighted she managed to slip that lead into the conversation, she said, "I want to interview the two girls who were with Lewis at the mall."

"What do you hope to find?"

"Um … I'm not certain, but maybe the detectives missed something in their interviews. It's worth a try." It had suddenly occurred to her, they may have seen the man. With the right questions, she should be able to prompt the description. She added, "In the morning, I'll call the Vicksburg police chief and set up a meeting."

"Let me do it. We're friends. There will be less resistance if I call and tell him we are coming into his jurisdiction and why."

"We?"

"Yeah, we. I'm going to Vicksburg with you."

Damn! She didn't want him along. She was stuck since she couldn't tell him not to go. But it would be a lot easier without Kevin sitting there listening to every word.

The waitress set steaming plates of enchiladas, beans, and rice on the table. The spicy aroma tantalized Cat's taste buds.

"Do you want another margarita?" he asked, before forking up a bite.

"No, one's my limit."

Cat laid the napkin on her lap and sighed. *How fun this could be if it were a date, no stress, no investigation, no killer, just two people getting to know each other.*

It seemed he had read her mind when he asked, "Tell me. Who is Cat Morgan? At times, you appear to be a mystery woman."

She laughed. "Devil, blind squirrel, and now mystery woman, you have quite an imagination."

"Nope, just wanting to find out what makes you tick. So, tell me."

"It's all pretty standard. I grew up in Bristol. After college, I applied to the FBI and worked in Texas until I transferred to the Tracker Unit. Nothing unusual or mysterious."

"I think there's a whole lot more, and—unusual and mysterious is a very apt description. Something … I plan to explore."

"Sounds like a challenge," she replied.

"Might be. Why did you join the FBI?"

Cat took the last sip of the margarita. *How do I answer a simple question that had a very complicated answer?*

Finally, deciding a generic response would have to suffice, she said, "Same as most officers, I guess, a desire to make a difference. A lot of bad going on. I like stopping it." It was time to shift the attention off her. "So, what's your story?"

"Oh, I grew up in Clinton, not far from here. I attended LSU on a football scholarship and became a cop after I graduated."

"Same question back at you. Why a cop?"

An expression of grief crossed his face as his eyes shifted downward. "A grim turn of events. My best friend was my next-door neighbor. Kyle and I grew up together and were tagged the terrorizing duo for our antics at school. I look back at the pranks we pulled, and it's nothing short of a miracle we didn't end up in jail. Anyway, we both got scholarships to LSU. One night, he stopped at a convenience store not far from the dorm and walked in on an armed robbery. He was killed."

Kevin glanced at her. "A good man, dead because a dopehead wanted money for a quick score. I had to do something, and short of becoming a one-man vigilante, I switched to a major in criminal justice and became a cop."

"Did they catch him?"

"Yeah, he's serving a life sentence. It's still not enough."

To ease the tension, she shifted to another topic. "An article I read said you were the youngest person to be hired as the police chief."

"What! You researched me?" he said with a note of enthusiasm in his voice.

Delighted her ploy worked, she gave him one of those 'don't mess with me looks.' "Hunter, don't let it go to your head. Routine fact-finding, that's all."

A smirk crossed his face as he picked up where he had left off. "After graduation, I hired on with the PD. I worked my way up from a patrol officer to Lieutenant. A couple of years ago, the chief retired. I decided, what the heck, why not apply for the position, and I got the job."

"You attended the FBI academy. Did you ever consider going federal?"

"More research?"

"Um ...not really. I saw the diploma in your office the day you shoved me out the door. You know, you really were obnoxious."

He laughed, then said, "Yeah, I was—wasn't I?" His tone was unrepentant.

Cat sent a glare his way, then pushed back her plate. "That was delicious, but I can't eat another bite. You didn't answer my question about joining the FBI."

"How about I would rather be stripped naked and whipped with a knotted rope than join any federal agency. Besides, Clinton has always seemed to be the right place for me."

"Wow, that bad."

"Yep!"

"So, what happened?"

"That's another story for another day."

The waitress dropped the check on the table. They both reached for it. Kevin beat her to it, saying it was his treat.

At her car door, she turned to say goodbye. She looked up at him, and his penetrating gaze caused a surge of longing to pierce her body. His hand gently pushed the hair from her forehead. Fingers lightly trailed down her cheek and over her lips, sending shivers along her spine. When his eyes moved to her mouth, his intensity pulled at her.

Head tilted down, he skimmed his lips over hers. Stepping back, he smiled and said, "Cat Morgan, there will be another time and place."

Driving to the hotel, she knew her focus had to be on the investigation. It was difficult, however, to dismiss the quiver of desire rippling through her body.

JD meandered along the concourse leading to the food court. It was late, and only a few people still lingered. He spotted two women inside a shoe store. His eyes skimmed each one as his hand slipped into his coat pocket and fingered the vials of liquid and syringe.

No, they're not right. At each store, he stopped at the window, searching, before moving to the next. A security guard exited a door ahead of him. Frissons of chills raced down JD's back. *Don't panic, he doesn't know anything.* When the guard turned and walked in the opposite direction, he exhaled a sigh of relief. It was time to leave. Even the food court was empty.

Frustrated, he headed to the exit. He'd been here since early evening and only found one. Even though he had followed the pack of giggling girls, he couldn't get close to her.

Muttering to himself, he said, "I'll find one, just have to keep looking."

A couple walking beside him glanced his way. The woman tugged at the man's arm, and they slowed to stay behind him. *Damn, I don't need someone's attention.* JD pulled his ball cap further over his forehead, tilted his head down, and pushed open the door.

Hell, I just came out on the wrong side. Now, he'd have to walk around the outside of the damn place to reach his truck. Irritated, he zipped his jacket and pulled up the collar to cut the chill of the night air.

Should he try somewhere else or come back the next day? He liked the malls, especially after Vicksburg. The one he grabbed there … well, that one had been special. Oh, yes, so very, very special.

The recollection brought a smile to his face—the scent of her perfume that had hung in the air, the way her long red-gold hair swung gently across her back. He remembered how his hands had twitched as he envisioned his fingers sliding through the gleaming strands.

He knew his Master had sent a sign when he got the chance to dope her drink. Then he waited. That was always the best part of the hunt, exhilarating since he was in control.

He wished Ezra could have seen her. He could never convince the old man all it took was the right sacrifice. JD fingered the amulet around his neck. He missed Ezra. He was the only friend he'd ever had. *I did what I had to do.*

Anxious to reach his pickup, he picked up his pace. He might stop by the burger place on his way out of town. The last time they gave him a free hamburger. If he was lucky, he might get more than food.

Nine

She fought to waken from the depth of terror. Drenched in sweat, her legs kicked to free her body from the twisted sheets as she rolled to sit on the side of the bed.

This was unlike anything she had ever experienced. Owls had circled and screeched in protest. As the moon whirled across the sky, Cat was helpless to stop the flow of blood that flowed over its surface.

Dreams had always been a link to another level of awareness, but she never dreamed about the owls. Was their appearance a link to the killer's activities? What she was afraid to admit, yet had to face, was the killer was on the hunt, and she couldn't stop him.

Shaken by the vivid images, the room seemed to close around her. Even though only a faint light gleamed around the edges of the drapes, she needed to leave. Showered and dressed, she grabbed her gear and headed downstairs. A quick pass by the buffet to grab a cup of coffee and sandwich made with scrambled eggs, and she was out the door. As the first sip of hot brew slid down her throat, she thought, caffeine is just what she needed to jump-start her system.

As she pulled out of the parking lot, she called Nicki, planning to leave a voice message since she didn't expect her to be up this early. Instead, she answered on the second ring.

"Cat, you're up early, everything all right?"

"Yep, headed to the PD. I planned to leave a message for you to call before you left D.C."

"We're already on our way and should be in Clinton in a few hours. We finished the reports faster than Scott predicted and left late yesterday afternoon."

"Hunter and I will probably be gone when you reach the station. If he's able to make the arrangements, we're going to Vicksburg to interview the two girls who were at the mall with Janet Lewis. We should be back by late afternoon. When you arrive, check-in with Jessie Barnes in the chief's office."

"Anything else?" Nicki asked.

Cat hesitated, then said, "Uh … one other request. Run a search for any yellow Volkswagens, the bug type, registered to an owner who lives in or near Clinton."

"Okay. Any particular reason?"

"A hunch, and it may be nothing."

When Nicki disconnected the call, she looked over at Ryan. "What do you know about Cat?"

"Hmm ... not much, though, there have been rumblings for the last couple of years. I'm friends with a couple of Texas agents. They laughingly refer to her as the witchy woman."

"That's weird," Nicki said.

He chuckled. "According to my sources, she comes up with details that seemingly have no apparent connection to the case. Then it becomes a key element in the investigation. Cat also finds the bodies of murdered victims, and no one understands how she does it. It's why I questioned her on her discovery of Lewis's body. I'm not sure what you think, but I didn't buy into the noise explanation."

"It was a bit suspicious. I think I just got a request for one of those odd details. She wants me to locate yellow Volkswagens. Not just any yellow one, but a yellow bug. Where did that come from?"

"What'd she say when you asked her?"

"Just said it was a hunch."

He glanced at her and grinned as he drove down the road. *Witchy woman, maybe so.*

When Cat arrived at the PD, Jessie was already at her desk, shuffling a stack of papers.

She eyed Cat's coffee cup. "I set up a table with a coffee machine in the conference room, and there's a fresh pot. There's also another pot in the boss's office."

"Thanks, Jessie. Oh, there will be two other agents arriving sometime today."

"The Chief told me yesterday before I left. Those poor girls and the possibility of more. It's horrible. The news media hasn't made the connection yet. When they do, it will be a feeding frenzy around here."

At the sound of the door opening, Cat glanced over her shoulder. It was Kevin.

"Looks like I'm not the only early bird. Morning, Jessie … Cat."

"Chief, coffee is fresh and hot."

"Bless you, and all your pets. I need it."

Kevin headed to his office, telling Cat he would call the Vicksburg police chief. "If I can set up the interviews, we need to leave. I don't want to limit our time with the witnesses. I'd also like to talk to the detective who handled the missing person report."

"That's fine with me. I'll grab a couple of other folders I want to review and will be ready to go." She turned, then looked back at Jessie. "Pets?"

A broad grin popped up on Jessie's face. "Two dogs, three cats, and a parakeet."

"Oh … that's definitely in the plural," Cat said, chuckling as she walked out the door.

In the conference room, Ed and Roger were already seated at the table with a stack of papers in front of them. Cat lifted her eyebrows in question. Roger shook his head no, and said, "So far, nothing on missing drugs. As soon as they open, we'll start calling the vet clinics.

Are you and the boss headed to Vicksburg?"

"Probably, he's on the phone to the police chief. I hope we find something that was missed. Nicki Allison and Ryan Barr will arrive sometime today."

Ed replied, "We'll take care of it. There should be enough room in here for everyone to set up whatever computer equipment they need."

Cat laughed. "You might want to rethink that opinion after you meet Nicki. The woman is a walking computer store."

Kevin entered and said, "We're good to go. The chief will contact the girls and ask them to come to the station. Are you ready?"

"Flip for who will drive?" she said.

"Consider next time your turn. It'll be faster if I do. I'm familiar with Vicksburg and where the police department is located."

Before sliding into the passenger seat, Cat pulled her folders out of the briefcase, then tossed it and her black leather jacket on the back seat. The backpack was dropped on the front seat floorboard. The travel time would let her review the investigation notes since she still had a difficult problem—getting the PTC's description into the investigation without raising Kevin's hackles.

He glanced at her as he negotiated the turns to reach the freeway. She wore black cargo style pants with a multi-colored shirt and a black vest. Fancy clips held her curly hair away from her face. She looked professional and sexy as hell. Images of the tight athletic body, he was certain her clothes disguised, circled in his head. *Don't go there.*

"You look tired," he said.

"Yeah, a short night. It's difficult to stop thinking about this case, knowing another girl could be at risk."

"We have a couple of hours. You can kick back and take a quick nap."

"No, I'm too wired."

One by one, she studied each page of the reports, her attention focused on the details. When she reached the last page, frustrated, she sighed and slid the stack of paper into the file folder.

"Nothing?" Kevin asked, who had occasionally glanced at her bent head. He'd kept quiet, not wanting to break her concentration.

"No, nothing! There's no pattern in his timeline, he hits and then it's weeks before he hits again. Why did these women catch his attention, and what is the trigger that sets him off?"

Remembering the railroad case, she added. "If there is a pattern, we might be able to predict his next move. Maybe Ryan can find one."

She grabbed her cell phone, and since Ryan was probably driving called Nicki. She relayed her request and disconnected. In her mind, she replayed the images of the bloody moons from her dream and her premonition.

"Kevin, I believe he's already searching for his next target. If we don't find him within the next couple of days, another girl will disappear."

As he'd experienced the same feeling, he wasn't surprised by her statement. Reluctant to discuss what he'd considered as nothing more than a hunch, he hadn't said anything. There was always the possibility the killer had already moved on to another location.

"Any basis for that opinion?"

"No, not really." She couldn't bring herself to say anything about her dreams, as it would only lead to more questions she wasn't willing to answer.

"I think you're right. I also believe there are more victims, some we may never find."

Cat's eyes widened in surprise. Accustomed to having her odd flashes of intuition met with disdain by her colleagues, his response was unexpected. Staring at the papers in her lap, she smiled. *There is more to Kevin Hunter than meets the eye.*

"I'm curious, why the animosity toward federal agents?" Cat asked and shifted in the seat to look at him.

His eyes met hers, then flicked back to the roadway. "A few months after I became chief, two of my patrol officers arrested three men for distribution of drugs. Turned out, they were connected to one of the Mexican cartels, and Clinton was a drop point on their distribution route. My officers amassed an extensive number of details on truck routes, dates and times, and other suspects.

"The feds, who also were investigating the cartel's activities, found out the men were in custody, and the next thing I knew FBI and DEA agents swarmed the town. They took over. Demanded the results of our investigation and even took the prisoners into federal custody. I was informed it was their case now and to butt out. They didn't want any inept actions by the local cops to compromise their activities."

At Cat's gasp, he glanced at her. "Yeah, that is exactly what the team leader said—inept actions. Then they used the results my officers had compiled to make several arrests and seize a substantial quantity of drugs."

"It makes sense why you were hostile to the involvement of my team in this case."

"When I look back on the incident, my anger was at the contempt and blind arrogance of the agents. It could have jeopardized the entire operation, and that was inexcusable and unwarranted."

Reminded of the dilemma she faced, she said, "Kevin, I'd like to conduct the interview. The girls might be more comfortable with a woman."

"That's fine with me." He looked at the dashboard clock. "Right on time," and pulled in the parking lot.

Inside, a uniformed officer directed them to the chief's office. Jerry Porter greeted them as he motioned for them to have a seat. Kevin introduced Cat, who gave him a quick overview of the case. She explained Kevin and herself were in charge of the FBI task force formed to investigate the homicides.

When he heard Kevin was heading up the task force, he looked at him with raised eyebrows.

"Yeah, I was as shocked as you look," Kevin said.

A knock on the door and an officer stepped inside to say the two witnesses had arrived.

They followed the chief to a small conference room where two young girls, who appeared to be eighteen or so, waited. Tightly clasped hands rested on the table, and two sets of eyes nervously flicked between Cat and Kevin.

Porter introduced the girls, Amy Reynolds, and Nancy Davis.

Cat turned to him and said, "I'd like to talk to each girl separately."

"There's a break room across the hall," Porter said and escorted Amy out of the room.

They sat across the table from Nancy.

Cat said, "We're investigating the death of your friend Janet. If you concentrate on my questions, it will help ease your nervousness."

While Cat talked, she'd pulled her recorder from her briefcase and set it in front of her.

"I'm going to record the interview and take notes. Before we start, do you need anything to drink, water or soda?"

The girl's emotional state was apparent in her breathless and squeaky voice as she responded to Cat's inquiry. "No, I'm all right. What happened to Janet was … was horrible. If we hadn't left her alone, she wouldn't have been killed."

Cat stretched out her hand and laid it on top of the girl's clasped hands. "There is no way you could have predicted what would happen, and you shouldn't feel guilty. This was not your fault."

Nancy nodded though her eyes filled with tears.

Cat clicked the button to start the recorder and began by stating the date, time, location, and names of the individuals in the room. She asked Nancy to say her name and date of birth.

Once Nancy had complied, Cat asked, "Where were you on the day your friend, Janet Lewis, disappeared."

"At the mall."

Her interrogation took Nancy through her day, the stores they entered, what they bought, even the stops at the restroom.

When Nancy mentioned the food court, Cat probed their every movement and that of the other people around them.

Kevin sat back, content to let Cat handle the interview. While he listened to her skillful technique, his respect for her deepened.

When Nancy reached the part of finding Janet missing, tears flowed down the young girl's face. Cat turned off the recorder and pulled a packet of tissues from her backpack. She quietly talked to the young girl, helping her to regain her composure. When Cat asked if she was ready to continue, Nancy nodded her head yes.

By the time Cat finished, a clear picture of three young girls enjoying a day at the mall had emerged. They laughed as they strolled in and out of stores, trying on clothes for sheer fun, with nothing more pressing on their minds than studying for the next exam.

She stopped the recorder and asked Nancy if she needed to take a break. The young woman said no.

"Nancy, I want you to close your eyes, sit back in your chair, and relax. Concentrate on my voice."

As Cat's voice altered to a soothing, hypnotic tone, Kevin eyed her, wondering what the hell she was up too.

"Take a deep breath and let it out slowly. That's good, now another. Let your mind follow the path you took and look at the people. Does someone look out of place, maybe dressed in an odd or unusual style?"

Next to her, Kevin's body stiffened as he sat forward. Intuitively, she realized her ruse had failed. He knew she was up to something. Cat kept her gaze focused on Nancy. The concentration on the young girl's face was intense, her brow wrinkled, and lips pulled tight.

Her eyes popped open, and she stared at Cat. "Yes! The weirdo in bib overalls. Who wears bib overalls?"

"Tell me what happened," Cat said.

"We were inside a dress shop. Janet and Amy were in one of the dressing rooms. I was at the front of the store looking at clothes on a rack. This man stared at me through the window."

"Close your eyes, and this time picture him in your mind. What do you see?"

"He has a scruffy, dark beard and is wearing a ball cap with some kind of decal. He has on a jacket and ... hmm ... his clothes are dirty.

Her eyes opened as she said, "His eyes were the worst. His stare raised goosebumps on my arms, and I headed to the back of the store. When I turned around to see if he was still there, he was gone."

"What color was his hair?"

"I'm not sure."

"Can you estimate his height or weight?"

"I guess a little taller than me. I'm five-eight. He looked skinny."

"What was the length of time from when you noticed the man to when you stopped in the food court?"

"Fifteen, maybe twenty minutes. When Janet finished trying on a dress, we decided to get something to eat. The food court is around the corner from the store."

"Did you spot him in the food court?"

Nancy hesitated and then said, "No ... no, I didn't."

"I want a police artist to work with you on a sketch of the man."

"I'm not sure how much I'll remember. I only saw him for a couple of seconds. Did he kill Janet?" Her voice quivered, and tears formed in her eyes.

"I'm not sure," though she was certain this was the killer. She turned to Kevin. "I'll take Nancy to the break room and bring in Amy. Would you ask Jerry if they have a police artist?"

He nodded his head, stood, and marched out of the room. His rigid body made it all too obvious he was angry. Cat sighed; the explanations would have to wait. Right now, she wasn't too sure it would be possible.

Cat was explaining to Amy what would happen during the interview when Kevin entered the room. She stopped.

"Jerry said he doesn't have an artist on staff. When the PD needs one, he uses an art instructor at the high school. He'll call her."

Following the same format and line of questioning she had with Nancy, Cat used the relaxing technique to jog the girl's memory. When Amy couldn't remember anyone unusual, she asked, "Do you remember seeing a man in bib overalls?"

Amy pondered for a minute and finally said, "Yeah, there was. He was hanging around the food court when we were in line. His appearance made me uneasy. I hoped he wouldn't be in line with us. I paid for my food, and when I turned, he was gone."

Amy's description was similar to the one from Nancy. The only detail she could add was that his hair was dark and tied in a ponytail. Cat told her a police artist was on the way to the station and asked her to wait in the conference room. When they entered the hallway, Jerry walked toward them.

"We got lucky. Ms. Stafford, the art teacher, was available and is on her way to the PD."

Cat said, "Let's go back to your office." Closing his door, she explained, "Both girls noticed a man whose appearance was odd, and he may have followed them. Please have your artist talk to each one separately since I don't want their memories tainted by listening to the other describe the man. How soon will she be here?"

"In a few minutes. Is Amy still in the conference room?"

Cat nodded yes. "Nancy is in the break room. She may be able to provide a more accurate description. He stared at her through a store window."

"I'll have the artist start with her. We'll keep the girls separated until we finish the sketches."

Kevin asked to speak to Detective Brooks, who was in charge of the kidnapping investigation. Jerry directed them to his office.

As they walked along the hall, Kevin fought to suppress his anger. He'd listened in amazement when Nancy described a possible suspect, and his every instinct had quivered. Somehow, Cat knew about the man before she even began that hypnotic routine. *Son-of-a-bitch! The first break in the investigation and I'm kept in the dark.* So much for all that rot on interagency cooperation.

He couldn't say anything until they left, but once they were in the car—well, the feds did this before. He'd be damned if he let them do it again.

Ten

The meeting with Detective Brooks was the last item on their agenda. Kevin had specific questions regarding the investigation that might not have been included in the detective's notes. Unfortunately, Brooks was unable to add any details.

They'd just finished when Jerry entered the room. He placed two original sketches along with several copies on the desk. Eerily similar, the drawings depicted a thin-faced man with deep-set eyes, thin lips, and a straggly beard. A ball cap covered his head.

Detective Brooks said he'd show the sketch to the food court employees. One of them might remember seeing the man.

Cat thanked the two men and placed the drawings in her briefcase, and as they walked out the door said, "We need a meeting of the task force as soon as we're back at your office."

"I agree," Kevin said, his tone abrupt. He pulled his cell phone from his pocket. Jessie was still at the office, and he asked her to relay a request to the detectives to stay late.

Cat made a similar call to Ryan as she eyed Kevin's tight-lipped face. Evidently, the ride back was going to be a bit unpleasant.

While Kevin navigated their way through the city streets to reach the freeway, Cat stared out the window, her thoughts on the results of the interviews, and Kevin's attitude. How was she going to explain?

"We need to talk," he said, his tone harsh with anger.

Startled, she said, "Oh! Sorry, I was woolgathering. It's a bad habit of mine. I was replaying the interview with …"

Kevin interrupted. "Yeah, let's talk about that interview. Cat, you knew about the man before Nancy mentioned him, and don't try to convince me that you didn't." The resentment in his voice reverberated in the car. "And then … when you talked to Ryan, you didn't say you had a sketch of a person of interest. Oh, no, you didn't even say—A—suspect. You said—The!—suspect! That's a definite assertion. How did you find out, and why didn't you tell me? Hell, this is nothing but the feds playing games again."

Suddenly, it dawned on Cat. *He thinks I deliberately excluded him from critical details of the investigation, and I'm screwing him over like the other agents did. He doesn't understand it's not the information I'm hiding, it's how I got it.* This was worse than she expected, but damn, she should have anticipated it.

It was doubtful any attempts to pacify him, or her denials would be believed. Even if he did, his distrust would only deepen and would ultimately impact the investigation.

She'd always been able to fend off uncomfortable questions, but she'd never been in this position before. The relationship with Kevin had become complicated. Her unexpected connection to him was a sensation Cat had never experienced with a man. *I don't want to lie to him.* Once the lies start, they don't stop. How could she balance the disparity? *Can I take a chance and trust him?* Deep inside, she already knew the answer.

"What! Cat … got your tongue?" He snorted, then said, "You know, that line would really be funny if this didn't involve someone killing women."

Maybe pacifying would work. She twisted in the seat to watch his face. "Kevin, I didn't deliberately conceal evidence from you. It's … hmm … sometimes … oh, it's difficult to explain. I … uh … I get hunches, and this time it worked." *You stammered and stuttered your way on that one. That ought to really convince him.*

"You identified a crucial piece of evidence and—call it a hunch! From the minute I met you, you've done nothing but tell lies."

He stopped talking as he negotiated a pass around a slow-moving truck.

As she looked at a jawline rigid with anger, Cat sighed. She had known it wouldn't be easy. "Kevin, I haven't lied—not exactly. It's what I would call more of an evasion."

Back in his lane of traffic, Kevin glared at her. "Call it what you want. You knew—I didn't, and we're back to what happened today. How did you learn about the suspect?"

Ah, the infamous moment of truth. "I talk to the dead."

Shocked, his hands slipped on the wheel, and the car swerved to the right. "Whoa, say that again!" he exclaimed as he steered back onto the roadway, then shot a stare of disbelief toward her. Kevin had expected a feeble excuse. However, this certainly stretched the limits of credibility.

She took a deep breath and said, "When I was a teenager, I found out I could see and communicate with the dead. My grandmother, Nana Ruth, had the same ability. It's a family thing," waving her hand in the air for emphasis.

Kevin stuttered, "A ... uh ... family thing?"

Although she was sinking into a sea of disbelief, she had to finish what she started. "Nana Ruth helped me understand my gift and how I could use it to help people. It's why I joined the FBI and ..."

He interrupted. "That's what you were doing at the hotel last night! You were talking to a ghost."

Stunned, Cat stared at him. *Oh, my god, is it possible he believes me?* "Yes. I talked to Janet and ... Susan. Janet described a man she had seen at the mall, and Susan saw the same person at the Burger Grill."

"Holy hell!" *What do I say to a woman who tells me she talks to the dead—not only the dead but the victims in our investigation?*

The only sound was the car's engine. Cat's eyes flicked between Kevin and her hands tightly clasped in her lap. At least, his face had a thoughtful expression, not the earlier look of disbelief and anger. Cat shifted in the seat to ease the tension in her neck and shoulders.

"Did … uh, Janet … uh … the ghost—what the hell do I call her—tell you she was in the dumpster?"

The question did not surprise her. He'd already displayed an uncanny ability to connect seemingly random pieces of information. Who else would have an M.E. measure cuts on a body?

"Hmm—not exactly."

"Well, then, how did you know the body was there? And, I don't want to hear about some damn animal."

"Oh, boy, are you sure you want the rest of the story? If you don't think I'm crazy now, you might if I explain that part."

"I'm not sure. However, any information, no matter how crazy it sounds, if it helps catch a killer, I'll keep an open mind."

"It wasn't a raccoon but owls … great horned owls. They led me to her."

"Damn, Cat! I may take back my comment on an open mind."

"I'm a descendant of a Cherokee Indian who had unusual powers. She could connect to the dead and the owls. I inherited her abilities. Occasionally, the owls lead me to the victim of a homicide. As an agent, it has proven to be quite an asset."

He shook his head in amazement. "Owls! This explanation should be interesting."

"According to tribal myths, owls are the guardians of the night as well as the messengers of death. They are a link to the spirit world, and in death, the soul crosses the owl's bridge to the other side. Their screech is even a signal of death. Because of my link to the owls, I think it's why I can talk to the dead."

She paused and glanced at him. The good news was the frown hadn't reappeared, but she still wasn't sure if he was convinced. "Kevin, I've never told anyone what I just said to you. Can you imagine the reaction from the Bureau? I'd be fired."

Cat wasn't sure what else she could say. She was uncomfortable and apprehensive about what she'd already disclosed.

"I can't entirely disbelieve since I've seen the results. Don't worry, I won't say anything," Kevin said. "Besides, if I tried to explain this to anyone else, they'd think *I* was the one who was nuts."

The entrance to the PD's parking lot was a lifeline to a drowning man. He needed time to consider the unthinkable. The idea of communicating with the dead was irrational and crazy. The owls added another bizarre element. Yet, on a level deep inside his mind, he seemed to connect to the possibility there was more to death than he knew. Somehow, after being with this woman for the last few days, the idea was not so outlandish.

When he walked through the door, Jessie waylaid Kevin with a stack of messages. He strode into his office, and Cat headed to the conference room. Ryan and Nicki had arrived. Files and computer equipment covered the large table. To her amazement, two laptops sat in front of Nicki. Evidently, the detectives decided to also make it their temporary office. Their computers were added to the mix.

Cat greeted everyone and pushed aside a pile of folders to make room at the end of the table for her briefcase. She pulled out the sketches. "I need to make copies of these. Where is the copier located?"

"I'll take care of it," Roger answered. Grinning, he stepped to a machine she missed seeing in the corner of the room. "Figured it would be easier to bring the copier to us."

When Kevin entered, Cat introduced him to Nicki and Ryan. Picking up the coffee pot, he asked, "Anything on the vet clinics?"

Ed said no, they hadn't found any reports of missing drugs.

Cat tacked a copy of the artist sketches on the board. "We interviewed the girls that were with Janet Lewis at the mall. They both saw this man. A few minutes before they reached the food court, he stared at Nancy through a store window. Amy spotted him in the food court area. The Vicksburg detectives are showing the sketch to the employees that were working when Lewis disappeared."

Kevin added, "Roger, Ed, take a drawing and head over to the

Burger Grill. One of the employees might remember him. Before you leave, I want to hear what Ryan has to say about the profile."

Ryan had been studying the sketches and glanced up at Kevin's comments. "A remarkable likeness to my description," he said, passing a stapled set of documents to everyone. "This is an updated profile based on the Texas and Louisiana homicides." For everyone's benefit, he reviewed the basics of the profile to include the criteria for a disorganized-style killer and his theory that the murders were a ritualistic kill.

He picked up his cup and took a sip before saying, "Kevin snapped on a key point. The cuts on Lewis and Benson were almost identical in position, length, and depth. We don't have measurements for the new victims. However, the pictures show a substantial similarity. The PTC may have worked at a meatpacking plant or in the meat section at a grocery store."

Kevin's cell phone rang. He held up a finger to stop Ryan's discussion.

"Hunter."

"Chief, it's Detective Brooks from Vicksburg PD. I have some info for you."

"Detective, I'm putting you on the speakerphone. I'm in a meeting with the task force and would like them to hear what you have to say. Go ahead."

"I contacted the employees who were working in the food court when Lewis disappeared. I located two witnesses who remembered a man that helped a woman walk away from a table. She appeared to be sick, stumbling, and bent over. The woman was wearing a jacket and a ball cap. They didn't see her face and couldn't identify her as Janet Lewis. They did identify the man as the suspect in the sketch. I'll email their contact information in case you want to talk to them. The security tapes from the mall's parking lot were checked when Lewis disappeared. We didn't find anyone who matched her description. We're reviewing them again, this time looking for the suspect in the sketch. How solid is your information? Is this the killer?"

"Detective Brooks, this is Cat Morgan. Yes, I am certain this is the man that killed Janet Lewis and at least three other women. We also believe he is driving a pickup if that will help in your analysis of the security tapes."

Brooks said he would contact them if he came up with any further information and disconnected.

"Pickup? How did you come up with that?" Nicki asked.

Cat explained her and Kevin's theory.

"Makes sense," Roger said.

Kevin said, "One other point—Cat suggested he is drugging their drinks. That's probably how he's able to control them. Ryan, anything else?"

"No, that's the sum of it for now," Ryan said.

Kevin looked at his two detectives. "Call me if you learn anything, otherwise head on home when you're done."

Rolling down the highway, his hand thumped the wheel to the pulsating blast of drums and guitars. Tonight, he'd troll the fast-food joints. He'd find someone to give him a free handout. Then he'd start his hunt again.

Up ahead, a sign flashed for Taco John. That sounded better than another hamburger, and maybe it wasn't a good idea to stop at the Burger Grill again.

Inside, the place was full of kids in uniforms. They hovered over the tables and wandered in and out of the game room. JD hesitated, then the aroma of the food hit. Hunger pushed back the sense of apprehension. Shoulders hunched forward and head down to avoid eye contact, he waited in line.

"Hey! Can I help you?"

JD looked up. The kid behind the counter was talking to him.

"I … uh … don't have any money. Can you help me out and give me a meal?" he mumbled.

The kid stared at him for several seconds before walking to a man who stood by one of the grills. The kid pointed, and the man looked at JD. He couldn't hear what was said, but the kid picked up a wrapped taco and put it, along with a cup, on a tray.

When he set it down on the counter, he said, "The manager said you could have this."

You bastard, this isn't my idea of a meal. They could have given him more than one lousy taco. Picking up the two items, he left the tray on the counter and turned to move to the soda dispenser. Glancing at the woman behind him, a surge of exhilaration flowed through him. Another one.

Eleven

Turning off the engine, Cindy leaned her head against the headrest. She was exhausted. Her day had started at six in the morning. Twelve hours, most of which she'd been on her feet. A multiple car accident on the freeway resulted in nine casualties, all hitting the emergency room, one behind the other. Since it was touch and go for several of the victims, the day shift stayed late. Too tired to even think about fixing a meal, it was a Taco John night.

When she entered, a blast of teenage voices reverberated in a room full of band members. Several stood in line, waiting to order. A groan erupted at the idea of the added time on her feet. She turned to leave, then decided driving to another location would take longer than if she waited.

Then, if her day hadn't been crappy enough, she was behind a man who stunk. The foul body odor permeated the air. When he begged for a handout, she figured he was homeless, probably hadn't bathed in weeks.

The young man at the cash register took her order and gave her a number. Grabbing the cup off the counter, she filled it, then scanned the room for an empty table. When she sat ... no ... more like collapsed, she sighed with relief. *Oh, this feels so good. I may not move until tomorrow.* She wiggled her toes and wondered whether she could stay awake long enough to soak her feet once she got home.

JD sat at a table in the back of the room and studied her. He liked how this one looked. Slim, dressed in a loose uniform, the type they wore in a hospital, her red hair tumbled over her shoulders.

He swallowed the last bite of the taco as she crossed the room to a table on the other side. He'd already removed the bottle from his coat pocket. Opening it, he held it ready in his hand.

The kid behind the counter called a number, and her head turned. When she stood, he was on his feet. Tossing his cup and wrapper in a trash receptacle, he headed to her table.

No lid, another easy one. He leaned over the table to pick up the saltshaker. His body covered her cup, and he dumped the contents of the vial into her drink. After dropping the empty container in his coat pocket, he slipped it off, sat, and waited. A wave of anticipation flowed through him.

Picking up the tray, she turned and spotted the homeless man at the table behind hers. *Hell! I don't like this. Why'd he move from across the room?* Setting the tray on another table closer to the door, she walked back, picked up her cup, and took a long sip.

Cindy always carried a book tucked in the side pocket of her purse. After propping it open in front of the tray, she bit into the taco. As she chewed, the print began to blur. *I must be more tired than I realized* and rubbed her eyes. When she tried to refocus, everything on the table was warped. *What's happening?* The light in the room started to pulsate. Dizzy, her stomach churned. Panic seared through her as her medical expertise screamed in her head. *Drugged! I've been drugged!*

The distorted face of a man floated in front of her. A distant voice said, "Darling, you're getting sick again. I'll slip my coat around you and get you outside. Fresh air is what you need."

Something slipped over her shoulders. An arm slid around her, then pulled her from the booth. As she felt the touch of cool air on her face, the arm tightened, pushing her arms against her body. Her feet scraped the ground.

Dear God, he's dragging me across the parking lot. She couldn't stop him. Terror tore its way through her body and into her mind. She fought the black mist that circled around her. With her last remnant of energy, she screamed, "NO! NO! Don't touch me." As her mind faded into oblivion, she wondered—*did I even make a sound?*

Ed and Roger headed to the Burger Grill with the sketches. Kevin and Ryan were in a discussion on the criteria Ryan had used for the profile.

"Nicki, did you find any registrations for yellow bugs?" Cat asked.

"I found seven either in Clinton or the surrounding area. Yellow seems to be a popular color," Nicki said. "I printed the registrations for each," and handed her a stack of papers.

Cat thanked her and spread the documents in front of her. Studying them, she selected three owners who lived near the Burger Grill.

Kevin's phone rang.

"Hunter."

"Chief, this is Dolores in dispatch. I have two officers enroute to a disturbance at Taco John. The caller said a woman was being dragged across the parking lot."

Kevin had told the dispatchers to contact him on any suspicious calls involving a woman. "Any other information?"

"No. I've tried to reestablish the call, but there's no answer."

Kevin disconnected. He relayed the dispatcher's information to the agents while tapping the speed dial for Roger.

"Roger, dispatch called. There's a disturbance involving a woman in the parking lot of Taco John. Swing by there on your way to the Grill."

He listened for a minute and then disconnected the call. "It may not be related to our case. Still, they are only a few minutes from the location and can check for certain."

An icy chill started in Cat's chest as she listened. It's happened. The killer had found his next victim. "How do I get to the restaurant?"

When Kevin looked at her, Cat felt a momentary tingle as they stared at each other.

Kevin nodded his head as if to acknowledge her premonition and said, "I'll take you."

She powered down her laptop, picked up her files, and stuffed them into her briefcase.

"I need a minute to load up, and I'll go with you," Nicki said.

Ryan nodded in agreement. He scooped his reports off the table, and like Cat shoved them in his case.

As the four reached the parking lot, Kevin's phone rang again. As he listened, his face lost all expression, his eyes bleak and grim.

"I'm on my way," and disconnected. "That was Ed. They're at the location. There was an attempt to kidnap a woman. She's on her way to the emergency room. Her name is Cindy Arp. Ed showed the picture to the witnesses, and the suspect matches the sketch."

"I want to go to the hospital. Since you're headed to the crime scene, Ryan can go with me and Nicki with you," Cat said.

When Cat and Ryan entered the emergency room, medics were moving patients from two ambulances into the ER. They had to wait until a nurse was available. Holding up her badge case, Cat explained they were checking on the condition of a patient involved in an assault.

When she said,

Cindy Arp, the nurse exclaimed, "Oh, Cindy, she's one of our ER nurses. Her condition is critical. They are still running tests to find out what is wrong."

Cat said, "Tell the doctor to check for ketamine."

Though a look of disbelief crossed the nurse's face at the possibility Cat could identify the reason for her colleague's condition, she agreed to relay the information to the doctor.

Ryan leaned against the side of the nurse's station. Cat was too wired to stand still. Angry and frustrated, she paced. What seemed hours was around thirty minutes before a man in blue scrubs finally approached them.

He asked if they were the FBI agents. When they nodded, he stuck out his hand. "Dr. Carter."

Cat shook his hand and introduced herself and Ryan, then asked, "How is Cindy Arp?"

"She was unconscious when the ambulance arrived though she's awake now and somewhat lucid. She is still experiencing hallucinations and having difficulty breathing. We're moving her to intensive care."

"Did you find ketamine in her system?" Ryan asked.

"Yes, I did. I had already run a toxicology test but didn't have the results. After receiving your information to check for ketamine, I ran another test to detect its presence, and it came back positive. I immediately started her on a series of drugs to counteract its effects."

He stopped, a look of gratitude replaced his somber demeanor, then continued. "Without your information, it would have taken longer to identify the cause of her collapse. The delay could have been deadly. How did you know it was ketamine?"

"The man who attempted to abduct her uses the drug to subdue his victims. Somehow, she escaped. Can we talk to her?" Cat asked.

"Once the nurse gets her settled in ICU, you can go in. It should only be a few minutes. A nurse will escort you. I'm not sure what she'll remember."

Cat pulled her phone from her pocket and called Kevin.

His voice abrupt and impatient, he said, "Hunter."

"It's Cat. She's alive. She had ketamine in her system. The doctor is going to let us talk to her. What's happened on your end?"

"There are several witnesses, and we're getting their statements. It's definitely the suspect in the sketch. The manager and order clerk identified him. They gave him a free meal. Another witness said the PTC helped the victim walk out the door. He put his coat around her and called her darling. Because of the man's appearance, the witness thought it was unusual. But when the woman didn't protest, he didn't pay any more attention until she screamed. He and two others ran outside. The killer was dragging her across the lot. When he saw the witnesses, he dropped her and a purse, then grabbed his coat and ran behind the building."

"Did anyone spot his vehicle?" Cat asked.

"No. There's an exit to the side street from the back parking lot. By the time one of the witnesses thought to look, the man was gone, and there are no security cameras. Since I'm not sure how long we'll be here, let's plan on meeting early tomorrow morning," Kevin told her. "There's no reason to go back to the PD tonight."

A nurse approached them, and Cat said she'd call if she learned anything new.

Inside the ICU, cords and tubes connected the woman to an array of machines. Tangled red hair framed a pasty-white face. Beads of sweat glistened on her forehead. The doctor stood by her bed.

"It will be difficult for her to talk, so you need to keep it short for tonight. She should be more responsive tomorrow." Carter leaned forward. "Cindy, someone wants to talk to you."

Her eyes slowly opened. Glazed, they twitched as she stared upward.

Stepping to the side of the bed, Cat realized she was still under the influence of the drug. "Cindy, I'm Special Agent Morgan. Can you hear me?"

The woman's eyes drifted toward the sound of Cat's voice. "Yes."

"What happened tonight?"

The woman's eyes closed.

"Cindy," Cat said. When her eyes reopened, Cat repeated the question.

"Not sure … tacos, lights … drugged." Her voice, weak and raspy, trailed off as her eyes closed again.

Ryan stood quietly by the bed and watched Cat. Her calm and soothing demeanor was a stark contrast to the earlier agitation she had exhibited in the waiting room.

Her voice soft, Cat said, "Do you remember anything else?"

The woman's eyes opened, and she tried to focus on Cat's face. "Someone ... dragging me, not right ... not rig ...." Her head rolled to the side.

Dr. Carter stepped up and told Cat they would need to come back the next day. She handed him a business card and requested to be notified if there was any change in Cindy's condition.

An overwhelming sense of relief washed over Cat when they walked out of the room. This victim had escaped. They wouldn't find her dead and discarded like trash.

Panic churned as sweat rolled down his back. JD didn't understand. The drug always worked, and they did what he told them. None of the others had fought him. Now, his heart raced, and he couldn't catch his breath. His hands shook on the wheel. Excruciating pricks of pain pulsed in his head, making it difficult to think. Did anyone get a good look at him? He had to leave. It was time to move on anyway. Right now, he needed a fix as he parked next to the trailer.

Inside, he popped a Vicodin, then collapsed on the bed. Curled into a ball, he gripped his amulet and waited for the soothing relief of the drug. Through the small window, he watched the moon creep across the sky. He had failed. He couldn't let it happen again.

Twelve

A pale moon rose, rivulets of blood spilled over its surface. It spun against a black sky, and droplets fell like rain. The beat of wings reverberated in the night air, and the frantic screeches turned into the strident ring of the hotel phone. The canned voice said seven a.m.

While images of the nightmare replayed in her head, she rubbed her face, and a deep sigh signaled her frustration. *One victim escaped, but I know he will be on the hunt again, maybe even tonight.*

Ryan and Nicki were at a table when she walked into the hotel's buffet section. With a cup of coffee in one hand and a plate of eggs and a muffin in the other, she joined them.

She said, "I called the hospital. Cindy's condition's been upgraded. The nurse said if she continues to improve, they'll move her out of ICU today. The doctor left instructions I could talk to her this morning."

Nicki pushed her empty plate aside and said, "We were discussing what made her fight back. Ryan thinks it was her medical experience. She recognized the symptoms in time to react."

Cat said, "I would agree. Drugged was one of the few words she used to describe what happened last night."

"At least we have positive confirmation on the sketch. There was no hesitation in the witness identifications," Nicki said.

"Ryan, do you think this will spook him? Make him move on to another town?" Cat asked.

"It's highly likely. He has to be afraid that someone saw him this time."

For a few seconds, there was a depressing silence, then Cat said, "Damn! If we lose him, it could take weeks or even months to pick up his track again. How many more women will die?" Cat pushed her half-eaten plate of food aside. "Just wish someone had spotted his vehicle."

"Evidently, he was parked at the back of the lot behind the building. Kevin and his detectives hammered this point with the witnesses. God, what a mess that was. There were quite a few teenagers. They were part of some local band and boy, were they wound-up. Probably the most excitement they'd ever seen. Getting them settled down and keeping them separated wasn't an easy task."

Cat's phone rang. Kevin's icon appeared on the screen. "You're up early," Cat said.

"I'm already at the office. I wanted to finish the reports from last night. Did you call the hospital?"

"Yeah. Cindy's doing better. The nurse said I'd be able to talk to her this morning."

"I'll meet you at the hospital."

When she passed through the revolving doors, Kevin leaned against the front desk, talking to the receptionist. His smile sent a warm tingle through her limbs. Whether she wanted to admit it or not, the magnetism this man exuded enticed her, unlike anyone she had ever encountered.

"They've already moved her out of ICU," Kevin told her.

As they walked along the hallway, Cat said, "She was still under the influence of the drug last night. I couldn't get many details. I'm hoping she may remember more this morning."

When they entered, the young woman was semi-upright on the bed. While her face was tired and ashen, her gaze was alert and focused.

Cindy looked at Cat, her voice low and raspy. "I saw you last night. At least, I think I did. My memory seems to have gaps."

"Yes, you did, not long after you arrived at the hospital. I'm Special Agent Cat Morgan, and I'm sure you know Chief Hunter."

The woman turned her head toward Kevin. "Chief Hunter. You may not recall, but we've met. One of your officers was injured not too long ago, and I spoke to you in the emergency room."

Kevin smiled at her. "Yes, I do. I also recall how you helped the officer's family."

"Can you tell me what happened?" Cindy asked.

Kevin responded, "Before we do, tell us what you remember from yesterday."

"I've been lying here trying to do just that. A lot is a blur."

"Start with what you remember," Kevin said.

"We had all those victims from that horrific crash on the freeway. Everyone on the day shift stayed late to help."

Kevin said, "One of the worst we've had for some time. Several of my officers also worked overtime to finish the investigation and reopen the freeway. Where did you go when you left?"

"I was exhausted and headed home. The taco place is on the way, so I stopped. When I saw all those kids inside, I almost turned around and left. God, how I wish I had. I got my food, and after a couple of bites, my vision blurred. Then I got dizzy and nauseated. When I started to hallucinate, I knew I'd been drugged."

When she reached for the cup of water on the bed stand, her hand trembled. Cat picked up the cup and held the straw as Cindy took a sip.

"Thank you. My throat is raw from the tube used to pump my stomach."

She took another couple of sips, then said, "A man called me darling and pulled me outside. I knew it was wrong, but from there, it's a blank."

Kevin asked, "Can you describe him?"

She shook her head. "No, his face was wavy, distorted. After I got my food, everything is a blur."

"When you got there, did you notice anyone who looked out of place?" Cat asked.

Cindy frowned as she concentrated. "There was a man ahead of me in the food line. Terrible body odor and dirty. I ordered my food and sat at a table across the room from him. This sounds awful, but I didn't want to be close to the smell."

"I understand," Cat said. It's why she carried a small jar of mentholated ointment in her police kit. A dab under her nose helped to cover up a lot of foul smells.

"When I came back from picking up my food, he'd moved to a table behind me." She paused again. After a few seconds, she continued, "I'm not sure why it made me uneasy, but I went to another table."

"Can you remember anything else about his appearance?" Cat asked.

"A dirty coat and ball cap, beard ... oh, and a ponytail. It hung over his collar."

Kevin asked, "Did you get your drink with your meal or before?"

Cindy glanced at him with a questioning look on her face as she answered. "Since I had to wait for my food order, I went ahead and filled my cup."

"Where was it when you left the table, did you take it with you?" he asked.

"No, I left it on the table. Someone drugged it. That's what happened, isn't it? The one you're asking about, he did it," she exclaimed.

Kevin replied, "Several witnesses said you were outside in the parking lot and screamed. People ran out, and you were struggling with a man who fits the description of the person you described."

"Do you have any idea what drug was used?"

Kevin hesitated before saying, "We believe it was ketamine."

Distressed, her voice rose. "Ketamine! Oh, my god! That's the drug the M.E. found in the two women who were murdered." Tears trickled over her cheeks. "I was the next victim!"

Cat grabbed several tissues. As Cindy wiped her eyes, Cat held the cup of water. "Take another sip," then turned to Kevin. "Would you get a wet washcloth from the bathroom?"

He quickly complied, handing the cloth to Cat, who folded it and laid it across Cindy's forehead.

She moved it against her eyes and leaned her head back against the pillow. "Thank you, this helps. Chief, you might make a good nurse. You're good at following orders," she said as she struggled to regain her composure.

Kevin chuckled. "Nope, wouldn't have the patience."

After a few seconds, Cindy wiped her face and laid the cloth on the bed stand. "I'm okay, though I'm not certain I'll ever forget the terror I felt. Knowing what might have happened makes it even more devastating."

Cat pulled the artist's sketch from her briefcase. "Is this the man you saw in the restaurant?"

Cindy studied the picture for several seconds. "Yes, that's him."

Both agents glanced at the door when it opened. Dr. Carter greeted them as he walked to the side of the bed. "You've improved from when I last saw you. How do you feel?"

"Nauseous, and at times disoriented."

"Another day, and it should be gone. You can't lie around here forever, everyone in the emergency room is already wondering when you will be back," he said while peering into her eyes.

Cindy managed a halfhearted smile.

"Much better, I'd hate for you to lose that smile."

He picked up her wrist. "What set off your pulse?"

"Chief Hunter believes I may have been drugged with ketamine. Is he right?"

"Yes," the doctor replied. Cindy was one of the most competent and knowledgeable nurses at the hospital. He couldn't gloss over the details. If she didn't like his answers, she'd grab her chart.

"The last test showed a slight trace is still in your system. It's why

I want you to stay for another day. You can thank Agent Morgan for your quick recovery. She got to the emergency room right after you arrived and alerted me to check for ketamine. Her information saved considerable time in counteracting the drug."

Cindy looked at Cat. "How did you know?"

"Chief Hunter had his dispatchers contact him on any report involving a missing or assaulted woman. Two of his detectives were near the restaurant and arrived a few minutes after the ambulance left for the hospital. Based on what the officers found, we suspected you'd been drugged with ketamine."

Her look of gratitude now included Kevin when she said, "I'm not sure I can ever repay you."

"Seeing you alive is enough. One of my detectives will be here later today to get an official statement and to return your purse."

He laid his business card on the bed stand. "If you remember anything else, call me, day or night."

As they left the hospital, Kevin said, "He missed with this one. How long before he tries again?"

"It will be soon if we don't find him first," she said.

When they entered Kevin's office, Jessie greeted them and handed Kevin a message. "The mayor's secretary called."

With a grimace, he read it. He glanced at Cat and said, "I'll be gone for a while." He grabbed several files from his desk and walked out the door.

Surprised at Kevin's abrupt manner, Cat turned to Jessie. "Everything okay?"

Jessie sighed. "There have been problems since Mort Bingham was elected mayor. The Chief's never happy when he's called to his office."

She wanted to ask more questions then decided it wasn't her concern. Besides, it could make Jessie uncomfortable to answer her inquiries regarding Kevin.

In the conference room, Ryan and Nicki were on their computers. Both looked up and greeted her.

"How's our victim?" Ryan asked.

"She's doing great and should go home tomorrow." Cat dropped her gear on the table and walked to the coffee machine.

"Damn, that's good news. Did you learn anything new?" Ryan asked.

"She saw the PTC in line ahead of her. However, she couldn't say for sure he was the one that dragged her outside."

"Her cup was still on the table. The lab test came back positive for ketamine, which confirms your theory the killer drugs his victim's drinks. I'm running the sketch through a facial recognition program. So far, no matches," Nicki said. Her computer beeped, and she turned back to the screen.

Cat set the cup on the table and pulled out her laptop. "Where are Roger and Ed?"

Ryan replied, "They found a report of a burglary at a vet clinic near Monroe, Louisiana. Money and drugs were stolen. They left to talk to the owner and the detective handling the investigation."

"Guys, two more responses to the agency alert just came in. Both state they have a victim that matches our description. The reports are coming. One is from Monroe PD," Nicki said.

Cat pulled up Monroe on her laptop. "Damn! Monroe is halfway between Clinton and Minden, where another victim was found. Anyone want to take a bet the killer and burglar is the same person?"

"I'll pass on that one," Ryan said.

Cat still wanted to talk to the owners of the yellow Volkswagens. A few taps on the keyboard and she had phone numbers and addresses. The calls rolled to voice mail. If she didn't receive a response to the message she left, she'd try again that evening.

"Nicki, did you find any other registrations?" When there was no answer, she glanced to find out why. When the team first met, Nicki had warned everyone about what she laughingly called her 'computer zone.' From the intense look of concentration as she studied her screen, Nicki was in the zone.

"Bingo! I found the symbol carved on the forehead," Nicki said as the printer spewed paper. "This new program lets me overlay bits and pieces of pictures. It's like constructing a 3D jigsaw puzzle on a computer. I deconstructed the incisions on the forehead and reassembled them in a different pattern." She grabbed the paper and handed copies to Ryan and Cat.

As Cat studied the image, a crescent with the tips up that sat on top of a circle, she asked, "What the hell is it?"

"It's a horned god and is the symbol for the lord of the underworld who controls life and death. I found several references when I researched satanic rituals for the profile," Ryan said, picking up a file from the stack on the desk. "It's prominent in many religions, some date back hundreds of years. The symbol has numerous names."

He pulled several sheets from the folder. "Ah, here it is. The most common are the Old One and Master. One reference indicated the Horned God must shed blood, so life can continue and draws its power from the moon."

Cat gasped.

He stopped and looked at her. "What?"

To give herself a few minutes to think, she got up and refilled her cup. She didn't want to mention her dreams of bloody moons.

Ryan looked at Nicki, eyebrows raised. Nicki shrugged her shoulders and grinned. Both wondered if this was to be another witchy revelation.

With a thoughtful look on her face, Cat dropped into her chair. "You mentioned the moon, and that struck a chord in my head." Her fingers tapped the table. "Ryan, is it possible the ritual is tied to the moon?"

"It won't take long to set up a program to compare the abduction dates to the moon's cycle," Ryan said.

Nicki listened to the conversation while paper continued to print. This time, it was the reports on the new victims. She thumbed through them, stopping to study the photos. "You can add two more to your timeline. Glad I didn't take a bet on the Monroe victim; the other is in Weatherford, Texas," she said, handing the stack of paper to Cat.

While they reviewed the new reports, Nicki pinned the pictures of the latest victims on the murder board.

Cat summarized the details. "Same pattern as the other victims. Both abducted at night, one from a mall and the other was at a bookstore. Death was due to a loss of blood from numerous cuts on the arms, wrists, and forehead. There's no doubt, it's the same killer. My god, how many more victims are out there that we haven't located?"

Thirteen

Outside, the air was cool and crisp. Kevin drew in a deep breath and pushed back the anger that threatened to erupt every time he was forced to meet the mayor. With two unsolved homicides, he was surprised he hadn't already received a call demanding his presence.

Bingham was a malicious and vindictive individual. It started several years ago when one of his officers arrested Bingham's son for drunk driving. At the time, Bingham was on the city council, and Kevin was a Sergeant and in line for the next Lieutenant's opening. Bingham told him to get the charge dismissed, or there wouldn't be a promotion. Kevin had refused, and since then, the man took every opportunity to smear his reputation. When he applied for the chief's position, Bingham was the only councilman who vehemently opposed his appointment. After the man won the mayor's election, he used his position to harass and criticize Kevin's every action.

Since City Hall was only five blocks away, he decided to walk rather than drive. The sun warmed his face, and the light breeze lifted his hair, causing the tips to tickle his neck as he strode along the sidewalk. Though Kevin greeted other pedestrians with a friendly grin and wave, his thoughts centered around his suspicions over the election. He never understood how the man had won. The predictions favored his opponent. Instead, it was a victory for Bingham. Kevin suspected election fraud and had been investigating the results. So far, he'd found nothing. His cop gut told him to keep digging. Once he found the evidence, he planned to wrap it around Bingham's thick neck. A corrupt politician sat high on Kevin's list of dislikes.

His secretary, Liz Watson, told him to have a seat. The mayor was on a conference call.

Since there was always a reason to make Kevin wait, he was confident the call was a ploy. The man liked to play power games and never realized Kevin was aware of his petty tricks. The time wouldn't be wasted as he'd use it to review the reports on the investigation.

The secretary's phone buzzed. After a short conversation, she hung up and looked at Kevin. "The mayor will see you now."

"Thank you, Liz," and continued to read. He smiled to himself, *two can play this game.* After several minutes, he closed the case file, stepped to Bingham's door, and knocked.

The oversize desk the mayor had purchased filled the room. For some incomprehensible reason, the man believed the big desk added to his stature. Kevin had to admit he needed help. Five-eight, and at least two-hundred pounds, his face resembled a bulldog with its heavy jowls and short, thick neck. A spider web of broken blood vessels spread over his nose and cheeks, and he did the comb-over bit to hide the bald spot on his head.

When Kevin entered, Bingham said in a loud and abrasive voice, "What the hell is the FBI doing in my city?"

He slowly strode to the chair in front of the desk, sat, and crossed his legs as he stared at the mayor. The question surprised him. Bingham enjoyed forcing him to justify his department's actions, always looking for a reason to fire him. He expected a demand for the details of the investigation. Instead, Bingham was concerned about the FBI's involvement. *I wonder who told him?*

Impatient at Kevin's silence, he said, "Hunter, I asked you a question, and I expect an answer."

His voice calm, Kevin replied, "It's not unusual for a criminal investigation to involve multiple agencies. Two women have been murdered. The FBI is providing computer and forensic resources. I would presume your primary concern would be the capture of the man responsible for their deaths, not whether another agency is involved in the investigation."

Bingham's face turned an even deeper shade of red. "Who authorized it?"

"I did."

"You stepped across the line on this one. You should have gotten my approval before you went crying for help. The FBI has no business poking their noses into an investigation in my city. It doesn't look good that we can't handle our business. Tell them to get the hell out of my town."

Now isn't this interesting! Why does their presence bother you, and why do you want them to leave?

"I can't do that," Kevin replied.

"That sounds like insubordination and grounds for disciplinary action. Hunter, this is another example of your lax supervision and incompetence as police chief. Your personnel file will be so noted. Since you refuse to order them to stop their activities, I will. I am the mayor of this city. I decide who conducts investigations."

Bingham had threatened Kevin on numerous occasions. This was the first time he said he would tamper with Kevin's personnel file. It was a threat he couldn't dismiss.

Kevin stood, laid his hands on the desk, and leaned toward Bingham. A look of panic appeared on the mayor's face when he stared into Kevin's eyes. He rapidly pushed his chair back.

His voice cold and menacing, Kevin said, "Any negative information added to my personnel file will be sent to the Attorney General's integrity unit. If the audit proves there was malicious intent, civil or criminal charges will be filed against the person responsible for the alteration."

The mayor's voice squeaked. "You sorry bastard, no one walks into my office and dictates terms to me! I'll have your badge for this."

A surge of rage rolled over Kevin. Picking up the files he'd left on his chair, he moved to the door.

Bingham shouted, "Don't you walk out of this office! Damn it, I demand to know what's going on."

Kevin glanced over his shoulder. "I'll provide the specifics of the investigation when they can be made public and not before," and walked out.

He was glad he had a few blocks to settle his anger and frustration before reaching his office. He hated to disclose the controversy with the mayor. Still, there was no choice, he had to inform the agents. His main concern was not to let the mayor impede the search for the PTC.

TV trucks were pulling into the PD's parking lot as he turned the corner. *Hell, this is all I need.* The news media was an unavoidable hazard. When he strode across the lot, the reporters converged as they jostled for position to stick a microphone under his nose while shouting questions. He pushed through the crowd and moved to the front steps.

He held up one hand and waited. When they finally shut up, he said, "We have two women whose deaths appear to be connected. Our investigation is ongoing, and I cannot release any details."

A reporter at the back of the pack shouted a question. "Chief Hunter, why is the FBI in town? Is your department not competent to handle the investigation of the homicides?"

Kevin recognized the man. He worked for the local newspaper and covered City Hall and the mayor's office. *A planted question. I have Bingham to thank for my sudden popularity.*

"The Clinton Police Department's detective unit is more than qualified. Their closure rate on cases is higher than the national average. What the FBI adds to this case are computer and forensic resources. The issue is the apprehension of the individual responsible for the death of two women, not who is involved in the investigation."

He turned and walked into the building. When he opened the outer door to his office, Jessie looked up from her computer and grinned.

She knew he hated press conferences.

"They didn't trickle in, they hit in mass," she told him.

"I suspect someone tipped them off to our investigation. Is everyone in the conference room?"

"Ed and Roger are not back yet. The three agents are there," Jessie said, reaching to answer the phone.

Kevin paused when he heard Jessie tell the caller that Chief Hunter had just arrived. Putting the call on hold, she said, "It's Scott Fleming with the FBI."

Great, I bet Bingham's already called him as he strode to his desk. "Chief Hunter."

"Chief, Scott Fleming. I just received an unexpected call from Mayor Bingham."

His voice harsh, Kevin said, "I bet you did."

"He demanded I withdraw my agents and claims the investigation has been compromised because of difficulties between your officers and my agents."

"I'm not surprised he contacted you. Bingham ordered me to terminate your personnel's involvement in the homicide investigation. I refused. His accusations are false. There's not a problem between my department and your agents."

"I know. I informed Bingham he was out of line, and my agents were staying. If he had any further complaints, I would have the governor call him."

Before ending the call, Kevin provided an update on the investigation, most of which Fleming knew. It reaffirmed Kevin's first impression of the man. He was a supervisor who stayed informed without hindering his personnel.

Kevin leaned back in his chair. Incensed, he pondered the mayor's interference. *Son-of-a-bitch!* Another attack on the integrity of his department and officers. It wasn't until he considered the phone call from Fleming that the anger faded. Scott telling Bingham to stuff it was more than he could handle. The laughter rolled out of him as he headed to the conference room.

Cat and Ryan both looked up and greeted Kevin. Nicki was deep into her computer program and unaware someone had entered the room.

"The media are camped in the parking lot," Kevin told them.

Ryan said, "Bound to happen, though I wish it could have been later. It's their task to report though it can complicate an investigation."

"Yeah, you're right, since this case just got worse," Cat replied.

Eyebrows raised, Kevin's look questioned her. He wondered if her boss had already called about Bingham.

Cat said, "Nicki received information on two more victims. One in Weatherford, Texas, the other is in Monroe. There may be a connection between the burglary at the vet clinic and our PTC. If Roger and Ed are still there, it would be a good idea to have them talk to the homicide detective."

"Damn, do we have the police reports?" Kevin asked.

"Yes. The victim's pictures are on the board," Ryan answered.

Kevin stepped up to the murder board and studied the new photographs. "It's the same killer. Those knife wounds are almost identical to our other victims."

Pulling his phone from his shirt pocket, he keyed in a number. "Roger, it's Hunter. Are you still in Monroe?"

He looked at Cat and nodded his head yes.

"There's another victim, and it happened in Monroe. Check your laptop. You should have the reports in a few minutes. Contact the detective that handled the case. See what you can find out."

He listened and then said, "Do you have Cat's number? Good. If you can't reach me, call her."

He disconnected. "Just caught them, they were leaving town. They'd given a copy of the sketch to the detective handling the burglary but will make sure the lead investigator on the homicide has a copy."

Cat said, "Give me their email addresses, and I'll forward the reports."

Jessie stuck her head in the door. "Wanted to let you know most of the TV and news trucks are gone. Anyone interested in lunch? There's a deli that delivers."

Cat tapped Nicki's shoulder.

"We're ordering sandwiches. Do you want one?" Cat asked.

Nicki looked up and saw Kevin. "Oh, hi. When did you get here?"

Ryan and Cat looked at each other and grinned.

Jessie wrote everyone's request on a small pad. Kevin told her to charge it to the department.

"Nicki identified the symbol on the forehead," Ryan said.

Kevin looked up from the reports spread across the table as Ryan handed him a drawing. "What the hell is it?"

"Glad someone else doesn't know what it is. I don't feel like such an idiot," Cat said.

"A horned god," Nicki replied.

"Okay, who is going to explain what a horned god is?" Kevin asked.

Ryan ran over the details, saying, "I've added the info to the profile."

"Kevin, do you have a chalkboard we can use?" Cat asked.

"Uh … yeah." He dropped the drawing on the table. "There's one in the detective's office. I'll get it."

"I'll go with you," Ryan said.

Cat pulled up the telephone number for the Weatherford Police Department and put in a call to the police chief. He was in a meeting. She left a callback message.

The two men rolled the chalkboard into the room, pushing it against the only wall that had any space left.

"Six locations so far." Grabbing a piece of chalk, she wrote across the top—Texas with two towns, Weatherford, and Canton. Then Minden and Monroe, Louisiana, and finally the two in Mississippi,

Vicksburg, and Clinton were added. "What's the date for the Weatherford murder and the abduction and dump site?"

Searching in the stack of files, Ryan said, "Texas ... where is ... here it is, Lori Taylor, September of last year, bookstore and left in a bin at a rest stop."

Cat wrote the details on the board.

Nicki had grabbed the next file. "Canton, Naomi York, November, and mall. Another dumpster, this time behind a restaurant," she said.

Ryan was ready with the next one. "Minden, Donna Landon, March, mall, and dumpster." He waited while she wrote, then added, "Monroe, Carrie Williams, fast food, July, and a county dump site."

Cat added the Benson, Lewis, and Arp information under Vicksburg and Clinton. She looked at Ryan. "This is our base timeline."

"He's traveling the interstate. Considering the time gap between the victims, I bet there are more we haven't located. I suggest we send out another alert to every agency within a hundred-mile radius of the freeway," Kevin said.

Turning to her computer, Nicki said, "I'm on it."

"A bookstore. How the hell did he drug a drink in a bookstore?" Cat asked.

"Here's how. I pulled up the store's website. They have a cafe," Ryan answered.

Jessie entered with a large sack and a cardboard tray filled with cups.

While everyone grabbed their sandwich and drink, Kevin pondered the problem with Bingham. Airing what he perceived was dirty linen did not sit well with him.

"This morning, Mayor Bingham ordered me to terminate the FBI's involvement in this case. He wants you out of town. When I refused, he called your boss, claiming interagency friction had interfered with the investigation. Scott didn't buy into his argument and told him his agents were staying."

Startled, the agents stared at Kevin.

"This is a first. Never knew a civilian official to object," Ryan said.

Kevin added, "There are issues between the mayor and me."

Cat's cell phone rang. It was the Weatherford police chief. Since Nicki had already talked to him, she didn't have to go into a lengthy explanation when she requested a search for any unusual or unexplained deaths in the past five years.

When she disconnected the call, she intercepted the grins Ryan and Nicki exchanged.

"What!"

"Wondering why the search?" Nicki said.

"So far, Weatherford is the first location. We might find the trigger event," Cat said.

Her phone rang again. This time, it was Betsy Miller, one of the yellow Volkswagen owners. She lived on the north side of Clinton and agreed to meet with Cat.

Kevin looked at her with raised eyebrows.

Cat shrugged her shoulders. "It's just a hunch, may turn out to be nothing."

Ryan kept his mouth shut. *No comments on witchy women from me.*

Jessie stuck her head in the room and reminded Kevin he had a staff meeting. Even though he had rearranged his schedule to allow time for the investigation, he couldn't miss this one. Personnel issues were on the agenda. He tossed the remains of his sandwich in the trash and headed out the door.

Cat packed up her case files, laptop, and left to meet the bug's owner. She'd forgotten reporters still lurked in the parking lot. Two made a beeline to intercept her before she reached her car. Microphones were shoved in front of her, and a camera crew filmed from behind. They wanted to know if she was one of the FBI agents, and what was the status of the hunt for the killer.

"Yes, I'm Special Agent Morgan. I can't discuss any elements of the investigation."

The two reporters continued to bombard her with questions as she got into her car.

On the way to the Miller residence, she received a call from Martha Anderson, another Volkswagen owner, and set up a second meeting.

She pulled in front of a bungalow style house. Parked in the driveway was a yellow Volkswagen. When Cat approached the front door, it opened, and a young woman greeted her.

"Are you Agent Morgan?"

Cat pulled her badge case from her pocket and identified herself.

"How can I help you?"

"I'm investigating an incident at the Burger Grill on Southside St. Have you ever eaten there?"

"Why, no, I haven't. What happened?"

"A young woman was abducted."

"Oh, how awful. Why did you contact me?"

"A yellow Volkswagen was seen in the parking lot. The driver may be a witness."

"I'm sorry. I wish I could help."

Cat thanked her for her time.

Martha Anderson worked for a real estate agency. A yellow Volkswagen was parked near the front door. Cat identified herself to the receptionist, who directed her to a desk near the front window.

The woman looked up when Cat approached. She introduced herself and flipped open her badge case. Seated in the chair next to the desk, she explained her investigation of an incident at the Burger Grill. "Have you ever eaten there?"

"Yes, two or three times a month. I have several listings in that section of town. If I have a showing, I usually stop and pick up a takeout order."

Cat's heart raced. *Oh, please, let this be the break we need.* She gave her the date and asked if she remembered stopping there that day.

The woman reached for her calendar. "I was there several days ago, but I can check my schedule and tell you for sure if it was the same day." She flipped the pages and nodded her head. "Yes, I met a young couple who were looking for their first house."

"A young woman was abducted ..."

The realtor interrupted. "Oh, I remember a news feature on a kidnapped woman who had been murdered. The reporter didn't mention a restaurant. Was it the Burger Grill?"

"Yes," Cat replied, handing the woman a picture of Susan Benson.

"Oh, how terribly sad, such an attractive girl. No, I never saw her. I was talking on the phone to a client while I waited for my order and wasn't paying attention to anyone else inside."

Cat handed her the artist sketch of the suspect.

The woman leaned back in her chair and studied it for several seconds. "Yes, I did see him. I was getting into my car. He came around the corner of the building and headed to the front door. There is additional parking behind the Grill. Dear God, did he kill her?" She handed back the sketch.

"He's a person of interest we want to locate. When you left, which way did you go?"

"I drove around the back of the building and exited on a side street."

"Were there any cars in the parking lot?"

"Hmm ... a white Honda was parked next to me. It caught my eye because I test drove one before buying my car."

Susan Benson's vehicle. "Any others?"

The realtor hesitated before continuing. "I think there were two others on the side, and I know one was at the back."

"Why do you remember that one?"

"I had to drive around it. Someone needed a lesson on how to park."

A ripple of excitement flowed through Cat. "What type of vehicle?"

"A beat-up old pickup. I think it might have been a Ford."

"Did you look at the license plate?" Cat held her breath, hoping against hope.

The woman shook her head. "No. I'm sorry, I didn't pay that much attention."

"What about the color? Two-door, four-door?"

"Uh ... two-door, I think, and it was black."

"Any other features that you remember?"

"No, it just an old truck."

"Would you be able to stop at the police department to give us a written statement?"

"Absolutely. I can do that today, though I need to wait until my associate returns. He is showing a property."

Cat handed her a business card. "Ask to speak with Jessie Barnes. She'll type the statement for you. Please call me if something else occurs to you."

Thanking her for her time and help, Cat turned to walk away. Elation over the details of the killer's vehicle was tempered with disappointment that she still didn't have enough to put out a BOLO, be on the lookout, for the truck. Her instincts told her time was running out. The killer would be on the move, or he'd grab a woman in Clinton. Either way, another woman would be at risk.

Fourteen

One miserable taco yesterday. There had to be something he could eat. After rummaging through the cupboard, all he found was the ends of a loaf of bread and a jar of peanut butter. Grabbing a knife from the pile of dirty dishes in the sink, JD wiped it on his pants. What was left in the jar barely covered the slice of bread.

Disgusted, he tossed the empty container in a sack filled with trash. The bag flipped. Paper, cigarette butts, empty cans, and bottles scattered across the floor, along with a few roaches that scurried out of sight. To hell with it. He'd pick it up later and kicked the garbage under the table. He had a bigger problem—money. What he had left wouldn't fill the gas tank, and he needed to get the hell out of Mississippi.

Damn, I should have kept her purse, swallowing a swig of beer to get rid of the dry bread and gummy peanut butter that stuck to the roof of his mouth. He didn't like to remember what happened yesterday. The terror he felt when the woman screamed, and the people who rushed outside still lingered.

He needed cash or drugs he could sell. He'd have to hit another clinic. But what if he couldn't find one in time? A gulp of beer pushed down another bite of bread. Where they already looking for him?

He hit the remote. Maybe there was something on the news. A reporter stood in front of Taco John, then a picture of a woman flashed on the screen. *Son-of-a-bitch! That's her. Cindy, huh.* He never bothered with their names, they weren't important.

As he listened, the reporter described the failed abduction and the interview of a witness who had run out to save the woman. His panic intensified. Sweat beaded on his forehead. They had a partial description. He stuffed the last piece of sandwich into his mouth and headed outside.

The park's office was in the front of a small house located near the front gate. The owner, unshaven with dirty white hair that hung over his shoulders, sat behind an old wood desk covered with gouges and stains. He glanced up from the magazine he held when the bell over the door tinkled. On the cover was a picture of a woman in a bikini astraddle a large motorcycle.

"What do you want?" His voice was deep and gravelly.

"Phonebook," JD said.

"On the table in front of the window. Look, but don't take." His gaze went back to his magazine.

Asshole! With his back to the owner, he thumbed through the yellow pages until he found the section for vet clinics. Tearing out the pages, he folded and stuck them in his shirt pocket. Even if the owner wouldn't let him have the book, he still had what he wanted. Whistling, he walked out the door.

Back in the trailer, he scanned the list of clinics, searching for one outside of town. Hell, he needed the map, but what did he do with it? He'd picked one up at a rest area when he crossed into Mississippi. It was probably still in the truck and found it lying on the dashboard.

Pushing dirty dishes aside, he spread it out on the table. One was only a few miles away. Tonight, he'd check it out. With any luck, he'd be on the road by daylight.

With his last bottle of beer, he sat on the front step of the trailer and scanned the park. Scattered along the gravel road were rundown trailers that hadn't been moved in years. It was the type of place where everybody minded their own business, none of this visiting and group cookouts like he had found in other parks. The space at the back had helped. It had made hauling them in and out of the trailer easy. *Damn, I hate to leave.* This was the best site he'd found since leaving Texas, and that was by accident—a small ad stuck on a bulletin board at a gas station.

He chuckled at the name, Almost Heaven. *Oh yeah, I've got the perfect spot, but not because it was near heaven.*

She nodded to the receptionist as she passed the front desk. Kevin and a group of officers exited his office. His personnel meeting must be over. It seemed to have gone well since everyone was smiling and shaking hands. Kevin caught her eye and nodded toward the conference room.

Nicki and Ryan glanced up when she entered.

Cat assumed her face had a smug expression, when Nicki asked, "Okay, what's up?"

"I located a woman who was at the Burger Grill the night Susan Benson was abducted. She saw the PTC walking toward the front door. And ... she saw an old pickup parked at the back of the lot."

Ryan asked, "How'd you find her?"

"She owned the yellow Volkswagen parked next to Susan Benson's car."

Cat turned as Kevin walked into the room.

Behind her back, Ryan mouthed, 'witchy woman.'

Nicki shook her head and grinned.

"Did your meeting go well?" Cat asked.

"Yeah, it did. At least, everyone seemed to be satisfied with the results. So, what's happening?"

Cat explained about the witness. "She'll stop on her way home from work and give us a statement."

Kevin asked with a note of incredulity in his voice. "You located a witness who had parked her yellow Volkswagen next to Susan Benson's car?" Cat nodded yes.

Ryan asked, "What made you search for yellow Volkswagens?" *Okay, witchy woman, like to hear you explain this one.*

"Hmm … not sure where, but someone mentioned a yellow bug parked at the Burger Grill." She wasn't about to mention it came from a dead woman.

Kevin gave Cat a long stare but didn't make a comment. His phone rang. "Hunter." He listened and said, "Thanks, Doc, appreciate the call."

Sticking the phone back in his pocket, he said, "That was Doctor Carter. Cindy Arp is going to be released tomorrow morning."

"Hey, great news, she is one lucky woman," Nicki said, echoing the thought in everyone's mind.

Kevin said, "I talked to Roger. He and Ed are on their way back from Monroe. Since they didn't find anything that wasn't in the reports, I told them to go home."

Jessie stuck her head in the door to say Martha Anderson was waiting in the chief's office.

Cat said, "I'll talk to her."

After she left, the two agents looked at each other and chuckled.

"You were right," Nicki said.

"Right about what?" Kevin asked.

"Cat's nickname is witchy woman. She either finds bodies or odd details and never has a rational explanation," Ryan explained.

Kevin grinned and followed Cat to his office.

After the realtor left, Cat headed back to the conference room to gather up her computer and files.

"Anyone interested in supper?" she asked.

Nicki zipped her computer case, which was large since it contained two laptops. "I'll pass. I am going to the hotel and will order something from room service."

Ryan said he planned to spend the evening expanding his research on cycles of the moon and satanic rituals. Room service sounded like a good idea.

Jesse came in as the two agents left and handed Cat copies of the woman's statement. Cat stuffed one in her briefcase and tossed the others on the growing mound of documents.

Reluctant to leave, yet not having a reason to stay, Cat stacked, then restacked the folders on the table. She wasn't ready to go back to her hotel room though she was still hesitant to risk further interaction with Kevin. Law enforcement and relationships were often an unpleasant combination. *Besides, you idiot, he probably has plans, maybe even a girlfriend. That's depressing.*

Kevin filed the reports from the personnel meeting. It was busy work to delay leaving that could have waited until the next day. *Admit it, Kevin, you're just waiting around to talk to her again.* Every time he saw her, a warmth spread through his body that was more than sheer lust. Hell! There was no doubt he wanted to take her to bed, yet there was another unfamiliar longing to spend time with her. Something he had not experienced before, even with his ex-fiancée. What harm was there in asking if she wanted to have dinner? His inner voice laughed, *you fool. Who are you kidding?*

Before logic took control, he headed to the conference room. Cat was pushing a stack of folders across the table.

"There's a restaurant a couple of blocks from here if you would be interested in Italian and maybe a glass of wine."

"Italian and wine sound great."

Her delight surprised him since he expected she would say no. "Then, you'll love this place. Mama Lorenzo uses family recipes her grandmother brought from Italy." Kevin suggested they take his car.

"No, I'll follow you. I don't want to leave my vehicle at the station."

As they walked across the parking lot, his eyes darted over her. Damn, she looked good. The snug black pants, red top, and black leather jacket that skimmed her hips seemed familiar though he couldn't remember why. He had to laugh at himself over the thoughts that had periodically flashed in his mind all day. He seemed to have reverted to his teenage days when all he could think of was sex. *Kevin, she's not someone for a quickie in the back seat of your car. Any relationship with this woman would be serious.*

When her enticing perfume, the fresh, clean scent of rain drifted in the night air, an image popped into his mind. That's the outfit she wore that first day in his office.

Lost in his thoughts, it was a few seconds before he realized she had stopped. When he glanced back, she stared at her car. A puzzling tug pulled at his thoughts. He twisted to see who was near him. No one behind him, then he spotted two owls perched on the hood of Cat's car. Large, yellow eyes locked onto his. Their unwavering gaze sent chills racing through him. When they lifted off, Kevin turned toward Cat. "Your owls?"

Troubled, she nodded her head yes as she watched them disappear over the roof of the station. She wouldn't be ordering that glass of wine.

Fifteen

gitated, JD paced. His bag of tools and the bolt cutter were by the front door, but he couldn't leave, not with someone outside. Peering through a slit in the blinds, he checked again. The two men still leaned against a pickup parked in front of a nearby trailer. Each held a beer bottle in their hands as they talked. Damn, how long were they going to hang around as he stared longingly at the six-pack on the tailgate?

Turning from the window, he combed through the drawer, where he occasionally stashed his weed and found enough for a joint.

Taking a deep drag, the rush muted his anxiety. Flipping through the channels, he stopped on one with a cooking show. The chef talked nonstop while he demonstrated the proper way to chop vegetables. JD snorted in disgust. The idiot didn't know the first thing about how to handle a knife. He could give him a lesson or two and chuckled at the thought.

He watched for another couple of minutes before changing the channel. The news was on, and reporters were at the police department. Someone asked a question about the FBI. The picture shifted to a woman walking out of the building. Her hair glistened, a red halo shimmering in the sunlight and the strands the color of blood.

Transfixed, he leaned forward. The camera followed her as she crossed the parking lot. As she opened her car door, she glanced over her shoulder. A surge of elation shot through him when he stared into her eyes. The newscast switched to another story and broke his trance. JD took the last hit from the joint. Damn, he couldn't leave town, not when he had just found the perfect sacrifice.

A large woman wearing an oversize apron stood in front of the open style kitchen when they entered the restaurant. Spotting them, she weaved her way through the tables. Amazed, Cat watched her grab Kevin and hug him.

"Chief, I wondered when you'd be back." She looked at Cat. "Welcome to Mama Lorenzo's."

Kevin laughed and said, "Cat, meet Mama Lorenzo. She makes the best lasagna you'll ever taste. Mama, this is Cat Morgan."

She gripped Cat's hand and gave it a vigorous shake. Mama told the waitress standing next to her that she'd take care of their order. Escorting them to a table, she handed each a menu and took their drink order. When Cat said iced tea, Kevin gave her a questioning look, then said he'd have the same.

When she left, he asked, "What happened to the wine?"

"Hmm ...oh, just changed my mind."

Kevin leaned back in his chair, a thoughtful expression on his face.

As he continued to eye her in silence, she finally said, "What's rolling in your head now?"

"The owls. That's why no wine. You're concerned something is going to happen."

She sighed before saying, "Yes. I'm afraid the PTC struck again, and there's another body out there." As the images of the pictures on the murder board flicked in her mind, a chill raced through her at the idea of adding another.

"Hmm ... that's what I thought. How does this link work?"

She idly shifted the utensils on the table. Discussing the owls was still a surreal topic despite Kevin's intuitive sense and seeming acceptance. She glanced up to find his gaze intently focused on her face.

"Whenever they appear, I know someone is dead, and I'm about to find a body …with their help, of course. But still, tonight was odd. I didn't get a sense someone had died. My last case had a strange …" Her voice trailed off as the memory flashed in her mind. The birds' warning had been more than a sensation, it was a word that had ricocheted in her head, and she still didn't understand how she could have heard it.

"What was so strange?" Kevin asked.

"Uh … oh, the owls saved my life and probably my partner's as well. We were chasing a serial killer in a railroad yard. He climbed on top of a car to ambush us. The birds warned me."

"How?" he asked, with a note of skepticism in his voice.

Should she mention the odd message, if it could be called that, of danger? No, best to leave it alone. "Two plummeted straight at my head. Anyone else, it would have scared the living bejesus out of them. It made me look up, and I saw the man. I hollered at Ben and got to cover. Even then, his shot was too damn close. If it hadn't been for the birds, I'm not sure … well, it didn't happen, so no point dwelling on the what-ifs."

"And that's never happened before?"

"No. Never." She sighed. "Though, this isn't the first time their actions have mystified me. I've never found a pattern. My grandmother's answer was human behavior is unpredictable, so why would the owls be any different. It would be funny if it weren't for the tragic results."

"How long has this been going on?"

"Since I was ten. I was playing in the backyard when two weird-looking birds, with what I thought were horns, settled on the edge of the fence. I was so scared, I tried to run, but my legs wouldn't move, which scared me even more. Before I could scream for mom, the fear vanished. Somehow, I knew they wouldn't hurt me. Then a sadness flowed over me."

She stopped when Mama, followed by a waitress holding glasses of iced tea and a basket of homemade rolls, approached their table. The tantalizing aroma of fresh-baked bread rose in the air. Mama asked if they were ready to order. Following Kevin's recommendation, she selected the lasagna. Kevin ordered the same.

When she walked away, Kevin asked, "Did someone die?"

"Oh, yes, my aunt. She'd passed away that morning. I didn't see them again until a couple of years later. They were perched in a tree outside my bedroom window. When they stared at me, I felt that same terrible sadness. This time it was my best friend; she was killed in a car accident."

Picking up a roll, Cat tore off a chunk and slathered on the butter. "Over the next few years, I'd occasionally see them and then find out someone I knew was dead." She added another glob of butter, then popped the bite in her mouth.

Kevin laughed. "Why bother with the roll, just eat the butter."

Cat glared at him as she chewed and decided to ignore the comment. Swallowing, she picked up where she had left off. "It changed after I graduated from the academy."

"Is that when you started finding bodies and talking to the dead?"

Once again, she was astounded by his quick uptake. "You know, Kevin, you really ought to consider another line of work. As a psychic, you could make a ton of money," she chided him.

His laughter erupted again. "Nah, no one would believe me. If I tried to sell the idea of owls and ghosts, I'd be laughed out of business."

"Now you know why I've never told anyone. But to answer your question, yes, that's when it happened. I'd been assigned to a drug investigation ..." Buttering another bite of bread, she frowned at Kevin, daring him to comment. When he just grinned, she said, "A witness came up missing. The owls appeared, and I sensed they wanted me to follow them. Which I did and found my witness stuffed in the trunk of an abandoned car."

"So, they don't talk to you?"

She glanced to make sure he wasn't laughing at her before she said, "Nope, just a feeling I get." At least it was until the Rail Killer took a shot at her.

Kevin's face turned grim. "Then, their appearance tonight means another girl has died?"

"Since they led me to Janet Lewis, it would seem to be the most likely reason. But I really don't know. All I can do is wait, and that's always the worst part."

The waitress set plates of lasagna and the extra sauce Kevin ordered on the table.

When the flavors from the first bite erupted in her mouth, she almost groaned with pleasure. It was every bit as good as Kevin had said.

Wanting to switch subjects, she asked, "What's the deal with the mayor?"

Kevin glanced at the nearby tables to make sure he wouldn't be overheard before he explained the incident involving the man's son. Then added, "Bingham won the election a few months back, and the interference and harassment have increased. He'll fire me if he can find a reason. I don't know how the man got elected. A couple of people have suggested the election may have been rigged, but so far, I haven't found the proof. Last week, I received an anonymous letter suggesting I check into the construction contracts the mayor signed. I haven't been able to follow up because of the homicides."

Cat said, "That reminds me of a case I worked in Texas. A district attorney had received complaints about the county's bid process. A couple of companies were getting most of the contracts. I was sent into the city inspector's office as a clerk." Gesturing with a hand that held the remains of another roll, she added, "It was my one and only undercover assignment. It took a few weeks, but after delving into the construction contracts and permits, I discovered the owners had bribed a couple of inspectors to sign off on substandard construction—which is why they could low ball the bid."

"What was the outcome?"

"We arrested the inspectors and several employees, including the owners of the construction companies. I think we can help. Get me copies of the contracts the mayor has signed. I'll pass them on to Nicki. If there is something, she'll find it."

Her plate empty, she leaned back, and despite their conversation, relaxed.

When Mama stopped to ask if they were interested in dessert, both looked at her, then laughed before uttering an emphatic no.

He was still smiling when his phone rang.

"Hunter." His face turned grim as he listened.

"On my way," he said and disconnected the call.

Rising, he pulled out his wallet. "I have a hostage situation. Two armed men are holding several people inside a convenience store. I'll see you tomorrow."

Sixteen

Mama had heard Kevin's comment and told him the meal was on the house. He thanked her, then rushed out the door, his thoughts already focused on the lives of innocent people at risk.

When he pulled out of the parking lot, he activated the red lights and siren. Grabbing the dash-mounted radio mike, he asked for an update.

The dispatcher said, "The hostages are still alive."

Cars immediately gave way as he raced along city streets. His call sign came over the radio. It was Mason, his patrol supervisor.

"Chief, two armed men are inside the store with the store clerk and two customers. SWAT's command center just arrived. The hostage negotiator is attempting to contact the suspects by phone. So far, they're not answering."

Kevin's insides twisted into a knot as he listened. It didn't sound good. "Where is the command center parked?"

"Kay Street."

"I'll be there in a few minutes."

Kevin cut over on a cross street and parked behind the SWAT van. When he exited that odd tug pulled at his thoughts again, a sense someone watched him. He stopped and scanned the sidewalk and cars parked on the street. The only movement was an approaching vehicle. Otherwise, there was nothing to set off the unexpected sense of disquiet that rippled through him. He shrugged and entered the van.

Lt. Grayson, the team commander, greeted him.

Two officers sat in front of a display panel that controlled the communication and computer systems. One, the hostage negotiator, was on the phone. The rings on the other end of the call were audible over the speakerphone.

"Any contact?" Kevin asked, reaching into a cabinet to grab a tactical radio and headset.

"Not so far," Grayson replied.

"What happened?" He positioned the headset over his ballcap.

"Officer Higgins pulled into the parking lot as the robbery was going down. When the suspects saw his car, they shoved the clerk and two customers to the back of the store. Instead of rushing inside, Higgins used his head, pulled back, and radioed for help."

"Where are the perimeter officers located?"

Grayson stepped to the white drawing board mounted on the wall and quickly drew the store and surrounding streets. He marked each officer's location with an X. Patrol had effectively cordoned off the surrounding streets to block any unauthorized entry.

"The manager should be here in a few minutes with a diagram of the interior."

"Is your entry team ready?" Kevin asked.

"They will be in a few minutes. They are suiting up and will be on standby behind the building. But we've got a major problem. The entry will have to be through the front door. The back door cannot be opened from the outside."

Kevin didn't believe the knot in his gut could wind any tighter until he heard Grayson's words. The store had windows across the front. Once the entry team turned the corner of the building, the suspects would see them. The breach would turn into a suicide mission.

The door opened, and Kevin looked over his shoulder. He was not surprised to see Cat, who had somehow changed clothes. Dressed all in black, her tactical pants were tucked into combat boots, and a lightweight jacket covered a T-shirt. A black ball cap covered her hair.

The gun belt that circled her slim waist had a tie-down holster strapped to her thigh.

"Everybody, this is Special Agent Cat Morgan." Further introductions could wait until later.

Kevin radioed Sgt. Mason to confirm the surrounding streets were blocked. The radio and TV stations monitored the police bands. When they showed up, he'd have another problem. He told Mason to make sure the reporters didn't break through any of the police barriers.

"Do we have an 'eye' on the front of the store?" he asked Grayson.

"Brent Stockton, 104."

Kevin keyed his radio. "104, what's your status?"

Stockton replied, "I'm on a roof across the street with a clear view of the inside of the store. Two men with pistols. Three hostages, two men and a woman, are on the floor at the back of the store. One of the men has a bloody face. I can't spot any injuries on the other two. The suspects have been arguing since I got into position. If you're going to deploy the snipers, this is the best location."

Kevin acknowledged. He studied the diagram on the board. "Do you agree with using the roof for the snipers?" he asked Grayson.

"Yes, but Sutton is the only one we've got. That's one rifle to cover two suspects. Greg Rainey and Stan Ames are at the SWAT school in New Orleans. I can pull in Doug Branton from patrol. The only problem is he still needs to take the final test for sniper certification, and he's off today."

The missing snipers, especially Rainey, the best marksman in the department, added more unwelcome news on top of what had rapidly become a nightmare situation.

"Call Branton. Let's hope we can talk them out of the store and not need him."

The phone continued to ring. Grayson turned to the officer and told him to use the loudspeaker.

The officer flipped two switches on an overhead panel and picked up his microphone. "This is Officer Newsome with the Clinton Police

Department. Answer the telephone." He repeated the instructions several times while the ringing continued over the speakerphone.

The radio crackled, and Stockton's voice said, "I think they are arguing about the phone. One's going to answer."

Heavy breathing replaced the ringing. Newsome introduced himself. There was no response. A click and dial tone echoed over the speakerphone.

Stockton's voice came over the radio. "The other suspect grabbed the phone and hung it up. They are arguing again. One suspect has a gun to the head of a hostage."

"Get Sutton on the roof," Kevin said.

Cat had leaned against the wall. They probably wondered what the hell she was doing here since the FBI would not typically be involved in this type of incident. Her gut instinct had told her to follow Kevin when they left the restaurant. Listening to their discussion, she realized why.

She straightened and stepped forward. "Chief, I'm a certified sniper. I have my rifle and equipment in my car."

Surprised, Kevin stared at her, then quickly recovered. "What do you need?"

"A spotter."

Kevin looked at Grayson, who answered. "Greg's spotter is on the entry team. I'll pull him off and tell Turner to have another officer replace him."

"I'll be outside." She had to get out of the light and let her eyes adjust to the darkness.

As she approached her vehicle, the screech of the owls echoed overhead. They landed on top of her car. Heads turned in unison to watch her approach.

Cat eyed them, but nothing pinged in her mind. "What!"

Four large eyes blinked.

Still nothing. "I sure wish you could talk. If this isn't about another murder, why are you here? Trying to figure out what you are doing is really getting a bit difficult," she muttered.

Another blink.

"That's not an answer. No one's dead, at least not yet. Wait a minute … is that it, someone's going to die?"

They blinked again.

"Damn!" If she was right, this was another change in their behavior. No point in speculating about it now.

Popping the trunk, she unlocked a metal case and pulled out the scoped rifle, then slid it into a soft case, commonly known as a drag bag. Constructed of heavy canvas material, it became a mat when unfolded. Small zippered compartments held miscellaneous equipment and two boxes of ammunition.

A flap of wings caused Cat to look up. They were gone. She hefted the rifle bag over her shoulders and positioned the carrying straps like a backpack.

Footsteps crunched behind her. It was Kevin and another officer. He introduced her to Steve Jones, who would be her spotter. After acknowledging the introduction, she asked about the department's procedures.

Kevin replied, "If the hostages are in imminent danger, take the shot. The negotiator is still trying to make contact. We won't authorize a green light unless we believe the situation has deteriorated, and there is no other option. If we send in the entry team, I expect you to cover one suspect and Sutton the other. The team will be exposed before they can reach the front door."

He handed her a radio and headset. "Your call sign is two-hundred. From Stockton's description of the suspects' actions, they may be high on drugs, which will increase the probability of violence. If we can stall and let the drugs wear off, we might be able to reason with them and make them understand they are in a no-win situation."

"Got it," Cat said as she attached the radio and slipped on the headset.

The screech of owls resonated in the night air. Looking up, Kevin saw the birds circling above them and felt the mystifying pull in his mind. He glanced at Cat, eyebrows raised in a silent question.

Kevin's thoughts seemed to flow into her mind with the same question. Was it a warning? Uncertain, she shrugged.

Steve asked, "Ready?"

Cat nodded.

Taking the lead, he circled the block to approach the building from the back. Mounted on the wall was a metal ladder. Though the rifle's weight pulled on the straps over her shoulders, it was an easy climb.

At the top of the building, two metal rods were embedded along the edge. *That's handy* as she grabbed them to pull herself onto the roof. To avoid being silhouetted against the faint light from the surrounding stores and streetlights, Cat crawled until she reached the front edge. Stockton was on his belly, elbows propped, as he stared through binoculars. He turned his head and nodded. Kevin had alerted him four officers were making their way to the roof. Steve moved up beside her and duplicated Stockton's position while he studied the building.

Sliding the straps off her shoulders, Cat pulled her binoculars from the bag and surveyed the store. Huge windows, ceiling to floor, covered the entire front of the building. Surprisingly, stacks of boxes or signs did not block the view.

Stockton's recommendation for the snipers' location was a good one. The building they were on was smaller and more important, not as tall as the convenience store. She could see all the way to the back. The checkout counter was to the left of the front door and rows of shelves on the right. A walkway extended between the counter and the end of the shelves to the coolers at the rear of the store.

Two men and a woman huddled on the floor in front of the coolers. One had his arm around the shoulders of the woman. Two men stood in front of them, arguing. When one waved a gun in the direction of the hostages, the woman cringed.

Faint sounds caused her to glance over her shoulder. Two officers were on the roof. Dragging the rifle bag, she slid backward and identified herself.

One said as he slid his case from his shoulder, "I'm Ted Sutton. I want to look at the building." He crawled to the edge of the roof and studied the store as Cat had done.

After several seconds, he scooted back. They quickly agreed to set up on opposite ends of the roof with Stockton between them and which suspect would be their primary target. Each team moved to their position near the edge of the roof.

Cat pulled the rifle bag alongside her. Steve crawled to the other side and with elbows propped, began to watch the store with his binoculars. He'd handle the radio communications and alert her to any changing conditions that could affect the accuracy of her shot. After removing a box of ammunition from a side pocket, she unzipped and spread the bag open.

The purchase of a drag bag instead of a standard rifle case had been a smart decision. It provided protection from a variety of ground conditions, in this case, a tar and gravel surface.

Picking up the rifle, she flipped down the legs of the bipod, and set it in place, then rolled onto the mat. Once the elevation and wind settings were verified, she shouldered it to check her view through the scope. Satisfied, she loaded the rifle. Even though the weather was calm, she wanted an object to signal a wind shift. An advertising flag hung limp on a pole down the street.

During her setup, Steve had whispered a running commentary on the actions of the two suspects. She tapped his leg with her boot. He looked over at her. Cat said, "Flag on building to the right, a block down, keep an eye on it. If the wind picks up, tell me. I'm ready."

Nodding, he keyed his radio. "Four-twenty in position."

He received a quick acknowledgment from Kevin. A couple of minutes later, Sutton's spotter informed the command center they were ready.

Focused on her view through the scope, she watched the suspects argue. Her target angrily waved a gun in the air, then jerked open the door to the cooler and grabbed a bottle of beer. Through her earpiece, she heard Stockton relay the information to the command center.

With the beer in one hand and the gun in the other, he bent over the female hostage. The scope magnified the terror in her face as she gazed up at him. She flinched and pushed back against the door of the cooler, bringing her knees tight against her chest as she shook her head no. The second suspect grabbed the man's shoulder and pushed him back, setting off another intense argument.

Adrenaline pumped through her system at the violent and unpredictable scene unfolding. Based on hundreds of hours of training, her reaction was immediate. Deep breaths helped to control her heart rate and ensure an adequate supply of oxygen to her eyes. The darting glances away from the scope refreshed her sight picture. When her target moved, the crosshairs moved with him.

Stockton's quiet voice came over the radio. "They're still arguing. One suspect continues to threaten the hostages. The woman is the primary target. He's more violent than the other one who tries to calm him down. They're both drinking beer. One's lit a cigarette. No, it's a joint. They're smoking weed!"

Inside the command center, the atmosphere grew exceedingly tense as the situation in the store deteriorated. Stockton's reports portrayed the escalation of violence and the potential for injury or death for the hostages. The use of drugs and alcohol added fuel to the volatile confrontation.

The manager had arrived and drew a layout of the building.

As the men studied the drawing, Grayson said, "Kevin, there isn't any way we can take them by surprise."

His face grim, Kevin replied. "I know. A frontal approach, and we've got injured or dead officers. Plus, the hostages will be in the line of fire. Goddamn, it will be a carnage."

The ringing of the phone stopped, and a voice came over the speakerphone. Fear radiated in the shrill tone as a man said, "Give us a car. Uh … fifteen minutes or we shoot someone."

In the background, another voice had become loud and abrasive. It was the second suspect telling the female hostage how he would rape, then kill her. A high-pitched scream echoed over the speakerphone—then the line went dead.

A slight tremor in Stockton's voice betrayed his tension. "The suspect has grabbed the woman. He's hitting her ..."

Kevin reached to key his mike and order the green light. Before he could complete the motion, the crack of a rifle shot covered Stockton's voice, followed by a second, and then a third.

Grayson shouted over the radio to his entry team supervisor. "Go! Go! Go!"

Seventeen

Cat's target grabbed a handful of hair and jerked the woman off the floor. Struggling to break free, she blocked Cat's shot, and the man's quick movements prevented a head shot. She could miss or worse, hit the woman. Forced to endure the sight of the butt of the gun slamming into the woman's face and head, she waited for an opening. When the woman fell to the floor, the crack of her shot ripped through the air along with the sound of breaking glass. The suspect slumped to the floor.

Cat didn't hear the sounds, her only thought, *he's down*. Instinctively, she shifted the rifle to track the second suspect who stood in stunned disbelief. Suddenly, he moved to grab one of the other hostages. Cat fired, and a third shot echoed—Sutton had fired.

Stockton radioed. "Both suspects down!"

Through the scope, Cat scanned the men for any further threat as the SWAT team raced to the front door. Once inside, two officers ran to them. When they stood, their body language told her both men were dead. A voice came over the radio, "Stand down, building secure, repeat, stand down."

Cat flipped on the safety while she continued to watch the scene through the scope. Officers surrounded the hostages. One knelt beside the woman lying motionless on the floor. He keyed his radio and requested the paramedics. *She's alive.* Cat did not realize she had been holding her breath until her lungs heaved in relief.

It was over. She rolled onto her back and gazed up at the night sky. It was quiet on the roof. The only sounds came from the parking lot below. *You had no choice. The lives of three innocent people were at risk,* she told herself. Knowing and accepting were two very different states of mind, as she had learned in Beaumont.

Hoots echoed. The owls circled above her. They dipped and soared, dancing on the night air as if to reassure her, and then—they were gone.

Kevin's voice over the radio broke the pensive silence. Stockton responded and was told to have everyone report to the command center. A clink of metal sounded from the other side of the roof as Sutton loaded his gear.

Cat sat up and unloaded the live rounds from her rifle. Steve picked up the two ejected cases and handed them to her. She stuck them in her pocket. They would be part of the evidence in the subsequent investigation.

"Need any help?" he asked as she refolded the mat.

"No, but thanks for asking."

He started toward the ladder and then turned. "It could have been worse." He hesitated as if searching for the right words. Finally, he shook his head and said, "Hell of a couple of shots!" and walked off.

Back on the ground, her gear stowed in the car, she tapped the speed dial for her boss.

"Fleming," his voice groggy.

"Scott, it's Cat. I have a bit of a problem."

Instantly, he was alert. "Hell, Cat, the last time I heard those words, you'd found a body in a dumpster."

"Yeah, this one's not any better. Hunter had a robbery turn into a hostage situation; two armed men inside a convenience store with three victims. He needed a second sniper, and I volunteered. We had to take down the suspects. Both are dead."

"Are the hostages okay?"

Cat liked that his immediate concern was for the victims. "Two were hurt. I don't know the severity of their injuries. The third, aside from substantial trauma from being terrorized by two doped-up, armed men is probably okay."

"Cat, how many shots did you fire, and how many hits?"

"Two suspects, two shots, two hits."

There was a moment of silence. The implication of her words screamed in her mind as she waited for Scott to reply.

"Where are you now?"

"Still at the scene. I expect I'll be at the police department most of the night."

"Send me a report detailing the circumstances as soon as you can. Call me in the morning."

By the time Cat reached the command center, the officers who had been on the roof had already arrived. They all turned to look at her as she entered the van. For a moment, she felt like the proverbial bug under a microscope.

Kevin walked up and quietly asked if everything was all right.

As she handed him the radio equipment, she said, "Yes. Sorry for the delay. I had to call my boss."

Understanding, Kevin nodded, then turned to address the officers. "Report back to the station for debriefing. You know the routine, written statements from everyone. Cat, you're included. We'll need your rifle for a ballistics test."

"For how long?" she asked.

"You'll have it back tomorrow." He looked at his watch and added, "Hell, it's already the next day, so make it this morning. If you want, you can meet the tech at the rifle range and pick it up."

As the officers filed out of the command center and Cat turned to follow, Kevin tapped her shoulder.

"Don't leave yet."

"I'll be outside."

Cat stood on the street corner and stared at the store. It was controlled chaos. The barricades were still in place, along with several squad cars and the medical examiner's van in the store's parking lot. Officers and medical personnel paraded in and out of the building. TV crews and reporters lined the barricades. She was glad she didn't have to face the cameras and microphones.

Kevin walked up and gazed at the hectic scene. He sighed. "I can't leave yet. I have to talk to them." His head twisted as he glanced at her face. "Ted Sutton told me what happened on the roof, that the first two shots were yours, and likely took out both suspects."

"I didn't have a choice. I knew it as soon as he grabbed the woman. I could see the rage on his face. He was going to kill her."

Footsteps sounded. It was Grayson. "Agent Morgan. Thank you for your help. From what I have already pieced together, your swift action saved lives tonight. Ready Chief?"

"No, but let's get it done," Kevin responded. He looked at Cat and told her he would talk to her later. It would be a long night for everyone involved.

Back at the station, Cat met with the detectives, handed over her rifle case, and dictated her statement. She fielded several questions regarding her training and certification. After the detectives were finished, she headed to the conference room to type her report for Scott. Once it was sent, she had no excuse to linger at the station.

When she reached the sanctuary of her hotel room, she dropped her gear on the floor and collapsed on the bed. Damn, she was tired. The aftereffects of the adrenaline dump had sent her system spiraling down. It was a familiar sensation.

Images from the convenience store rolled in her head. She'd killed one, possibly two men. In Beaumont, she would have been shot if she hadn't fired first. This was different. She hadn't been in imminent fear of her life. Still, the fear had been just as real, only it was for the lives of the hostages. She'd told Kevin she didn't have a choice, but did she? With her arms crossed under her head, every detail was replayed in her mind, all with one question—*could I have done anything differently*? The recurring answer was no.

With a sense of relief, she got up, stripped and left her clothes in another heap on the floor, and headed to the shower. The tension faded away as hot water flowed over her body, and muscles relaxed.

Desperate for sleep, her system crashed as soon as she crawled into bed. The exhaustion, though, did not suppress the dreams. In the deepest regions of her subconscious, she dreamt of a full moon. It was bright and alluring before the blood flowed, and the owls screeched.

Euphoric from a drug-induced high, JD's eyes shifted to the two sacks filled with an unexpected quantity of drugs on his front seat. The old-style lock on the drug cabinet had only taken one snip of the bolt cutter. As the door swung open, he had stared in disbelief at the number of vials and boxes stacked on the shelves. The money from selling them would last for weeks. The cash was a surprise. Usually, the cash register was empty, not this time. There had to be at least two hundred bucks.

Ahead, the lights on a sign for an all-night restaurant pulsated. Food, and he had money to pay for it. When was the last time he ate? The memories jumbled in his head.

Parked at the back of the building, he clung to the door as he climbed out of his truck. At the sound of a voice, he glanced toward the source. A cell phone to her ear, a woman came out of the restaurant. Under the lights, her hair gleamed bright red. A jolt of exhilaration shot through him. He'd found another one, but could he get to her in time.

Reaching across the seat, he grabbed a bag. His hands trembled as he searched for the box of syringes. Tearing it open, he grabbed one, then fumbled through the vials for the ketamine.

He glanced over his shoulder. The woman had stopped on the sidewalk, her voice raised in anger. Shifting his body to let the light hit the bottle, he filled the syringe. His eyes wouldn't focus, and he had to guess. *Hell, that should be enough.*

At the corner of the building, he hugged the wall, staying out of sight until he could move behind her.

Dropping the phone in her bag, she walked along the side of the building and stopped at a car parked near where he stood. As she unlocked the door, her phone rang. Turning her back to the sidewalk, she reached into her purse, unaware of the approaching danger.

An arm came around her face, his hand covered her mouth and pulled her head back. The needle struck deep in her neck. He pushed the plunger with his thumb. Tossing it aside, he held her tight against his body as she struggled. The purse and keys fell to the ground. As the drug took effect, her resistance weakened until her body slumped against him.

Holding her under the arms, he dragged her to his truck. Shoving her onto the floor between the seat and dashboard, he covered her with a tarp he kept behind the seat.

Excitement coursed through him as he pulled out of the parking lot. Gleefully, he glanced at the hump on the floorboard. This one didn't get away, and there was still time to perform the ceremony. *The Master will be pleased.*

Even though it was late, and no one should be awake, he still parked on the side of the trailer that was out of view of the other residents.

He unlocked the door to his trailer and left it ajar. Startled by a rustling sound, he spun to look around him. When he heard a screech, he spotted the birds on a tree branch near the truck. *Those damn owls are back.*

Several times over the last few days, he'd heard their calls and noticed them perched in the trees, even during the day. They seemed to watch the trailer, and the sight of them sent trickles of fear racing through him. A sensation he didn't understand. *Why the hell should a couple of birds scare me?* This time, their glowing eyes watched his every movement.

Ignoring them, he opened the door and tossed the cover aside. JD grabbed her and began to pull the woman out of the truck.

Damn! Stunned, he dropped her, then pressed his fingers against her neck—cold skin and no pulse. She's dead. How can she be dead? *You sent me a sign. How can I offer her if she's already dead?* Confused and angry, he paced as the furious rant whirled in his head.

Nothing he could do but get rid of her. No blood, so he didn't have to wrap her in the trash bags. After pushing her back down on the floor, he slid into the driver's seat and cranked the engine. There was a place he had spotted on the way back from the clinic.

As he neared the location, he slowed to park on the shoulder. Trash bags littered a field next to the road along with rusty appliances and a couple of old couches and mattresses. JD dragged the body to the back of a large pile of rubbish. After kicking trash over it, he surveyed his handiwork. It was a good spot. No one could see her from the road. It would be a long time before anyone found this one. Overhead, the owls circled.

Eighteen

hand groped for the receiver as the unpleasant sound of the phone, her wake-up call, pulled Cat from a deep sleep. A momentary flash of a bloody moon instantly brought her awake. *Damn, I hope this doesn't mean another woman is dead.* Her instincts said it did.

Swinging her legs over the side, she felt as tired as when she went to bed. Three hours wasn't enough to purge her body of the aftereffects of the adrenaline rush from the convenience store crisis.

A groan erupted at the sight of the clothes she'd tossed on the floor. Well, they are not going to pick themselves up, so get with it. With only an hour to get to the range, she had to get her butt in gear.

While she bagged the dirty clothes, she listened to a local news channel. Hearing Kevin's voice, she glanced at the screen. It was the broadcast from the night before, and Kevin stood in front of the convenience store with Lieutenant Grayson at his side. He didn't waste any words. His voice low and calm, he competently explained the hostage takeover and why two men were dead.

Relentless, the reporters hammered him with questions trying to identify who had fired the shots. Kevin refused to provide any additional information citing the ongoing investigation. The picture switched back to the TV studio, and the morning news personnel continued the discussion. The only significant detail was the status of the injured woman. She was in stable condition though she had not regained consciousness.

Walking out of the elevator, she dropped the bag at the front desk and made a pass by the buffet table, then headed to the parking lot. Setting her cup in the console holder, she took a bite of the scrambled egg sandwich and programmed the address for the police range.

When Cat pulled through the gate, there were already several squad cars in front of the building. Ted Sutton was getting out of his vehicle and waited while she parked. Inside, he introduced her to Bill Clifton, the crime scene tech.

"I've already test-fired both rifles," Bill said, motioning with his hand toward the two rifle cases on a nearby table.

"When do you think your report will be ready?" Cat asked and picked up her case.

"I should have something in a day or two. The bullets we recovered are badly mangled, and I don't know yet if I can match them to a specific rifle."

"Would you mind if I use your cleaning room to run a few patches through my barrel?"

"It's the small building next door. Help yourself to any of the cleaning equipment," Bill said.

Ted picked up his rifle case. "I'll go with you."

Inside the building, Cat gathered up several patches, a cleaning rod, and solvent. Alongside her, Ted did the same.

"Last night, that was a rapid transition from one suspect to the other. How long have you been shooting?" he asked.

"About eight years, and I've shot a lot of competitions. I qualified as a sniper when I was in the academy. One of our speed drills used square cardboard targets set at different distances. Each had a small white dot somewhere on the target. The idea is to hit the dot. If the bullet doesn't touch the dot, points are deducted. It's accuracy versus time. The exercise improves the speed of moving from target to target."

"Well, no one can argue with your expertise. Anytime you need to use the range, it's available. Let Jessie know, and she'll set it up with the range officer," Ted told her.

"Thanks." Acceptance between officers was not a given, it had to be earned. Ted's comment told Cat she'd made the cut.

Kevin was parking his car at the station when his phone rang. The screen showed it was Jessie. He answered, saying, "I'm on my way inside."

"Chief, the mayor's secretary called. The mayor wants you in his office immediately."

Several swear words ran through his thoughts before he said, "I'm on my way. Let the task force know I'll be late." This was probably going to be another waste of his time.

The mayor's secretary looked up from her computer as he stepped into the office. Since she had worked for the previous mayor, Kevin had known her for several years. Though Liz never said anything, Kevin had the impression she disliked Bingham and even suspected she might be the source of the anonymous letter he had received on the construction contracts.

She turned her head to glance at the door to her boss's office. It was closed. Her gaze swung to Kevin as he reached her desk.

She whispered, "Chief, I think you should know something before you walk into his office. He wants to file criminal charges against you and the agent for that shooting."

Stunned, Kevin stared at her. What the hell! Criminal charges! That's insane. He was rarely at a loss for words, but when Liz shifted in her chair, seemingly uneasy at his continued silence, he realized all he had done was stare at her.

"Thanks for the heads up, Liz."

She nodded. "I'll let him know you are here."

Expecting Bingham would make him wait, as usual, Kevin headed to a chair. For once, he was thankful for the additional time. He needed to assess what Liz had said. Whatever happened inside the mayor's office, Kevin had to maintain control of his emotions. But, how in the hell did he come up with criminal charges?

When the door opened, Bingham had a sly smirk on his face. *He's like the cat who believes he has the mouse cornered.* Kevin had never hated anyone more than this sorry bastard!

"Hunter … in my office," he said as he turned and strutted to his desk.

Seated and seemingly relaxed, Kevin's every instinct was on high alert.

Once Bingham had settled his oversized butt in his chair, he said, "Last night was a damn fiasco because of your bungling and illegal actions. Oh, and you can include the female FBI agent."

"I'm not sure how you decided anything we did could even remotely be construed as illegal."

"Yeah, I just bet you're already scrambling to cover your backside on this one," he gloated as he eased back in his chair and rested his clasped hands on his plump stomach. "That agent overreacted, and now two men are dead. She should never have been involved in the first place. It seems to me that you can't do your job if you have to rely on the FBI."

Who the hell was planting ideas in this idiot's head, and how did he find out Cat was involved? "Who told you this?"

"I have my sources, and they tell a different version of what happened to the victims last night than you touted in your press conference."

Kevin's hostility shot up another level at the use of the word victim to describe the dead criminals. "I need their names so my detectives can interview them."

"You're not getting them. I won't jeopardize the safety of the witnesses. And," he looked at his watch, "I've already scheduled a press conference to address the city's response. I expect the news folks are already outside."

His voice tight with suppressed anger, Kevin said, "I strongly advise that you wait until my department's investigation is complete before talking to the media."

"I don't need to. I'm sure your results will have been doctored to make your department look good and justify your actions."

"Is this more information from your alleged source?" Kevin asked. He couldn't control the sarcasm that crept into his voice.

"Not saying, but it's why I've requested the State Attorney General investigate you, Agent Morgan, and the Clinton Police Department personnel involved in last night's homicides. Once they've completed their investigation, I expect criminal charges will be filed."

In disbelief, Kevin stared at the man as the absurdity of the accusation punched him in the gut.

Gleefully, the mayor chuckled. "Yeah, I knew that would get your attention. I ordered you to put a stop to the FBI's activities, and you didn't, and this is the result." Another smirk crossed Bingham's face. "Once her boss finds out she killed two men without cause, I bet he'll rethink whether he wants to keep his agents in town."

Kevin's anger rolled over his good sense. "Don't you understand that women are being stalked and killed in our city? And you want to waste my time and that of my staff, all because of your petty vendetta!"

"Hunter, it's not my fault you can't do your job and catch this guy. I told the city council not to hire you as the police chief. They didn't listen. Now, I have proof. They will realize I was right. And that petty vendetta, as you call it, was my son convicted of a crime because of you. It will give me intense pleasure to see you standing in court facing jail time."

He had to get out of the man's office before he lost what little control he had left. Standing, he said, "Just remember ... I warned you. I'm done here."

"You bastard. This time, thanks to that FBI agent, I've got you. Your days as police chief are numbered."

Bingham's laughter followed him out the door.

Kevin pulled his cell phone from his pocket and called Jessie.

When she answered, he said, "The mayor scheduled a press conference. Call the news stations and find out when it will air and then record it. I want to make sure we have a copy of his remarks. Also, have Roger and Ed meet me in my office."

Kevin would have the detectives track down the mayor's so-called sources. But Bingham's vindictiveness had added an inordinate amount of extra work for his department, and there was still a killer on the loose.

Rush hour traffic, no matter what city, was always a royal pain. This morning was no exception as Cat left the range. She mentally reviewed her agenda as she inched her way forward in the stop-and-go traffic. Her memory of the red moon still clung to the back of her mind. She'd asked Ryan to compare the dates of the kills to the cycle of the moon. She believed there was a connection. *If he has found a link, could we use it to catch the killer?*

The parking lot was full of news media vehicles. *What triggered this?*

She parked in the section reserved for police cars, grabbed her backpack and briefcase, and headed to the front door. A reporter tried to cut her off. His microphone inches from her face, he asked, "Are you the agent that shot those men last night?"

Another reporter shouted, "What are your qualifications?"

A third asked, "Why were you there? The mayor said you exceeded your authority."

Holy hell, what's going on? She didn't let the shock over the questions show on her face as she pushed her way to the front door. "There is an ongoing investigation, and I cannot comment." She reached for the door as another voice shouted.

"Are you aware the mayor has requested a state investigation, and you could face criminal charges?"

"No comment," was her only response as the door slammed behind her.

Jessie stood next to the reception desk. A sympathetic grin crossed her face. "Judging by your stunned look, I would say you hadn't heard about the Mayor's press conference."

"I was at the range, and the only newscast I saw was Kevin's interview from last night. Is he here?"

"Yes, and in a closed-door meeting with Ed and Roger."

Cat headed down the hall to the conference room. Ryan tapped his keyboard, and Nicki was pinning pictures on the murder board.

Ryan saw her first and greeted her with a short whistle before saying, "You had a rough night."

"You don't know the half of it," she replied and dumped her gear on the table.

"We've only gotten bits and pieces," Nicki added.

Pouring a cup of coffee, Cat quickly recapped the events of the night, then added, "Have you heard what Bingham did?"

"No," Ryan answered.

"The parking lot is full of reporters. One said the mayor ordered a state investigation of the shootings. Apparently, Bingham claims I could be facing criminal charges. I don't know how much is true until I can talk to Kevin."

"It's true." Kevin stood in the doorway, his face reflected the anger that pulsated in the abrasive tone of his voice.

After covering the gist of his conversation with Bingham, Kevin added, "The state police will have to investigate, or the news media will scream cover-up. Once the facts are known, the case will be dismissed. In the meantime, he has managed to effectively smear my department and everyone who was involved last night."

"I need to call Scott," Cat said.

"If you need privacy, you can use my office."

"No, I'll call from here. We're all involved."

Cat hit the speed dial. When he answered, she explained the mayor's action.

"Where are you?" he asked.

"At the PD. Ryan, Nicki, and Kevin are here. They're listening."

"I've read your report, and don't see anything that I should question. Kevin, do you have anything to add?"

Kevin said, "Scott, I'm waiting for a callback from the state homicide unit. My officers will do everything possible to facilitate the investigation. I'm certain the case will be dismissed once they are aware of the facts. However, I don't want this to drag on. For a number of reasons, it needs to quickly be resolved. My chief concern is the impact on the task force. Our time will be expended on the mayor's accusations instead of the search for a serial killer."

"I agree," Scott replied. "I'll make a few calls, including one to the Attorney General."

Cat breathed a sigh of relief as she disconnected the call. As the saying goes, her boss had her back.

"Roger and Ed will be here later. They are finishing up the interviews from last night's events, plus trying to find the mayor's so-called witnesses. I'll be in my office. Jessie has informed me there is a stack of paperwork on my desk, not to mention a pile of phone messages that cannot wait."

Though deeply disturbed by the mayor's action, the certainty the killer had found another woman had slowly grown in intensity. Cat walked to the board to study the printed diagram of the satanic symbol and the cuts on the forehead of the women. Nicki stepped next to her.

"Have you found any more links to the symbol on their forehead?"

"Nothing I consider pertinent to the PTC, though I am still searching," Nicki answered.

Cat turned to Ryan. "How about a connection to the moon? Is there a tie-in to the symbol on their forehead?"

He glanced at Nicki and grinned. They believed Cat's request for a timeline against the cycle of the moon was another witchy hunch that paid off.

"Good call, Cat. I finished the timeline this morning, and there is a link." He motioned to a graph on the screen of his computer. "This is a chart of the moon cycles and dates of the murders. They have all occurred around a full moon."

Ed and Roger entered the room as Ryan talked. The grim look on their faces brought an abrupt halt to his discussion.

"Another woman, Lindy Denton, is missing," Roger told them. "She disappeared early this morning from a restaurant parking lot. Her car is still there."

Ryan asked, "Who reported her missing?"

"A couple left the restaurant and found her purse and car keys on the ground next to her car. The county sheriff put out a BOLO early this morning."

A shiver raised the hair on Cat's arms. The premonition from her dream was real. The killer had struck again.

Jessie stuck her head in the door. "Roger, you've got a phone call. It's from a veterinarian. He said you had called earlier and asked if he had any drugs stolen. Someone broke into his clinic last night, and he wants to talk to you."

Cat stared at the four officers in the room and knew each had the same question. Did the PTC just acquire another supply of drugs to support his killing spree?

The detective left to take the call. Cat gazed at the murder board and the pictures of the dead women and one survivor. It was only a matter of time before another was added—Lindy Denton.

Nineteen

Cat, asked, "Ed, do you have the address of the restaurant?"

"Yeah, I do. It's in the BOLO on my desk. I'll get it."

"Also, the address for the vet clinic." Cat booted her computer and pulled up a map of Clinton and the surrounding counties while she waited.

When Ed handed her the two addresses, he said, "Roger is still on the phone with the vet. From his end of the conversation, a substantial quantity of drugs was stolen."

She plugged the locations into the search engine. Ryan, Nicki, and Ed looked over her shoulder at the computer screen.

"Damn!" Cat said as the pins dropped on the map. The two locations were only five miles apart.

"That's too much of a coincidence. A burglary and a woman missing. Either on his way to the clinic or on his way back, he stopped, and my money is on a stop after the burglary," Nicki observed.

"I have to agree," Ryan replied as he studied the computer map.

"Ed, what time where her keys and purse found?" Cat asked.

He examined the BOLO and said, "The 911 call came in at 1:20 a.m."

Suddenly, her sense of trepidation was amplified by that riveting tug on her thoughts. Cat had planned to head to the hospital to check on the victim from the robbery. Now, she felt compelled, pushed to take a trip to the restaurant and vet clinic. "I want to check both locations. Anyone interested in tagging along?"

"I can't. Roger and I have interviews with the hostages from last night," Ed said.

Ryan glanced at Nicki. "I'll flip you for it."

"No, you go. I have another search program running and need to stay here," Nicki said.

"My car's in front unless you want to drive," Cat said.

"No, but I do need to grab some gear from my car."

Cat stepped into Kevin's outer office. His door was closed, and Jessie wasn't at her desk. She headed back to the conference room.

"Ed, would you tell Kevin where we're going? His door is closed, and I don't want to interrupt. I'm sure he's knee-deep in trying to fix the mess the mayor handed him."

It didn't take long to reach the restaurant. A sheriff's patrol car was parked in front of the building. A wrecker was leaving the parking lot with a vehicle hooked to a tow bar. Probably the victim's car, Cat thought.

A deputy sheriff walked out as they exited the car. After the introductions, Cat explained the missing woman could be connected to their investigation of several homicides.

Unfortunately, he had little information to add to what they already knew, though he provided the names and addresses of the two people who had found the woman's purse and car keys.

Ryan, followed by the deputy, went inside to interview the staff and obtain a list of employees who had worked the night shift.

Cat began a search of the small parking lot that was edged by bushes and several trees. Leaves of burnt orange, crimson red, and shades of green all mixed for a visual wonderland of color. A light breeze stirred the falling leaves. Fall was one of her favorite times of the year, and under other circumstances would have enjoyed the cool, refreshing touch of the wind on her face.

At the back of the lot, a few pieces of trash blew across the blacktop.

When she knelt to examine a small white object caught in the stems of a bush, Cat realized it was an empty packet for a syringe. She pulled her phone from a pocket and snapped several pictures.

At the sound of voices behind her, she stood and turned. Ryan and the deputy strode towards her. "Deputy Hayes, did anyone find a syringe?"

"A needle? No, I don't think so."

"What'd you find?" Ryan asked.

Cat motioned to the object in the bushes. "It's an empty syringe package. I bet syringes were stolen from the clinic."

"Do you have evidence bags and rubber gloves in your car?" Ryan asked.

"Yeah, there's a container in the trunk labeled evidence." She tossed him the keys. "There's also an envelope with evidence transfer forms." If Cat was going to keep the empty wrapper, she had to transfer custody from the sheriff's department.

As Ryan walked away, Hayes stared at Cat, his face confused.

"The killer uses drugs to subdue his victims. Where was Denton's car parked?" Cat asked.

Hayes indicated with his hand.

Once the evidence had been bagged and the form signed by Hayes, she said, "Ryan, would you and Deputy Hayes search for a needle? I want to finish checking the other side."

Cat strode along the edge of the lot. At the corner, limbs from a large tree hung over the outer edge of the pavement. When she walked under them, the leaves rustled. Glancing upward, two large owls sat on a branch. The sight of the birds removed the lingering hope they'd find the Denton woman alive.

Ryan shouted, "I found it."

Cat rushed toward him. He knelt near the edge of the sidewalk. The needle was wedged in a crevice. She snapped a few quick photos.

Ryan pulled another evidence bag from his jacket pocket. With a pen, he pushed on one end and slid it into the bag. "Deputy, I'll have another form for you to sign."

Once Hayes had signed, he asked, "Do you need anything else?"

Cat said no, thanked him for his help, and handed him a business card.

As they headed to her car, Cat glanced at the tree where the owls had perched. They were gone.

"Do you mind driving? I want to watch the terrain on the way to the clinic."

As he sat behind the wheel, Ryan wondered if he was about to experience another of Cat's hunches.

When they pulled out of the parking lot, the birds circled overhead, though Ryan was oblivious to them. When she asked him to slow down, he thought, *Yep, this is going to be a witchy happening.*

The county road to the vet clinic meandered through the woods southwest of Clinton. As they discussed Denton's disappearance, Cat kept an eye on the owls. Suddenly, they dipped behind a bend in the roadway, and she lost sight of them.

As the car rounded the curve, she spotted a large pile of debris. It was a sight too often seen on county roads. Trash bags, cast-off furniture, and appliances littered the area. The owls sat atop an abandoned refrigerator behind a stack of plastic bags.

"Pull over! Let's check that dump."

As he stopped on the shoulder, he said, "How about telling me what's going on?"

Cat stared out the window at the birds that patiently waited for her to acknowledge their presence. *Oh boy, here I go again. How the hell do I explain that I know her body is here?*

"Cat, I'll try to make this easy for you. I think everyone in the unit realizes there is something … should I say unique about us. The problem is we've learned to hide our abilities, even lie out of self-preservation, if nothing else. There are secrets we don't discuss. Am I getting close here?"

She sighed. "You're right. Scott referred to our special skills as the reason for being selected for the new unit. I wondered at the time. Yet … it's like you said, secrets and what would happen if someone finds out."

"While you think about it, I'm going to examine your trash pile."

Cat watched him slowly walk along the shoulder as he studied the site. She had opened up with Kevin, because, deep inside, she felt she could trust him. Yet, *I'm hiding information again, this time from a member of my team. If we are going to rely on each other, there must be trust and no secrets;* something that had never been a problem with her former colleagues.

Scott's words echoed in her head, *"you must be willing to be open and honest with each other. I expect it will be disconcerting and even uncomfortable."* Well, he was right, it was damn uncomfortable, even downright scary.

Her decision made, she popped the button to open the trunk. Grabbing the camera, she stuck a couple of evidence bags and rubber gloves in her jacket pocket. She called out, "I think she's over here, by that old refrigerator."

Cat walked a short distance down the road and circled to approach the trash heap from the back. Ryan had turned at the sound of her voice and followed her.

On the ground, hidden from the view of anyone on the road, was the body of a fully-clothed woman. Several bags had been tossed over and around her. The familiar sense of pain and anger swept over her. This woman should not be dead.

Ryan stopped beside her and stared at the body on the ground. "Holy hell! Witchy was right. How did you know she was here?"

"Meet my informants. They told me." Cat motioned with her hand to the two owls who still sat atop the rusted-out refrigerator. Recognizing her acknowledgment, the birds took flight and disappeared over the surrounding trees.

"Holy hell, this is incredible! Owls! Whatever I thought, it certainly wasn't this. Uh ... hmm ... just how does it work?"

"I've never really figured that one out. I just know when they show up someone has died, though I don't know who."

Moving to various positions, Cat snapped several pictures of the body.

"So, all that happens is that they appear?"

"Hmm ... no, it's more than that. They have a way of plucking at my thoughts if I don't notice them. Many times, just like now, they will lead me to the body."

She stepped to the side and took several more shots. "You didn't notice, but they have been ahead of us since we left the restaurant. It's why I had you slow down so we could follow them."

Cat dropped to one knee to examine the woman. "She hasn't been mutilated like the other victims. I wonder why?"

"Probably because she died before he could conduct the ceremony. It's all about the blood. If she died first, that couldn't happen," Ryan said.

"I bet you're right, that is the only answer that makes sense."

Standing, she scanned the surrounding field and woods. There was no ghostly presence.

"Let me try."

Astonished, Cat watched him kneel, lightly touch the back of the woman's hand, then close his eyes.

Several minutes later, he said, "I'm picking up a swirl of chaotic and delusional thoughts—fear, confusion, rage. It's not her, it's from the killer. Since his master, the old one, sent her to him, he doesn't understand why she's dead. He can't use her for his sacrifice and is afraid the master will be angry and punish him. He needs the perfect one."

"What!" she exclaimed in amazement.

Ryan stood up and shrugged his shoulders. "Sometimes, when I touch the body, I'm able to tap into thoughts and emotions." He glanced at her with a sheepish grin. "Trust and openness, right? Well, this is my ability. I'll call this in."

Wow, but any further discussion of their individual talents would have to wait as she surveyed the ground around the body.

Finding nothing, not even a footprint, she snapped a couple of additional pictures, then headed to the car. After dropping the camera in the trunk, she leaned against the side of the vehicle and called Nicki.

"We found the woman. The killer dumped her body at a trash site not far from the restaurant. This one is different, fully clothed, but we're certain the PTC killed her. We located a syringe at the restaurant. Let Kevin know if you see him."

"I will, though he has been tied up in meetings since you left. How long are you going to be there?"

"I don't know. We're waiting for the sheriff's department to arrive. Can you meet the medical examiner at the morgue? We need to put a rush on the autopsy, especially the toxicology report. You might be able to expedite the process if you're there in person. Since I'm not certain where we are exactly, I'll text you the coordinates."

As she hit the send button for the text, the rising wail of a siren signaled the response to the 911 call. Hearing the sound, Ryan moved to stand beside her as Deputy Hayes pulled behind Cat's vehicle.

When he approached, he asked, "Did you call 911?"

"Yes. We found a woman's body behind the trash pile and believe it's Lindy Denton," Cat explained.

The officer grunted, "Huh!" and gaped at her in disbelief. His eyes flicked to Ryan, who nodded his head.

Cat explained how they had approached the location of the body, and the deputy followed the same route. As soon as he spotted the woman, he radioed and requested the homicide unit and medical examiner.

After receiving the dispatcher's acknowledgment, he continued to scan the area. His eyes flicked between the road and the body. After several repetitions, he walked to the car, where the two agents waited. "How the hell did you find her? It's impossible to see the body from the road."

Cat responded before Ryan could say anything. "As I said earlier, we're investigating a series of homicides. The killer drugs the victim and then dumps the body at a trash site. Last night, someone burglarized a vet clinic a few miles from here and stole a number of drugs. We believe the burglar and killer are the same person. Finding the syringe at the restaurant connected the abduction to our killer. On the way to the clinic, we spotted the trash dump. It was just a hunch to stop and search it."

"Damn! That was some hunch." Another squad car pulled up, and Hayes left to greet the other officer.

Ryan leaned in to whisper in her ear. "Oh, you're good."

"Yeah, well, I've had lots of practice."

They watched the two officers talk and the number of times they glanced their way.

"I'd bet they are discussing our …hmm … your hunch," Ryan said.

Cat chuckled.

Other vehicles arrived. The county's homicide unit took numerous pictures and conducted a ground search before allowing the M.E. to approach the body. Once he had finished his examination, he motioned for the gurney.

As the attendants bagged and then loaded the body, the doctor stopped to speak to the agents. Cat recognized his name. He had performed the autopsies on the other victims.

"Based on my preliminary exam, death occurred between midnight and four a.m. this morning. I'll be able to be more definite once I can run a few tests."

"Any idea of the cause of death?" Cat asked.

"Not yet, though I did spot a possible injection site on the side of her neck."

"Dr. Morris, check for ketamine," Cat told him. "We believe this is connected to the other women who have been killed."

"Thought so when I heard two agents were waiting to talk to me. Have you figured out why this one wasn't carved up like the others?"

"We think she died before he had a chance," Ryan said.

"Well, I'll know soon."

Cat said, "Another agent, Nicki Allison, is going to meet you at the morgue."

"I'll put a rush on the reports," he said and headed to his van.

Twenty

Cat glanced at her watch. It was getting late, and they still had to visit the vet clinic. Her phone rang. It was Kevin.

"I talked to Nicki. She was headed out the door to the M.E.'s office. You can tell me later how you located the body, though it probably involved the owls. Where are you now?"

A surge of warmth flowed through her at his easy reference to the birds. He even made it sound quite ordinary. "We're headed to the clinic."

"I'll be working late if you want to stop by the station on your way back to town. How does dinner sound?"

"Great idea. I'll check with Ryan and Nicki. They might like to join us."

Disconnecting the call, Cat told Ryan about the late dinner.

"Yes, we have a lot to discuss, the killer, and the status of the mayor's investigation. I'll call Nicki."

Back in the car, there was an awkward silence. Uncomfortable with their earlier conversation, Cat wasn't sure what to say. *I hope I didn't make a mistake.* This was new ground in a working relationship with a team member.

"I was eleven when I had my first encounter," Ryan said.

Engrossed in her thoughts, his voice startled her.

She glanced at him. "What happened?"

"A friend of mine and I were roaming through the woods behind his house one Saturday afternoon. We were playing war games. Matt climbed a large tree to ambush me. He didn't know the tree was rotten, and the limb he crawled onto broke. When he hit the ground, his neck snapped. The doctor said death was instantaneous."

The voice on the navigation system said to take a right at the next road.

Ryan made the turn and continued with his story. "I ran to him, screaming his name. He didn't move. I touched his shoulder to shake him, and then—he stood in front of me. His body was on the ground, yet he stood there and stared at me. 'Don't be afraid it will be okay. You are going to save lives,' he said, then vanished."

He paused before saying, "It was one of the worst moments of my life. When I tried to tell my parents and friends what happened, they all believed I was traumatized by Matt's death. I finally shut up and accepted they were right."

"So, when did you learn they were wrong?"

"After I joined the FBI. There was an incident. How about you? When did you learn, you had a special ability?"

Certain there was more to the story, she still appreciated his sharing his experience. She explained the first time she'd seen the owls and the family legacy.

"Fascinating, a family legacy. I'm the only one in my family with this gift, and it's a total mystery how I got it." He turned into the driveway of the clinic.

It was a small building with a large barn and enclosed paddock in the back. Two horses stuck their noses over the wood fence and watched the approaching car. The door on the side of the clinic, its frame and several panels broken, had been nailed shut.

"That's how he gained entry. No cameras, perhaps some are inside though I doubt it. I bet this is the first time there's been a burglary," Cat said.

When they exited the vehicle, the horses whinnied to make their presence known. Ryan stepped over and rubbed their heads.

"Someday, I'd like to buy a small spread and have a few horses. I grew up on a farm. It will have to wait until I'm not so transient."

Footsteps crunched on the gravel. A large, grey-haired man dressed in jeans and a long-sleeved plaid shirt walked towards them. His eyes twinkled as he extended his hand. "I'm Doc Foster. You must be the FBI agents."

Cat introduced herself and Ryan as she shook his hand. It was large, the palm and fingers covered with calluses.

"Let's go inside, though I see you've already made friends with two of my patients." He reached to run his hand down the necks hanging over the fence. One butted his head against Foster's shoulder. Cat took an immediate liking to the man.

Inside, a small reception room had a few chairs and a counter. They followed Foster into an office. Settling into a chair in front of the desk, Cat glanced around the room. It was cluttered yet clean. Stacks of paper and magazines covered his desk and two cabinets. Diplomas hung on the wall along with a multitude of pictures of animals and people who were probably their owners.

"How long have you been here?" Cat asked.

His voice was mellow and soothing as he said, "I've been taking care of animals around here for the last thirty-five years. Those pictures you're looking at are my patients from over the years. Got some coffee in the pot over there. Help yourself."

Both shook their heads to decline his offer.

"I run a small and large animal clinic though most are of the large variety. I occasionally treat cats and dogs, which are mainly strays. Never understood why city folk think they have to drive into the country to ditch their unwanted animals. Anyway, how can I help you?"

"We know you've talked to the Sheriff's Department personnel. However, we wanted to examine your clinic," Cat said.

"You got any ideas on who broke in, and why is the FBI involved?"

"We believe the burglary may be connected to an investigation we're conducting." Cat wasn't about to tell him his drugs were used to kill a woman, and unless they could stop the PTC, they would be used to kill again.

"Has anyone ever broken into your clinic before last night?" Ryan asked.

"Nope, it's a first. Have to say, it was a shock when I arrived this morning."

"Do you have cameras or an alarm system?" he asked.

"Never needed them. Like I said, I've never had a dang bit of trouble before."

Cat asked, "Did you notice anything unusual over the last couple of days? A car parked on the road, someone watching your building?"

"No, nothing at all. As I explained to the deputy sheriff who took my report, I got here earlier than normal, but I'd been up all night. A neighbor's mare was ready to drop her foal, and there were complications. Rather than go home, I came to the clinic. I found the side door broke open. The lock had been cut off the drug cabinet, and the drugs were gone along with some cash."

"I'd like to look at the cabinet," Ryan said.

Foster led them through an open doorway to another room off the reception area. In the center was a large metal table, and medical equipment and cabinets lined the walls. Yips came from an adjoining room. Intrigued, Cat followed the sounds. Cages lined the walls, and several were occupied with dogs of varying sizes. The vet followed Cat, and as soon as the animals spotted him, the yips turned into barks. He walked to each of the cages. Reaching inside, he'd pat their head while a tail wagged in ecstasy.

"They love the attention." Straightening, he glanced at Cat. "Don't suppose you're in need of a pet? I need to find a home for a couple of these guys," he said as they moved back into the treatment room.

She chuckled, then said, "No, not with my schedule."

Ryan stood in front of a wall cabinet, his hand on a door covered with fingerprint residue. His gaze was fixed on the interior.

"As you can see, the lock was cut. Whoever did this had a bolt cutter with him, since I don't have one," Foster said, with a curious glance at Ryan who didn't seem to notice their presence.

Wanting to divert Foster's attention, even though she also wondered what Ryan was up too, she asked, "Where was the money kept that was stolen?"

"In the cash register in the front room. There was over two hundred dollars. I don't normally leave money. What with the emergency call yesterday, I just locked the door and left."

Cat followed him to the reception area. The vet motioned toward a small broken drawer under the counter. "That's where I kept the cash."

"Do you have a list of the drugs and quantities that were stolen?" she asked, as she stooped to take a closer look.

"Sure, got a list I wrote up for the deputy and kept a couple of copies. I thought I might need one for insurance. It's in my office."

While she waited, she glanced over her shoulder at Ryan, who still stood motionless in front of the drug cabinet.

Foster handed Cat a stapled set of papers. She scanned the long list of drugs. "This is a lengthy list. Do you always keep this volume of drugs in the clinic?"

Ryan walked up in time to hear Cat's question. His face lit up with a broad grin.

A twinkle glinted in the doc's eyes. "Young lady, you ever lived in the country?"

"No, sir, I haven't."

"Well, you learn to stock up as there is no store around a corner. That applies to the drugs. I never know what will come through the door and what I might need. It takes time to order in supplies, so I keep extra on hand."

Cat laughed. "It makes sense." She handed him a business card and told him to call if he remembered anything else.

They had reached the door when she remembered. Turning back, she asked, "Where any syringes stolen?"

"As a matter of fact, there were—two boxes. I didn't know they were missing when the deputy sheriff was here. It didn't occur to me to add it to the list. Is it important?"

"Could be." As with the drugs, she wasn't about to tell this kind and compassionate man the reason for the theft of the syringes.

Twenty-one

For the drive back, they swapped places. Ryan had brought his laptop and planned to plug the burglary data into the profile program he had developed.

Instead, the laptop sat in his lap, unopened while he stared out the window. Cat glanced at him a few times and mulled over what he was up to inside the clinic.

Well, the only way to get an answer was to ask a question. "What happened back there?"

There was a pause before he responded. "More to my story than I told you. It's not just bodies, but also objects. Usually, it occurs once I have connected to someone's thoughts and carries over to objects handled by the person. In this instance, the PTC touched the cabinet door."

Suddenly, Cat felt an unexpected empathy for Kevin's reaction to her owls and ghostly revelations. "Holy hell, you actually do have a way to link to the killer's mind. What did you pick up?"

"That's what I've been sorting in my mind. The degree of erratic feelings, the constant swirl of conflicting emotions and shifting thoughts, is a new experience. The chaos makes it difficult to filter a rational thought. I wonder if this is what it means to be insane?" He stopped again, his face furrowed in concentration.

"I detected elation over the drugs and money. He'll sell some of the drugs. He's also spooked by what happened with Arp and that the FBI is involved. He wants to leave town, yet he can't until he does something for his master, something special. That's about all I could get." He glanced at her. "These were his thoughts before he grabbed Denton. When I touched her, I picked up the rage, the fear he would be punished, and again that overpowering fixation to please his master."

Cat said, "Well, there's only one thing—another sacrifice. He can do that in another town. What could be so important he would risk staying here? Was it Denton?"

"No, I don't think so. Whatever it is has become an obsession, and Denton just happened to cross his path. It's not her. I need time to process what I learned today, plug the details into the profile, and study his behavior," Ryan said.

"Earlier, you mentioned another incident. What happened?" she asked, trying to understand his strange talent.

"Hmm … my partner and I responded to a homicide call related to a drug investigation. I touched the body, and suddenly, I sensed inexplicable thoughts that weren't mine. At first, I believed I'd gone crazy. Once I got past that notion, I realized I'd somehow linked to the killer's thoughts and emotions. The details I picked up led us to him. We were able to arrest him and shut down his drug operation."

Ryan sighed. "Like you, I had a hell of a time explaining how I obtained the information without divulging that it came from a dead man. This is the first time I've told anyone. How unexpected; this sense of relief someone not only understands but has similar experiences."

"I feel the same way. Do you remember what Scott said about the need to be open with each other? This must be what he meant. Do you think he knows?"

"I've wondered a few times. It doesn't seem possible. Yet, it accounts for his curious remarks. There is something inexplicable about Scott. I think working for the man is going to prove to be very interesting," he said.

"Any ideas on our fellow team members?"

Ryan laughed. "No, but I'm sure we'll find out."

Cat pulled into the parking lot of the station. *No media trucks, no gauntlet to run to reach the door. How nice.*

Jessie stepped out as they climbed the steps. She grimaced as she said, "It's been a hell of a day. I'm going home, pop a cold can of beer, prop my feet and forget that son-of-a-bitch even exists. By the way, that's the mayor. See ya tomorrow."

In the conference room, Ed and Roger were busy on their computers. Both looked toward the door as Cat and Ryan entered.

"We heard you found the body of the missing woman. What happened?" Roger asked.

Ryan started on the day's events, and Cat headed to Kevin's office. His door stood open. His fingers tapped the keyboard. A couple of raps on the doorframe caught his attention. When he looked up, a smile lit up his face.

A similar sense of joy rushed through her. A sensation she had come home.

"Rough day?"

Kevin sat back in his chair. "One of the worst, still probably not as bad as yours. I'm ready to get out of here. Are you?"

Cat realized she had missed lunch again. "Absolutely. What did you have in mind?"

"Want to try Italian again? We can sit in the back and have some privacy."

"God, it sounds good. Tonight, I'll have that glass of wine. Ryan's going to join us. Nicki's at the morgue. I'll call and let her know where to meet us."

Per Kevin's request, Mama Lorenzo seated the group at a corner table. He said they'd wait to order since there would be one more person joining them. Mama took their drink orders. For Cat, it was the long-awaited glass of wine and for the guys, beers.

Cat's phone rang. When she hung up, she said, "Nicki's on her way.

She stopped at the hotel to shower and change clothes."

Everyone could relate to the odor of a morgue. Antiseptically, it was probably the cleanest of medical facilities. There was, however, an aroma even the most potent disinfectants couldn't disguise.

While they waited, a conversation about sports flowed between Kevin and Ryan. Cat sipped her wine and listened.

Their talk turned serious once Nicki arrived.

Kevin said, "Let's get Bingham's activities out of the way. My homicide unit completed their investigation today. The detectives have taped interviews from two of the hostages who, of course, refutes the mayor's allegations. Mrs. Tilden is still unconscious. Also, there is the physical evidence from inside the store. Fingerprints on the guns match the dead men's prints. We have the recording from the open phone line; when one threatened to rape and kill Mrs. Tilden."

Mama Lorenzo walked up and dropped baskets of hot bread and small bowls of butter on the table.

Once she left with their orders, Ryan asked, "Any luck on locating Bingham's source?"

Kevin eyed Cat as she piled a gob of butter on a roll. "What is it with you and butter?" Sliding his bowl in front of her plate, he said, "Wouldn't want you to short yourself."

She grinned, popped the morsel in her mouth, and chewed.

Kevin turned to Ryan. "To answer your question, it's the brother of the man who assaulted Mrs. Tilden. Says his brother wanted to walk out of the store, but the cops wouldn't let him. There is a call on the dead man's phone to the brother's phone. The timestamp is just before the hostage negotiator began calling the store. We still haven't located any other witness. The District Attorney, though, is satisfied with the results and plans to send the case to the Grand Jury tomorrow."

Cat swallowed another bit of bread and asked, "Have you heard anything more from the mayor?"

"No. Two state detectives will be here tomorrow morning and plan to meet with him. That should be an interesting confrontation. I'd like to be the proverbial fly on the wall."

"How can Bingham even believe he could get away with such outrageous accusations?" Nicki asked.

"He's not the brightest star on the horizon, but he has money and has successfully used it to flimflam his way through the political arena. He won't hesitate to use bribes or threats, and if it doesn't go his way, he's good at setting someone else up to take the fall. In this case, someone handed him a line of BS, and his obsession to get rid of me overrode what little common sense he has."

"Kevin, tell Ryan and Nicki your suspicions of the election. And, I still need those contracts," Cat told him.

Kevin explained the reason for the bad blood between him and the mayor and his concerns over the election. He added, "Recently, I received a tip the construction contracts Bingham approved may be tied to his election. I haven't had time to follow-up because of the homicides."

"Give me that list of companies. I'll run a background on their financials," Nicki said.

"I'll look into the funding for Bingham's election campaign," Ryan added.

Kevin's face reflected his amazement at their comments. "I didn't expect your support for a local issue. Especially when I don't have any evidence, just a gut instinct that says Bingham is dirty. But, when he made a big deal about kicking you out-of-town, his attitude added to the red flags."

Waving a knife with another glob of butter in the air, Cat said, "After today's stunt, he's got my attention."

Kevin stared at the knife, then the two empty butter bowls, and grinned before taking another swig of beer. He said, "Bingham made an odd comment about Scott's reaction, that he might rethink the decision to keep his agents in town. I'm beginning to wonder if that's the motive behind his accusations."

Ryan said, "You might be right, get rid of you and us at the same time. What he doesn't understand is that we aren't going away, and if he thinks our boss will knuckle under," he chuckled, then added, "He's in for a rude awakening."

Considering enough time had been spent on the mayor's activities, Kevin said, "Bring me up to date on what happened today."

Cat covered the day's events, ending with, "Ryan and I are absolutely certain the burglar is the PTC, and now, he's stocked with drugs and money. It was only a matter of time before he struck again."

"What made you stop at the trash pile?" Nicki asked.

Cat glanced at Ryan, who seemed to be engrossed with his bottle of beer, and Kevin's eyes gleamed with laughter. It suddenly struck her that Nicki was the only one at the table who didn't know about the owls. This certainly wasn't the time to enlighten her.

"The site was on the way to the clinic, and the killer would have seen it. It was just one of those freakish ideas that paid off."

Hoping to divert Nicki's attention away from any more uncomfortable questions, she asked, "Anything new from the autopsy?"

"There's an injection site on her neck. The M.E. is waiting on the toxicology report though his preliminary finding is an overdose. The deputy sheriff who investigated the initial call found a prescription bottle for anti-depressants in her purse. If she was injected with another drug, the combination could have killed her."

Ryan said, "We suspected she died before he could perform his ceremony."

Kevin asked, "The injection is a change from doping a drink. Ryan, any thoughts on that?"

"Denton was headed to her car in the parking lot. He had an opportunity and took it. Does that mean he may change his M.O.? Possibly."

Ryan paused, took a sip of beer, then added, "He may be spooked by what happened with Arp. She fought back. Injecting means there's a faster response to the drug, less of a chance they would fight him like she did. He might decide it's easier than sitting around, waiting for the drug to take effect."

Cat said, "It's time to go public with the sketch."

"I agree, but we need to be cautious in the wording. I don't want to start a panic," Kevin said.

"Can we get one set up for tomorrow?" Cat asked.

"Shouldn't be a problem. I'll have Jessie make the arrangements as soon as she gets to work."

"I'll work on the press release tonight, so it will be ready. Tomorrow, I want to go over every detail we've found so far. We might have missed something," Cat said.

Their plates of food arrived. Kevin switched the conversation back to football, and Nicki eagerly dived into a debate with the two men over which team would be headed to the super bowl.

Cat listened and watched Kevin. He liked to gesture with his hands when making a point. A sudden image of those long fingers stroking and caressing her body flashed in her mind. The heat rose. *Hell, here I go again. What is it about Kevin that sends me straight to lust-land? I've been around sexy men before. My god, look at Ryan. He's one good-looking guy. Yet, he doesn't generate even the slightest spike in my temperature. As soon as I am near Kevin, it's fever time. It's pathetic.* She sighed and turned her attention back to her food.

Since it had been a long day for everyone, there was no disagreement when Ryan suggested they call it a night. When they filed out of the restaurant, Nicki and Ryan went ahead. Cat waited for Kevin as he had stopped to talk to Mama.

Walking out, his hand touched the small of her back as if to steady her down the steps. As light as the contact was, she felt the warmth through her jacket. She longed to just lean back, let his arms wrap around her. Instead, his voice brought her back to the events of the day.

"I suspect there is more to the story than you were saying, just didn't want to ask. How did you find the body … or was it the owls that found her?" Kevin asked.

Her eyes flicked up at him. "Yes. They led me to her."

He chuckled. "I knew from that 'oh, it was just a freakish idea' comment you were in your vague explanation mode."

Cat clicked the remote to unlock the door. When she reached for the door handle, Kevin put his hand on her shoulder and turned her toward him. The lights in the parking lot illuminated his face. What she saw sent another wave of heat flowing through her. A man had never gazed at her with such intense desire. She leaned into him, her eyes locked on his. His hand gently brushed her face, his thumb stroked her lips.

"Kevin ... um ... not ... not certain …"

"Hush. Let's enjoy the moment. Tomorrow will take care of itself," he said as his lips closed over hers.

As the kiss deepened, Cat's arms circled his neck, her fingers slid through strands of hair. His arms tightened, pulling her closer to his body. The honk of a car horn suddenly intruded, reminding them they stood in full view in a parking lot.

Cat nervously stepped back. "I should head to the hotel."

"Yeah, I guess so," he said and lightly trailed his fingers down her cheek. "I'll see you in the morning."

Her thoughts as she drove out of the parking lot were all Kevin. *I don't want to leave. Still, it's not what I want, but what I have to do. The man has enough trouble without giving the mayor additional ammunition.*

In her room, it didn't take long to write up the press release. She tried to review the case files and finally gave up when she caught herself rereading the same paragraph. She fell asleep, reliving the kiss.

Images of a blood-red moon drifted in her dreams. As it rose, she soared on the night wind. The beat of wings, then the screech of an owl echoed. Odd, the sounds seemed to come from her. Drifting downward, she flew over a small trailer park. As drops of rain fell, she circled the trailers. No! Not rain—blood, and it coated her wings until she plummeted to the ground.

Twenty-two

errified, she fought to break free of the sheets that again entwined her body. Gasping for air, she came awake. Pushing the covers aside, she sat on the edge of the bed. With hands braced on each side, she stared into the darkness. *What the hell is happening? I've never had dreams like this, and they are getting worse.* It was the first time she was an active participant.

Cat took several deep breaths to slow the stabbing beat that pounded in her chest. The lingering fear left a bitter taste in her mouth.

There was still an hour until her wake-up call. It was a waste of time trying to go back to sleep. *At least, I got a few hours* as she stripped off the sweat-soaked nightshirt.

With her forehead pressed against the shower wall, the hot water cascaded over her. The warmth eased the tension in her neck and shoulders. *Nana, oh, how I wish I could talk to you.* The loneliness brought tears to her eyes as her mind slipped into the past.

The day she learned about her gifts was one she would never forget. It was the same day her best friend was killed. She had been at her grandmother's house when her mother called with the news. Devastated, her body shook from uncontrollable sobs. Seated on the couch, her grandmother's thin arms had enclosed Cat in a tight embrace. Fingers stroked her back as Nana Ruth lightly rocked her.

She never knew what prompted her to mention the birds outside her bedroom window, but it set off a conversation that changed her life forever.

Ruth had tipped Cat's face up and wiped away the tears. "Sweetie, is this the first time you've seen the owls?" she'd asked.

"No. I saw them the day Aunt Hester died."

Her face troubled, and with a deep sigh, her eyes took on a distant look as she stared over Cat's shoulder. "It's time, she has to know, but this will be difficult. I wish she were older, but what is done is done."

Her tone had scared Cat. Who was she talking too? She had even glanced behind her to see if someone was there. "Nana, I don't understand."

At the sound of her voice, Ruth's eyes had refocused on Cat's face. "I know you don't. It's a story about your ancestors. Long ago, a group of Scotch-Irish immigrants settled in Bristol. One of the immigrants, Conall, married a Cherokee Indian, Avita. She was an extraordinary person and revered by her people. She could communicate with the dead and owls that were considered sacred by the tribe."

Her attention diverted from the loss of her friend, Cat learned about the mysterious powers of the owls and what it meant when they appeared.

Then her grandmother had added, "But Avita wasn't the only one with a special gift. Conall could see and hear what others couldn't. Today, most people call it a sixth sense. We are their descendants, and their gifts have continued to be passed down to family members. As you grow older, other abilities may develop."

Frightened, she'd asked, "What else is there?"

Nana had patted her hand. "There's nothing to be afraid of. But you might see people who have died, or it may be dreams or a feeling that something will happen. It's different for each person who has inherited the gifts. Have you had any other odd things happen?" Ruth asked.

"I have dreams, sometimes they are really weird, but when I tell mom, she says I've just got an active imagination. She tells me it's better if I forget about them. Does she know?"

"Oh, she knows about the legends, but she doesn't have the gifts. If you experience anything unusual, I want you to tell me."

Suddenly, Cat realized what Ruth meant. "Nana, do you have the gifts?"

A smile lit her face as she answered. "Yes, I do, and I know your abilities will surpass mine."

Over the years, there were a number of inexplicable incidents. Cat relied on her grandmother to explain the unthinkable, especially after her first encounter with a ghost. Ruth also taught her how to disguise the source of her information … how to lie.

The first year she was at the academy, her grandmother had a heart attack and died. Cat always wondered why the owls never appeared.

She turned off the water and grabbed a towel. Nothing her grandmother had ever told her had prepared her for the dreams she now experienced. *Figure it out* as she chastised herself for the moment of weakness. *If you don't—another woman might die.*

The hotel staff had just started to set out the breakfast items. She grabbed her usual cup of coffee and egg sandwich. As she opened her car door, the distinct screech of owls sent chills running down her back. Over the years, she had learned the difference in the sounds they made. The screech was their warning. A sense of foreboding weighed on her as she scanned the sky. She knew but was powerless to act.

Jessie was at her desk when she entered the office. Her cheerful smile lightened the depression that had settled over Cat. Laughing, Cat said, "You sure work long hours. It seems you are here when I leave and when I arrive."

"Since I'm not married, you might say my job is my life, and I like working for the Chief. He puts in longer hours than I do. Besides. with the task force investigation, the workload has increased. It's good that I got here early since the Chief wants a press conference."

Cat handed her the press release. "I'm not sure how many copies we might need. What time is it set for?"

"Nine, and I'll take care of the copies. Are you okay? You look tired."

"Crazy dreams." Cat looked at Kevin's closed door. "Is he busy?"

"He's already on a conference call with the Attorney General's office and the District Attorney."

As she left the office, anger pulsed through her. Cat knew another woman was dead, and Bingham's interference in the task force investigation had resulted in a deep-seated hostility toward the man.

Nicki was in front of her computer. Ryan was unpacking his briefcase, and the aroma of freshly brewed coffee filled the air.

"I thought I'd be the first one here, but you two are really up early." She dropped her gear and headed to the pot to refresh her coffee.

Nicki said, "I set an alert on my computer to wake me. Good thing I did, because I received several emails with additional pictures of some of the sites where victims had been found. I wanted to get them posted."

Amazed, Cat said, "Your computer woke you? Oh, god, that is so funny." The laughter rolled out of her.

Ryan chuckled, then said, "Yeah, she called me. Told me to get my butt in gear, she had to get to the office."

Puzzled, Nicki eyed them. "Uh … what's the joke here? What's so funny about an alert on a computer?"

"Oh nothing, I guess, other than most people rely on an alarm clock or a wakeup call."

Nicki snorted in response, then nodded toward a stack of papers on the desk. "Kevin dropped off the construction contracts. I'll work on them today."

The thought of the mayor brought an abrupt halt to Cat's enjoyment of Nicki's discomfort. Anger rumbled as she said, "I hope you find the evidence to lock him away for a long … long time."

The whirr of the printer sounded as it spit out pictures. Nicki grabbed them. Since the murder board was full, she and Ryan spread them across the table. While they examined them, Cat sorted through the case files, picking up where she had left off the night before.

The next in the stack was labeled Martha Anderson. Easing back in the chair, she studied the woman's statement. "Damn!" she exclaimed.

Nicki and Ryan glanced at her. She stared up at them. "A hitch. The woman saw a trailer hitch."

"What?" Ryan asked.

"Martha Anderson, the bug owner, saw one of those large balls that mount on a bumper. She didn't mention it when I talked to her, but it's in her statement. My god, he is staying at trailer parks," she said. The trailer park from her dream flashed through her mind.

Kevin entered, followed by two individuals attired in business suits. He introduced them, Detectives Hall and Simpson, from the state homicide division. As he explained the task force investigation into the homicides, the men walked to the murder board.

"We received the bulletin and sketch you sent out. It's a bad case, and I wish we could help. Unfortunately, our caseload has overflowed," Detective Hall said.

Kevin said, "I can imagine if you have to deal with many cases like Bingham handed you."

Simpson replied, "Can't say we ever got one quite like the mayor's complaint. Unfortunately, we do have to investigate, despite whether we believe the case has merit."

Hall looked at Cat. "Agent Morgan, if you have a few minutes, we need your statement."

Kevin said, "You can use my office."

Detective Hall set up his recording device on Kevin's desk, and when prompted, Cat detailed the events that led to the shooting of the two men. When she finished, the detectives asked several questions regarding her rifle qualifications, Kevin's instructions, and what she observed when the entry team entered the building, after which he turned off the recorder.

"When will your investigation be completed?" Cat asked.

Simpson said, "Tomorrow or the next day at the latest. We've received Chief Hunter's reports and the taped interview of the hostages. We need to conduct interviews with the individuals involved and Mrs. Tilden. She regained consciousness this morning."

"Oh, that is good news," Cat said. A call to the hospital was on her agenda.

The detectives thanked Cat for her time, and she headed to the conference room.

Kevin's raised eyebrows sent a silent question when she came into the room. She simply nodded her head to indicate everything was okay.

"The press conference is scheduled to start in about twenty minutes. How do we play it?" Kevin asked.

"Kevin, I think you should take the lead, the three of us will stand behind you. It's up to you whether you want to introduce us," Cat replied.

Nicki and Ryan nodded their heads in agreement.

Ryan handed out several stapled pages. "This is an updated profile. I found a correlation between the cycle of the moon and the death of the victims. Based on the moon's current cycle, there are only a couple of days left. He could go after another victim, or he might go dormant. If he does plan to move to a new location, this is when it will likely happen."

Cat looked at each of the individuals around the table. Her voice was quiet but firm with absolute conviction. "I believe there is a short window of opportunity to apprehend the PTC, three to four days at the most. If we lose him ... well, it will have deadly consequences."

There was a short silence at the stark reality of her assessment.

"We've got another lead," she said for the benefit of Kevin. "Anderson saw a trailer hitch on the truck. It could mean he is staying at an RV park."

Ryan added, "A trailer is very likely and would fit the profile. Kevin, do you have any idea how many RV parks there are in and around Clinton?"

Kevin groaned. "A lot. Hunting and fishing are a major sport in this area of the state, and many of them are the mom and pop type locations. The problem is locating them. The Park Rangers might be able to help. We'll contact the sheriff's office and highway patrol. As soon as Roger and Ed have finished their interviews with the state detectives, I'll hand that task to them," Kevin said.

Cat asked, "Do you have a large map of the state? I want to pin each park location to establish a geographic relationship to our crime scenes."

"Jessie can find one," he said as the woman walked in and handed him a large envelope.

"This is from the M.E.'s office. What do you need me to find?" Jessie asked.

"A large state map," Kevin answered.

"I'll check the storeroom. If we don't, I'll locate one. How soon do you need it?"

"Within the next couple of hours. Also, a box of colored push pins."

He opened the envelope, removed several documents, and thumbed through them. "He sent all the reports, Lindy Denton and the men from the robbery."

Kevin handed the Denton report to Cat and sat at the end of the conference table to read the other two. When finished, he laid the reports on the table and stared at them. He did not realize until he looked up the room was silent.

He glanced at Cat, who held the Denton report, unopened. Though her gaze was steady, the rapid beat of the pulse in her throat gave her away.

Kevin had learned from Scott that Cat had been involved in a deadly force incident in her last case. He hadn't been surprised at her reticence to discuss it in the aftermath of the events at the convenience store. Being closemouthed seemed to be an ingrained habit with her.

He said, "The reports do not include the officer's name. The rifles are labeled A and B. If for any reason, this case goes to court, we'd have to identify the officers. Cat, rifle A is yours. Your first shot struck the heart. He was dead before he hit the floor. Your next shot clipped the aorta of the second suspect. Sutton's shot hit him in the shoulder. He was also dead within seconds."

Three lives saved—I have to focus on that fact. It was what it was, and there was nothing—nothing I could have done to alter the outcome. Suddenly, she realized no one else had commented. They all looked at her. *God, what do I say?*

Twenty-three

J essie stuck her head in the door. "The hordes await. The parking lot is full, and the mayor called. He wants you in his office."

Kevin looked at his watch. "Well, he'll have to wait. Everyone ready?" he asked.

Thankful for Jessie's timely arrival, Cat nodded her head yes.

The parking lot was jammed with vehicles and people. TV vans with raised towers ringed the lot. Reporters milled around the vans, and camera crews jostled for the best position. A crew filmed a reporter who stood in front of a marked patrol car.

Everyone turned toward Kevin when he stepped to a podium placed by the front door. He was in full uniform today instead of his usual casual attire. The morning sunlight reflected off the gold stars on his collar. Kevin had something that went beyond exceptional good looks. He exuded a sense of power and confidence.

Several of the reporters shouted questions. Kevin held up his hand and waited. When it became quiet, he said, "Behind me are FBI Special Agents Caitlin Morgan, Ryan Barr, and Nicole Allison. They are part of the Clinton Police Department's task force formed to investigate the murders of several women."

Over the next few minutes, he highlighted a few of the results of the investigation, then pointed to a small table near the podium. On top was a stack of papers. "I have a press release with a sketch. Anyone who has seen or knows the whereabouts of this man is asked to call the Clinton Police Department. I will take a few questions. Any further details of the investigation, though, are confidential at this time."

Most of the questions resulted in the same answer—no comment. Kevin said he'd take one more question.

The reporter assigned to the Mayor's office asked, "Two men were killed by an FBI agent. Mayor Bingham has filed criminal charges against you, your department, and the FBI for their deaths. Any comment?"

Though Kevin bristled at the failure to mention they were killed during an armed robbery turned hostage incident, his face showed no emotion. "The two men attempted an armed robbery of a convenience store and held three people hostage. District Attorney Marlin filed the results of the police investigation today with the Grand Jury. This is a standard procedure when a death involves the use of deadly force. As for Mayor Bingham's charges, the state homicide unit has initiated an investigation. Once their investigation is complete, I am confident the Clinton Police Department and officers who saved the lives of three innocent persons will be exonerated of any wrongdoing."

Kevin turned and stepped away from the podium as reporters continued to shout questions. The three agents followed him inside. Jessie looked at him with a sympathetic smile and said, "Fresh coffee along with an assortment of bagels and muffins are in the break room. The mayor's office called again."

Kevin headed to his meeting at City Hall. When he entered the mayor's office, Liz looked up and grimaced. She nodded her head toward her boss's open door. Kevin recognized her signal to be careful about what he said.

"I'm here for the meeting."

At his words, her shoulders dropped in relief.

"I'll tell him you ..."

Bingham's booming voice covered her response. "Hunter, get your ass in here."

Kevin walked in and asked, "What's this meeting for?" With difficulty, he managed to keep his contempt out of the tone of his voice.

"The state investigators canceled our meeting. I want to know why and what you told them."

"They're conducting an investigation. I answered their questions. As to why they canceled a meeting with you, I don't have a clue."

"I haven't seen any evidence of an investigation. I've been told all they did was pick up your reports."

"Which is part of the investigation. I'm sure the detectives will contact you when they are ready to discuss the case," Kevin said. *And—you just confirmed my suspicions that someone in my department has been feeding you information.*

"They damn well better. This city will not be responsible for any cover-up for your department's negligence. Your press conference will blow up in your face when they prove you and your officers screwed up."

He had heard enough. "I'll be in my office if you have any further questions."

Bingham shouted as Kevin walked out the door. "Enjoy it while you can. It won't be yours much longer."

Cat soon learned Kevin was right. Even with Roger and Ed working on the RV park lead, it would take time to compile the list. Many of the small rural parks didn't have websites. The detectives devised a plan to coordinate with the other agencies and started on another round of phone calls. Ryan and Nicki were running searches online.

Jessie rolled a second corkboard through the doorway. "I borrowed this from a nearby school." Tacked on it was a large map.

Cat helped to push it into place against the wall. Jessie pulled a box of pushpins from her pocket and handed them to her. "If you need anything else, let me know."

"Here are the online sites I've found so far," Nicki said and handed Cat a printed list.

As Cat marked the location of each park with a pushpin, her anxiety and uneasiness continued to intensify. Once she was done, she paced, picking up one file after another, or added a pushpin as someone found another location.

Nicki finally told her to sit down before she drove everyone nuts. Ryan looked up and silently mouthed, 'witchy moment' to Nicki.

When Nicki's phone rang, Cat's heart plunged. She knew. Hunched over the table, her face grief-stricken—she waited.

Within seconds everyone else realized there was another victim. Nicki made a few notes as she talked. Disconnecting, she said, "That was the Richland police chief. They have a body that matches our victims. Two city workers stumbled across it this morning in a gravel pit. His detective is sending the initial reports and pictures."

Everyone in the room felt the agony in Cat's voice as she asked, "Did he say when?"

"The preliminary time frame from the M.E. is between midnight and five a.m."

Kevin walked into the room. "What happened?"

"Another body, west of Richland," Nicki said.

"Where the hell is Richland?" Cat asked, her grief turning to anger.

Kevin stepped to the state map and pointed to the location. "It's southeast of Jackson, around fifteen miles from Clinton."

Nicki's computer beeped. "This may be the reports." Clicking her keyboard, "Yeah, it is. Pictures and reports are printing."

As page after page slid out, Cat grabbed them. Silent, she gazed at a photo of a naked woman, covered with dried blood and partially encased in trash bags. Multiple cuts disfigured her face. Deep incisions were on one arm, and plastic covered the other. The dread that had built since waking from the dream now had a name, Wendy Carson.

Ryan made copies and passed them out. Roger and Ed put their cell phones aside. For a few minutes, silence reigned as the investigators absorbed the information in the documents.

Cat broke the silence. "There's an injection site on her neck. I bet he grabbed her the same way he did Lindy Denton. Yeah, here it is," as she flipped a page in the report. "A parking lot at a local bar. Hmm … a bar, that's different as well as a gravel pit."

"Yeah, if the city employee hadn't stepped out of his truck to take a leak, the body might never have been found," Nicki said.

"He's escalating. This is five victims in and around Clinton. Before this, there's a distinct time difference between the victims. Ryan, any idea why?" Kevin asked.

Ryan shuffled the photos of the latest victim, examining each one before he said, "Participants in satanic rituals call on a demon or the devil to grant their request. The ritual makes them feel powerful. The use of drugs enhances the experience. The killer has probably been spurned all his life. Performing the ceremony would compensate for his inadequacies, make him feel potent and in control. His victims are the blood offering to obtain approval and power. He even marks them with the symbol of his deity, the horned god, his way of saying, here this is yours."

Dropping the handful of new photos on the table, he stood in front of the murder board and examined the pictures of the other women. "As Kevin noted, there is a separation of time and distance with his earlier victims. The gratification he received was probably in the performance of the ceremony itself, not from any results of the ritual."

Ryan tapped one of the Lewis pictures. "That changed with Lewis. Something happened. This is a psychotic, drug-addicted individual. If his delusions made him believe his master answered, and he had to repeat the experience or suffer the master's anger—well, fear can be a powerful motivator, maybe even more than success. It could be why he immediately went after another victim, then another."

He turned to look at the people seated in front of him. As he paused, he ran his hand across the back of his neck. Cat had noticed this mannerism whenever Ryan discussed a complex set of ideas. He reached and picked up one of the photos of the latest victim and stared at it.

"I've asked myself, why is he still in Clinton? He must know we are searching for him and even have his picture. He could easily move and pick up where he left off at a new location, but he hasn't. Why? I think it's because he has a new target. One he believes will satisfy his master. He can't leave until he gets her. Once he does, he'll be gone. And it's not our latest victim. Look at the carving on her forehead."

He tossed the picture in the middle of the table. Jagged incisions spread across the young woman's forehead, nose, and cheeks. "Unlike the others, her face, not just the forehead, has been mutilated. These are cuts of rage. He failed. Which means he will be on the hunt again and soon."

Twenty-four

The angry yowls of a catfight brought him out of a sound sleep. *Damn animals!* He had a solution to cure the problem, but it would probably piss off his neighbors, and he had to avoid calling attention to himself. Knowing he wouldn't get back to sleep, JD crawled out of bed. In the tiny bathroom, he took a leak and splashed water on his face.

Bright light flooded the living room, setting off sharp pricks of pain in his head. He'd forgotten to close the blinds again. The sunlight made the headaches worse. Grabbing a can of beer, he strode to the window, scanning the floor for any bloodstains. The rage he had felt when he knew he had failed resurfaced, setting off another round of agonizing pain.

He shook a pain pill from a bottle on the table, popped it in his mouth, and followed it with another swig of beer. With a plate of leftover pizza in one hand and the beer in the other, he settled in front of the TV. He rested his head against the chair for a few seconds, to let the pain and nausea ease before setting the can on the floor. He flipped channels to a midday local news program as he lifted a slice to take a bite. It fell back onto the plate. "Son-of-a-bitch! That's me!"

A reporter stood in front of a police car and held a drawing up to the camera. How did they get his picture? It was impossible, no one ever paid him any attention. Waves of panic and fear rolled through him. *I gotta leave, gotta get out of here.*

The picture shifted to the police chief who stood in front of the police building. As the camera spanned the group standing behind the cop, the image changed. For an instant, he saw a red moon, bright and glistening with blood. The vision faded, and it was a woman, her hair a glowing cloud of red around her face. *It's her, the perfect one. Damn, I can't leave. This is the one the Master wants.*

The picture switched back to the reporter who held up the drawing one more time. Pushing the plate onto the couch, he watched as the camera zoomed onto the sketch—his face filled the screen.

What if the prick that runs this place sees the picture, will he know it's me? I can't stay here. I'll have to move. Damn, where do I go? I can't go far until I have the woman.

JD's muddled thoughts twisted and tumbled from one to another. He'd ditch the overalls, switch to an old pair of jeans, though he wasn't sure what to do with his hair and beard. Hell, he'd push the hair under the ball cap. Since he was leaving anyway, no sense in cutting it or the beard. But where would he go? Finally, he remembered a location he spotted on one of his many trips prowling around the county backroads. *That'll work, no one will find me until I am ready to leave, and I'll have time to finish my plans.*

After changing clothes, he headed to the park office. The car belonging to the owner was gone, and a closed sign hung in the window. He stopped at the corner of the building and scanned the small row of trailers. It was the middle of the day, and most of the cars were gone. It was an easy task to jimmy open the old door lock, and he slid inside. *Hell, the idiot will never know someone broke in, he'll think he forgot to lock it.*

What he wanted was on a small table in the living room behind the office. He quickly disabled the TV set. Hopefully, they would stop showing his picture before it got fixed. *Too bad, I can't take it. I could sell it for a few bucks, but a report would bring out the cops.*

Searching for his registration card, he found a wad of cash in a desk drawer. For several seconds, he studied the bills before grabbing several. *What the hell, I just won't take it all.* The way it's stuffed in here, he probably wouldn't notice any was missing. Besides, if someone was going to steal it, they'd take all of it.

His form was in a stack of papers thrown into the filing cabinet. He still had two days left. *The bastard will think he came out ahead when he sees I'm gone.*

Back at the trailer, it didn't take long to hook up. Whistling, he drove out the gate as images of the perfect one lying on the floor consumed his thoughts.

Cat picked up the photo Ryan had tossed on the table. The image burned into her mind as she pondered Ryan's comments. Deep inside, she believed that if they didn't find the killer soon, they would lose him.

Kevin asked, "Where do we stand on the RV parks? This is our best lead right now."

"Roger and Ed issued another law enforcement bulletin with the sketch, this time requesting that all rural parks be checked. We also started a list, and the map is marked with the sites we found so far. How did your meeting go with Bingham?" Cat said.

He grimaced as he closed the door to the conference room. "Not well. This conversation does not leave this room," he cautioned as he looked at his two officers. Both nodded their heads.

"Bingham ranted and raved for several minutes, tossed out additional threats against the department and me. It's bluster. In his rage, though, he let a valuable detail slip. Someone is feeding him information on the department's operation and our cases. I hate to say it, but it's likely the person works for the PD."

"I've uncovered several facts I haven't had a chance to give you," Nicki said. "Ryan found that Bingham received large contributions to his election fund from dummy corporations. I discovered a connection between the corporations and two of the construction companies on your list. Both were awarded hefty contracts after he took office. And,

I found a link between several individuals who contributed to his campaign and those same dummy companies. It's possible they are straw donors, paid to contribute." She handed him a list containing the names of the contributors, dummy corporations, and the construction companies.

For a minute, Kevin was speechless. He suspected—still, evidence built a case, not suspicion. "No wonder Bingham was upset over your involvement. I wonder if he had a premonition his house of cards was about to come tumbling down?"

He quickly scanned the list. "I bet I just found the identity of the mayor's informant. The department has a ride-along program for civilians. One of the regulars is a young college student working on a degree in criminal justice. He rides with an officer in the evenings, at least a couple of times a week. His father owns one of the construction companies. Mike goes home and tells his dad the latest scuttlebutt, along with the details of our investigations. His dad passes the information to Bingham. I wonder if the kid is in on it or is an innocent victim?"

He glanced at the group. "It would explain several of my conversations with the mayor and his distorted version of events, like the convenience store takedown. The next morning Bingham's press conference aired before most people were even at work. The kid was riding with an officer and was at the scene. Several wild and absurd stories circulated that night. Be interesting if we could find a record of a call from the contractor to the mayor's home."

"There is another issue," Ryan said. "I'm running a program to compare the information on the petition that put Bingham's name on the ballot and the IRS records. It will identify any fake or invalid social security numbers."

A smile of unholy glee lit up Kevin's face.

Cat sat back and listened while Kevin discussed the details with Nicki and Ryan. Once they got past their initial shock at Kevin's suspicions, the detectives tossed in an occasional question. As she enjoyed watching the animation in Kevin's face, she suddenly realized that being in the same room with him improved her day. *Though I still don't understand this incredible connection, I'm not fighting it anymore. We'll find out where today and even tomorrow takes us. Well, now—how crazy is that?*

The knock on the door brought her attention back to the conversation in the room. Jessie opened it and handed Kevin several sacks.

"How much do I owe you?"

"I took it out of petty cash. Figured the mayor owed us lunch."

Kevin grinned and didn't argue. As he handed out the sandwiches, the conversation on Bingham's activities resumed. Details were added to the investigation, a search of phone records and bank accounts, and even the need to monitor the mayor's movements. Over Kevin's objections, Roger and Ed volunteered for the detail. It eliminated Kevin's concern about adding additional officers. The fewer involved, the less chance Bingham might learn he was under investigation. Kevin didn't want the bastard to know until he walked into his office and slapped on the cuffs.

No one quibbled over the extra tasks or the extended work hours. The first priority was stopping a killer. The Bingham investigation would be squeezed in whenever there was a lull.

By the end of the day, a lengthy list of RV sites had been compiled. Cat tossed out a question about the best way to check them.

"If we send the list to other agencies, there is always a chance one might get missed. We can't risk it. I think we need to handle the search," Kevin said.

He studied the sites on the map before saying, "If we divide into three teams, we should be able to contact all the locations in one day."

Using the map, she and Kevin set up a search grid to reduce the drive time to each location as several were in remote areas of the county.

Armed with their list, Ed and Roger headed out the door. Cat glanced at her watch; more than enough time to contact the locations on her list that were inside the city limits before it got dark.

She gathered her files and computer. While Nicki continued her internet search of sites, Kevin and Ryan were in a discussion on the fraud investigation.

When Kevin noticed she was ready to leave, he asked, "Are you headed back to your hotel?"

"No, I'm stopping at the parks that are in Clinton before it gets dark."

"If you'll wait for a few minutes, I'll go with you. I'm done here for the day."

Cat wanted to grin from ear to ear but didn't let the emotion show. "Your car or mine?" she asked.

"Let's use mine. It will take less time to reach the sites if I drive."

"I'm going to move my car to the parking lot. I'll wait outside." When she had arrived that morning, barricades had already been set up to close off the parking lot for the press conference, and she was forced to park on a side street.

As she strode along the sidewalk, an eerie sensation trickled across the back of her neck. Certain she was watched, she spun to look behind her. No one was there, and no owls were in view. There was nothing to account for the sense of uneasiness.

At the side of the car, she paused. Her gaze slowly scanned the streets and parking lots a second time. Cat should have been reassured, yet the disquiet hovered in her mind.

JD sat on a bench in the small park across the street from the police department. When the woman walked out of the building, her hair was a red-gold halo around her head. *She's perfect, and the Master will be pleased.* Suddenly, she stopped and looked around. A jolt of excitement rolled through him. *Yes, I'm waiting for you. Soon, you will be my gift to the old one. I will purify you for him. You will be washed clean with your blood.*

Kevin was tired. It had been a rough few days, too much stress, and too little sleep. Still, the elation over the preliminary results of the investigation of the mayor had kept his energy high. He hated corruption at any level, and the confirmation of his suspicions had been extremely gratifying.

Walking out the door, he saw Cat exit her car. His exhaustion faded away as if it had never existed. She was amazing. Her looks would make any man have wet dreams. However, she never played on her appearance and seemed unaware of the impact on the men around her. Even Ed and Roger, both happily married, sent a few glances her way. She was more than a pretty face or a sexy body. Cat was intelligent, cool under fire, and quick and intuitive.

"Hey, are you ready?" he asked. "Once we've finished, let's stop for dinner."

"Okay, sounds good."

It didn't take long to check the few parks. At each, the answer was no; the clerk didn't recognize the PTC. They left a copy of the sketch, in case the killer attempted to rent a space. Before leaving, Kevin drove through the park to check the trailers and vehicles. Most were new or only a few years old and didn't match their description of the truck, or Ryan's profile of the trailer.

It was dark when Cat crossed the last site off the list. "These were doubtful as they're not the killer's type of trailer park. Still, they had to be eliminated."

"Any food sound enticing, Chinese, barbecue, fast food?" Kevin asked as he exited onto the street.

"How about barbecue? Any place close?"

"You must have read my mind. There is one a few miles from here. The ribs are so tender the meat almost falls off the bone," Kevin responded. "My house is not far from here. I'd like to change out of this uniform before we eat. Dinner is more enjoyable when I'm not advertising the chief of police is out on the town. Do you need to stop by the hotel?"

"No, I'm good to go the way I am."

As Kevin turned into his driveway, his house surprised Cat. She imagined a bachelor would have a small house or even an apartment. Instead, his headlights flashed across a two-story home, with a full porch and even a couple of rocking chairs near the door.

Kevin hit the remote control mounted on his visor. "It'll be quicker to go through the garage."

He parked and came around to her side to open the door. She followed him up a few steps to a small mudroom and then into a large old-fashioned kitchen filled with glass-fronted cabinets. A granite top in brown, gold, and cream tones covered a center island. Walls painted a light golden brown, the rich tones in the countertops, and the green and gold accessories on the counters created a warm and inviting look. She stepped to the kitchen sink to peer out the window, but it was too dark to distinguish the layout of the backyard. Turning, she gazed around the kitchen.

"Wow, it's not my idea of a bachelor pad."

"It's really not," Kevin said as a sheepish grin crossed his face. "This is where I grew up, and after my dad retired, they bought an RV. Their goal is to visit every state. They gave me the house. Come on, I'll give you the grand tour."

"From what I've already observed, the interior is stunning. I bet it's your mom's doing, right?"

He laughed. "It's sure not mine."

The dining room connected to the kitchen by a large, arched open doorway and more windows overlooked the backyard. Another arched opening led into the living room that stretched across the front of the house. At one end was a small office. Windows in both rooms overlooked the front porch. The stairs to the second floor were near the front door.

As they walked through the rooms, Kevin said, "Mom likes open spaces, so dad removed the doors and widened the doorways."

Upstairs were four bedrooms and two baths. At each room, Cat paused to glance inside. "Lot of house for one person."

"The family pops in now and then, especially around the holidays. When my sister and her family are here, it suddenly seems a lot smaller. Kids can sure fill up the space. Here's the master bedroom. I moved in here when mom and dad hit the road."

Cat walked in, amazed at its tidy appearance. There were no clothes tossed anywhere, and the bed was covered with an exquisite quilt bedspread. She turned to comment on the room. Startled, she took a quick step back as Kevin was behind her. Her hand hit his chest as she reached out to brace herself.

Kevin's hand quickly grasped it. Desire simmered in his eyes and sent a rush of yearning through her body. Instinctively, she drew back, but he held her hand tightly clasped in his. His other caressed her cheek, and his thumb outlined the curve of her lips. Bending his head, his lips feathered kisses across her face, then moved to her mouth.

Her free arm came up and circled his neck. Lost in the sensation, Cat pushed her body tight against him. *This must be what it means to go down for the count.*

Needing to steady herself, she pulled back. She should leave, yet, for some odd reason, her feet refused to move. Something was in the air, alive and pulsating, a heat that made Cat want to crawl closer to him, feel his bare skin next to hers.

Words, uncontrolled, rolled out of his mouth. "I've wanted you from the first moment I saw you standing on the sidewalk outside the hotel, your chin tilted upward with that look of utter disdain. A vision of you in my bed, my hands stroking and caressing every inch of your body has been in my head, and it won't go away." The slight tremble in her body as she listened sent an overwhelming sense of satisfaction flowing through him.

The ring of a phone broke the intensity of the moment. He

hesitated, pondering whether he should ignore the call. "Damn, I need to answer this."

"Yeah, probably so," Cat said as she moved away, grateful her feet were no longer glued to the floor. She needed to get her feelings under control. Her emotions never ran amuck, and she didn't have a clue how to handle the raw intensity of desire.

While chiding herself for her reactions, she listened to his side of the call. His detective was on the other end. It had something to do with the surveillance of the mayor.

Kevin disconnected the call. "Bingham and Ron Sullivan are at a local bar."

Cat was aware Sullivan was the owner of one of the construction companies and the father of the student who rode with the officers.

The emotional momentum swung back to their investigation. Even though she had decided not to fight her feelings for Kevin, still, she was relieved. "I'll wait downstairs."

Reluctantly, he watched her walk out of the bedroom. How had his feelings become so entangled in such a brief time? This was new and unfamiliar territory, and he was fighting emotions that were already a lost cause. With a deep sigh, he stripped off the uniform, wishing they were Cat's clothes he tossed onto the chair.

She wandered around the living room, studying the pictures of Kevin and his family. They hung on the walls and filled the mantle. She picked up one. No doubt, the man in a uniform was his brother—the same mischievous smile and glint in his eyes.

"That's Adam. He should be home in about six months unless he decides to re-up."

Cat turned, and her insides turned to mush. A pair of tight jeans clung to his lean hips and long legs. The T-shirt was tight across his chest and biceps and did little to hide an impressive set of muscles. Collecting her wits, she knew she had to say something about what happened in the bedroom. "Hmm ... upstairs, what ..."

Kevin interrupted her. "Let's take it one day at a time. I want you to be absolutely sure before we take the next step." Moving closer, he cupped her jaw with his hand. "And ... Cat Morgan, there will be a next time." He lightly kissed her, then took the picture pressed tight against her chest and put it back on the mantle.

"Come on. I don't know about you, but I'm starved."

Twenty-five

The parking lot of Big Red's BBQ Pit was full. Kevin circled the block until he found an empty spot.

"Is it always like this?"

"With the dance floor, great barbecue, and a family atmosphere, it's a favorite for a lot of folks." He grabbed a leather jacket from the back seat.

Inside, people lined the walls of the foyer, waiting for a table.

"The wait should be short. It's a large building." He walked to the front to add his name to the list.

"Chief Hunter, good to see you," the waiter said. Kevin didn't recognize the young man.

At his questioning look, the man smiled and said, "You probably won't remember, but a couple of months ago, my mom and sister were in a car wreck. My mom went to the hospital. You took my little sister to my aunt's house." He glanced down at a layout of tables and checked a box.

"I remember the accident. How's your mom doing?"

"Good, though she's still in rehab for the broken arm." He picked up a set of menus and led them to a booth.

A waitress stood nearby as they slid into the seats. After she had left with their drink orders, Cat looked at Kevin and grinned. "Nice to have an in."

"Yeah, well, I try not to trade on the fact I'm the police chief, but sometimes it helps."

"I think in this case, it was not you as the police chief, rather you helping someone."

Kevin looked at his menu and cleared his throat a couple of times.

Cat grinned at his obvious embarrassment and his even more apparent relief when the waitress set their glasses of iced tea on the table. Both ordered the rib special.

When the food arrived, the plates were piled high with ribs, a loaded baked potato, green beans, and stacks of golden cornbread filled another plate.

The waitress asked if they needed anything else, and Cat scanned the table. "Extra butter, please." She shot a look at Kevin, daring him to make a comment.

He made a motion with his fingers as if zipping his mouth, though he couldn't stop the grin.

Ignoring him, she said, "So, do you normally work accidents?" as she buttered a slice of cornbread.

"Not really, but I do like to be involved with my officers. It usually depends on my schedule. Fortunately, we are a small enough department that I can spend time in the field."

Slowly, they worked their way through the mound of food and stayed away from a discussion of the investigations.

Cat pushed the plate aside and sighed. "That's it. I can't eat another bite."

Eyeing the remaining ribs on her plate, he asked, "Are you sure?"

"Yep." Then laughed when he reached for the ribs and dropped them on his plate. "Where are you putting all that food?"

His eyes twinkled as he gestured with the rib in his hand toward three empty bowls. "Same place you put all that butter."

The waitress stopped at their table and asked if they were ready for dessert. The young woman grinned when Cat groaned. As she left with their empty plates, Kevin's phone rang, and the light atmosphere changed.

After listening for a few seconds, he said, "I'll talk to you in the morning." He slid the cell phone back in the holder on his belt and glanced at the other tables around them. Even though no one was close enough to overhear, his voice dropped as he said, "Stetler, the owner of the second company, joined the meeting."

"Hmm … curious," Cat said. "Anything on their conversation?"

"No. Bingham knows most of my officers. Roger had to stay back, but he did notice one interesting item. Stetler handed Bingham an envelope. I'd give next year's pay to know what was inside."

She leaned back in her chair and considered the possibilities. "If it was money, Nicki will know as soon as it hits his bank account, assuming he does deposit it. Are there any open bids that haven't been awarded?"

"Good point. I'll have Roger check," and reached for his phone. He quickly relayed the request to his detective.

She glanced at her watch. "Time to call it a night. Tomorrow will be another long day." Despite her enjoyment of their evening, she still couldn't shake the urgency and apprehension that continually rode in the back of her mind. If she rechecked the files, maybe there was another detail they had missed.

The ride to the PD was quiet. The stress of the day, another victim, the emotional roller coaster of her feelings for Kevin, all weighed on her.

Kevin pulled into the parking lot. Turning off the engine, he looked over at her as he reached across the seat and put his arm around her shoulder. "We've too many complications right now. There will be a day when we will talk … about us."

"Kevin, I'm not a person who's into one-night stands though you're right, it's something we need to discuss."

As he exited his car, he felt that odd tug again on his thoughts. Uneasy, he scanned the parking lot. Suddenly, he was afraid to let her out of his sight. This must just be a reaction to his overwhelmingly desire for her. *I want to grab her, hold on, and never let go.*

He took the keys from her hand and hit the remote. Before she could open the door, he pulled her to him, locking his arms tight around her. Hot and demanding, his mouth crushed hers. Raw desire almost took him to his knees. He felt the pressure from her hands lightly push against his chest and let his arms slide from her body. Kevin stepped back as he fought to suppress the raging emotions. Fingertips caressed her cheek and lips. "Tomorrow then."

JD had followed them when they left the police station. When the cop drove into the second park, he knew they were looking for him. Another surge of panic ripped through him. *How the hell did they know to go lookin' in RV parks?* Despite the instincts that screamed at him to leave, just hook up and go, he convinced himself that he was safe. They'd never find the trailer where he had it hidden. He popped another pill as he drove away. The soothing narcotic washed away the lingering feelings of fear. Once he had her, then he'd leave.

Since her car was still at the police station, he'd wait there and follow her when she left. For his plan to work, he had to find her hotel. Parked on the side street, he headed to the same park bench. When the police car pulled into the lot, anticipation flooded him. *She's here, so close.* But when the cop pulled her into his arms, rage inflamed his senses. No! No! She isn't yours, you can't have her. She belongs to the old one. And knew, with absolute certainty, that before he left, he would kill the police chief.

Cat wanted Kevin on a level she didn't even know existed. If she said anything, the intensity of her emotions would betray her. Instead, she had just nodded and got into her car. As she pulled out of the parking lot, she glanced in her rearview mirror. Motionless, he stood in the middle of the lot and watched her drive away.

Common sense said she should leave, yet the emotional connection to Kevin tugged at her to stay. She almost stopped, but common sense won the battle. Caught up in her emotional struggle, she didn't spot the truck that turned from a side street to follow her.

Kevin waited until her car was out of sight before moving to his car. The screech of an owl caused the hair on the back of his neck to rise, and a chill raced down his back. He quickly looked up, but there was no sign of the birds.

Again, he felt that improbable tug, and, this time, his mind filled with an unfamiliar sense of foreboding. *Danger*—the word echoed in his head. He scanned the streets and parking lot. The only movement was the flash of headlights as a vehicle turned from a side street.

Twenty-six

She flew, soaring on the night wind over the trees below. Her frantic calls echoed in the air. Moonlight illuminated the night sky. Women, the killer's victims, floated in front of her. Their hands outstretched, they begged for help. As she flew across the countryside, blood flowed over the moon, and the ghostly glow of the women turned red. She plummeted toward a lake below her. No, not a lake—a pit of blood. As she sank into the abyss, the gore coated her, filled her nose and mouth until she couldn't breathe.

Terror, alive and coiled inside her, pulled Cat from the depths of the hideous dream. *Same as yesterday morning, only worse. God, how do I stop it?* When her mind began to think rationally, she knew it wouldn't end until the killer was behind bars or dead.

When she stood, her legs trembled. Cat grabbed the edge of the nightstand to steady herself before she staggered to the bathroom. The image that stared back at her in the mirror was a terrified woman, eyes dilated, skin pasty white except for the dark circles under the eyes. *I've always wondered when a person fits the description of death warmed over. I'm looking at one now.*

Under the shower, she let the hot water flow over her body for several minutes. While the terror of the dream receded, the images remained. Time was running out for another woman.

It didn't take long to dry her hair and dress. Her regular use of makeup was a light coat. Today, she added concealer to cover the dark circles. She opted for jeans, a long-sleeved shirt, and boots, attire more appropriate for the countryside than an office. While she dressed, she pondered what had happened in the dream. What clues did it hold to help her find the killer?

Cat grabbed her fleece-lined jacket, backpack, and briefcase, then headed to the breakfast buffet. She was early but preferred to wait in the dining room. Her room held too many reminders of the horrific nightmares.

Today the breakfast choice was simple, cereal, and fruit. Between the aftereffect of the nightmare and the heavy meal the night before, she didn't have much of an appetite. Clearing away her dishes, she spread the files over the table. She had overlooked something, but what?

It was tough to examine the photos of the victims and not reenact in her mind their last moments. The sound of footsteps broke her contemplation.

Ryan said hi and headed to the coffee pot. Dropping into the chair, he eyed the folders. "I did the same thing last night, went over every report. I came up with one item—red hair. I missed it because two of the victims had short hair, and it was heavily matted with blood, but reports state red. The color may connect to the initial trigger that set the PTC on his killing spree."

Cat looked back at the pictures. *Holy hell, is this what I missed, the connection to red.*

Ryan took a sip of coffee. "I've also got bad news. Nicki and I are headed back to Washington. Scott called this morning. He didn't want to pull us but said there wasn't a choice. Another case came in. We'll leave as soon as we finish breakfast."

"Damn, I hate to see you go. Did he say what the case was about?"

"No, just to get our butts back to D.C."

Nicki walked in, followed by Kevin, who immediately headed to the buffet.

"Hey guys," Nicki said and set her large computer bag on the floor.

Cat said, "Ryan gave me the bad news," and stacked the files to make room.

An empty plate in his hand, Kevin looked at the group with a look of apprehension. "Bad news?"

"No, nothing to do with our case," Cat said before explaining.

"I'm sorry you have to leave. You've been a big asset to this case." He chuckled as he piled a plate with bacon, eggs, biscuits, and gravy. "And … I never believed I'd admit to that."

When he set the plate on the table, Cat gave the food a long stare and shuddered.

"What?" A broad grin crossed his face. "I'm a growing boy and need my nourishment."

"Well, after the huge plate of ribs you devoured last night, the nourishment should last beyond an early morning breakfast. Anymore growing won't be up, it will be out."

Kevin's eyes twinkled as he munched on a piece of bacon.

Everyone followed their unwritten rule not to discuss the investigation until they finished breakfast. With a last cup of coffee in front of him, Ryan pulled a file folder from his briefcase and handed it to Cat.

"I updated the profile." For Kevin's benefit, he explained. "Last night, I went over the information on each victim. I realized there was a common trait, red hair. I believe it's connected to the initial event. A woman he was emotionally attached to had red hair."

Fear and a sense of impending danger jerked Kevin back in his seat. He stared at the reason for his terror. It was the woman across the table whose hair gleamed red. No one seemed to notice his reaction.

Ryan looked across the table at Nicki. "You ready?"

"Yeah, my gear is already in the car," Nicki replied. She handed Cat their list of RV sites. "Kevin, we're going to stay on the Bingham investigation. I'll contact you as soon as we have any results."

Kevin shook hands with the agents and thanked them for their help. Cat gave each a quick hug.

Once they were gone, she turned to Kevin. "Are you okay? For a second, you had a wild-eyed look in your eyes. I didn't want to say anything in front of Nicki and Ryan."

"Yeah, I'm fine. Let's go." His tone was abrupt since he didn't want to get into a conversation about the reason for his sudden panic. Just because Cat had red hair didn't mean she would be a target.

Following him out the door, she eyed his backside in disbelief.

Cat opened the car door, then stopped. A sudden chill raised goosebumps on her neck and arms. She looked around, but there was nothing to account for the unexpected apprehension.

"What's wrong?" Kevin asked as he looked at her over the top of the car.

After a few seconds, Cat said, "Just a weird sensation that we're being watched, but I don't see anyone."

He glanced around as he said, "I've had the same feeling several times over the last couple of days and couldn't account for it."

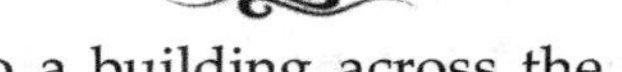

He'd parked next to a building across the street from the hotel. Daylight was risky, but still, if he got a chance, he was ready. A syringe filled with ketamine was on the seat next to him.

When she came out of the hotel, JD slid down behind the wheel. The sight of the cop next to her set off a surge of rage. As long as they were together, he couldn't grab her. Once they had driven away, he cranked the engine. Not much he could do now. He'd catch a few hours' sleep and be ready to start the hunt again. He had to try, even if it wasn't the agent. His master waited.

When Kevin pulled into the parking lot, Roger and Ed were getting into their car. He tapped the horn to get their attention. "We need to divide Nicki and Ryan's list," he said as he stepped out of the car.

In the conference room, Kevin explained the absence of the other two agents. He checked off several locations, then made a copy.

As Ed scrutinized the new list, he said, "We should be able to contact all the sites today, though it may be late before we're finished. It might affect the surveillance on Bingham."

"Who has the shift to follow him?"

Roger said, "I do. I had planned on being back before he left for the day. My source will let me know if Bingham leaves early."

"Oh, who is your informant?" Kevin asked.

A wide grin split Roger's face, "His secretary."

Kevin chuckled. "If you can't get back, don't worry about it. We'll pick it back up tomorrow. The search for the PTC is more important than tagging along behind the mayor."

Kevin glanced at Cat. "I won't be long, just a couple of administrative matters I need to handle," he told her, then followed the detectives out the door.

Cat stared around the room. It seemed empty without Nicki and Ryan. Walking to the murder board, her eyes slowly scanned the face of each victim. Once again, terror sent ripples of chills down her back, as visions of the women in her dream filled her mind. The dead cried out for retribution.

"Good news!"

Kevin's voice pulled her thoughts back from the brooding contemplation of the pictures.

Standing in the doorway, he waved a document in the air. "The state's homicide unit completed their investigation. The report finds no misconduct or malfeasance in the actions of the law enforcement officers involved in the convenience store incident. What's even better is the report severely censures the mayor."

Cat felt an immediate sense of relief. While she did not believe any of the officers had been at fault, it was reassuring to learn they were vindicated of any wrongdoing.

Kevin's laughter echoed around the room. "Gotta love this part," and read a section of the report. "'*This complaint was unwarranted, and the facts should have been investigated before filing said action with the Attorney General's office.*' In other words, he wasted their time, and the

AG didn't appreciate it. The District Attorney received a copy and will forward it to the Grand Jury."

"I'd like a copy to send to Scott."

"He's already received one from the AG," Kevin replied.

"When do you expect to hear from the Grand Jury?"

"Today. I'm not finished with the stack of documents Jessie handed me. She insists they must be signed today. Another few minutes, and I'll be done."

Her phone rang. It was Scott. He called to say he had received the state's report. She brought him up to date on their search of the RV parks before she hung up.

Cat had acquired another map from Jesse. Within a few minutes, all the locations were marked with an X. She was refolding it when Kevin asked if she was ready to leave.

Jessie stopped them in the hallway.

"The mayor called and wants you in his office," she said.

"Bet he received a copy of the report from the Attorney General. I imagine he is livid. Call his office and tell his secretary, I am involved in an investigation and not available."

Jessie grinned. "I'll be happy to pass that message to him." She never bothered to hide her dislike of the man.

As they headed out of town, Cat was strangely silent. She couldn't shake the ominous feeling she had experienced in the parking lot, and the remnants of her dream still lingered in her mind. A couple of times, she looked over her shoulder at the cars behind them and caught the quick looks Kevin shot her way.

"Want to talk about it?" he finally asked.

"No, I am still trying to sort out my thoughts. If I tried to explain, it would sound disjointed and bizarre. This time you really would wonder if you had a crazy woman on your hands." She laughed, though the sound was weak, even to her ears.

"Disjointed and bizarre, I might understand, crazy—never. Cat, you have an unusual ability. You detect what others don't. If it would help to discuss it, I'm willing to listen. I've learned talking can put a different spin on all those thoughts that rattle around in our heads."

Cat eyed him, still in awe of his easy acceptance.

Kevin glanced back, cocked one eyebrow and grinned.

God, the man, is incredibly irresistible. There should be a law against letting him run amuck in the female population. The distraction caused her mind to veer into the what-ifs of a committed relationship.

Kevin pulled into the first RV park. It was a small, run-down place with only a few spaces for trailers. It was typical of the parks on their list, used by full-time residents with the occasional hunter or fisherman. Most didn't even advertise, and the locations had been pieced together from information provided by other agencies.

Armed with a folder containing copies of the artist sketch of the killer, they entered the small office near the entrance. The man seated behind a desk stood to greet them as they came through the door. Kevin introduced himself and Cat.

"Artie Johnson, I own this place. How can I help you?"

Kevin removed a sketch from the folder and handed it to him as he said, "We are looking for this man. He'll be traveling with a trailer. It's probably a small older model that he is towing with the bumper of his pickup. Anyone rent a space from you in the last couple of months that looks like this man?"

Johnson looked at the drawing for a couple of minutes, spit a wad of tobacco and juice in a cup before he said, "Nope, ain't seen him. What'd he do?"

"He's a person of interest in a case we are investigating. I'll leave this copy with you. If you spot him, don't confront him. Call the number on the sketch. Are there any other RV parks in the area?"

Kevin compared the sites Johnson provided to those on their master list. Cat wandered around the office, looking at brochures and ads posted in various places on the wall. One, Berber's Propane Service, caught her eye. She pulled a small notepad and pen from her jacket pocket and jotted down the address and telephone number.

Kevin finished his conversation and stepped next to her to find out what had caught her attention. He looked over her shoulder at the notes she'd made.

Cat turned and looked at him for a minute. When his eyes shifted from the notebook to the brochure tacked on the wall, she knew he'd grasped the significance of the ad. Looking at Johnson, she asked, "Do most trailers use propane bottles?"

"Yeah, they do."

"I'm not familiar with travel trailers. What is the propane used for?"

"Could be any number of reasons—refrigerator, furnace, hot water heater, stove."

"How do you get one refilled?"

"Depends. You can trade the empty for a full one or refill the empty. Around here, most everyone goes to Berber."

They thanked him for his help and headed to their car.

"Good spot on the propane issue," Kevin said. "It hadn't occurred to me the PTC would need to fill a propane bottle. Berber's only a couple of miles from the next place on the list. I'll swing by there first."

Cat pulled out her laptop and started a search of propane dealers as Kevin drove out of the park. When the list popped up on the screen, she exclaimed in amazement. "Do you have any idea how many places fill or sell propane bottles?"

"I imagine quite a few though I've never gone looking. I've got a gas barbecue grill and trade mine out at a hardware store not far from the house." He hesitated for a few seconds before continuing, "He might use a place in town. My gut says otherwise. Select the ones outside the city."

Cat found a half dozen sites in the radius they had established around Clinton and added the addresses to their list.

Berber's was a small building with an attached shed that housed the refill connector from a sizeable above ground propane tank. A pickup truck with a couple of bottles sticking up in the bed pulled in ahead of Kevin and parked in front of the shed. As the driver exited, it only took a quick glance to identify he wasn't the PTC.

"You check inside, and I'll show the picture to the employee handling the refills," Cat said.

A receiver to her ear, the young woman, seated at a desk behind a long counter, gave him a decided look of interest when he entered. While he waited, he wandered around the barbecue grills on display. One piqued his interest. As he inspected the components, a man stepped out of an office.

"Victor Berber. Can I answer any questions? That grill has several nice features."

Though it might be time for an upgrade, Kevin shifted to the reason he was there and pulled his badge case from a back pocket. "Chief Kevin Hunter, Clinton PD. I'm looking for a suspect in an investigation. I'd like to find out if you or any of your employees have seen this man?" He pulled the sketch from his folder and showed it to Berber.

The man studied the picture for several seconds, then slowly shook his head. "No, I've never seen him. I have three employees. Todd is outside, and Beth is on the phone. Seth has the day off."

Beth hung up as Berber walked over. Leaning over the counter, he showed her the picture. "This is Chief Hunter from Clinton. He wants to know if you've seen this person?"

She scrunched her face as she stared at the image. "He's one creepy-looking dude, but no, I haven't seen anyone who looks like him."

That's the understatement of the year. "I'll leave the sketch and would appreciate it if you'd show it to your other employee. When will he be back?"

"Tomorrow. Do you want to show it to Todd?" Berber said.

"An FBI agent is with me and is outside talking to him. If you see him, don't confront him. Call the number on the picture." Kevin took another lingering look at the grill as he turned to leave.

"If you're interested, they go on sale next week."

Kevin grinned. "I may have to give it some serious consideration."

Cat was walking to the front door as he exited. She looked at him, her eyebrows raised in a silent question.

"Nada, anything from the guy at the pump?"

"Nope."

In the car, Cat checked the list for the next location. "Sunset Park is five miles away. It is the closest on the list."

Kevin's phone rang. He listened for several seconds and said, "Thanks for letting me know. I appreciate your help in expediting their verdict."

He disconnected. "That was District Attorney Marlin. The Grand Jury returned a no bill on everyone involved in the convenience store shootings."

A no bill meant criminal charges would not be filed. Cat, while not surprised by the ruling, was relieved.

As Kevin drove out of the parking lot, he said, "This place has some great barbecue equipment. The owner said they'd go on sale next week. I may have to come back."

As he enthusiastically described the features of the one that caught his attention, Cat's laughter rang out.

"What! Barbecue grills are an essential piece of equipment."

"You and my dad would be soulmates when it comes to a grill. Mom may be the queen of the kitchen, but my dad rules when it comes to his barbecue equipment."

"Sounds like a man I need to meet."

A dilapidated sign advertising Sunset RV hung on a pole next to a dirt roadway. As they bumped their way over the potholes, the park came into view.

"Not many trailers parked in this one," Cat said.

"I imagine it's more for hunters or fishermen. There is a small lake nearby."

The mention of the lake sent a sense of anticipation soaring through Cat. Could this be the place in her dreams? As she stepped from the car, she searched for the owls, but there was no sign of them.

Once again, they went through the routine, with no luck. It was the pattern for the day. Not wanting to lose the time, they skipped lunch as they worked their way down the list of stores that sold propane and the RV parks. At each stop, there was a faint hope it would be the place where they would find a solid lead on their killer.

"How far is the next location?"

Cat scanned down the list to the next one and then looked at the map open on her lap. "Ten miles."

"What's the name?"

Cat grinned before saying, "Almost Heaven."

Twenty-seven

A burst of laughter erupted from Kevin. "Oh, that's a good one," he said as he considered the rundown and ramshackle parks they had already visited.

The lane leading to the park was narrow with deep bar ditches on each side. "Be difficult to pull a trailer down this road." He slowed to negotiate a sharp curve in the roadway.

The entrance to the park was even more unkempt, weed-infested, and full of potholes. As a tire dropped off in another deep hole, Cat said, "Just because of the road, this place should be named—Almost Hell."

The office was near the entrance, and Kevin parked in front of the door. The twang of a country-western song could be heard. "Someone's here."

A bell over the door tinkled as they entered. It was a small office, cluttered and dirty with a wide opening at the back that led to a living room. The stink of alcohol and smoke permeated the air. The blaring radio sat on a battered desk, amid piles of magazines and a large ashtray heaped with cigarette butts.

The man seated behind the desk hit a button on the radio as he stood. Unshaven, his face was puffy, and his eyes were bloodshot. Stringy white hair fell across his shoulders. His gut hung over a belt that rode low on his hips, and the dirty shirt failed to cover the flabby belly. Cat figured what showed on the backside would be worse.

A slight slur in his voice, he asked, "Wadda you want?"

Cat pulled her badge case from her pocket and held it up. "Agent Morgan, FBI. This is Chief Hunter, Clinton PD. We're searching for a man that may live in a trailer park. Are you the owner?"

When the man saw the badge, he backed up, hitting the chair behind him. "I'm Charlie Dent, and yeah, I'm the owner. I run a clean place, don't ever have any kind of trouble here. Cops never have a reason to come snoopin' around."

Kevin handed him the picture. "Have you seen this man?"

At first, Dent eyed it with suspicion, then a look of recognition crossed his face.

Kevin's tone turned sharp and authoritative. "You've seen him! Where?" he demanded before the man could collect his thoughts and deny he knew him.

"He rented a spot a few weeks ago."

They'd found him. A surge of elation shot through Cat—until his next words.

"He's gone, though. Pulled out yesterday. Why are you lookin' for him?"

Kevin said, "He's a suspect in an investigation. What's his name, and do you keep records of who rents your spaces?"

"JD ... something. Don't remember his last name. I got a card filled out on him." He stepped to a filing cabinet and pulled a stack of cards from a drawer. Dent thumbed through them, then went back and started over. This time, he dropped each card on the desk. Perplexed, he scratched his head as he stared at the pile. "Uh ... it's not here. I know I filled it out, but it's gone. Don't understand that."

The dismay on his face convinced them he was telling the truth.

"Tell us what you remember," Cat said.

"Not much. He pulled in one day and wanted to rent a space at the back of the park. Said he needed somewhere quiet."

"What kind of vehicle and rig?" Kevin asked.

"An old trailer, bumper pull with one slideout. It's not in very good shape. Same with his pickup—black Ford, single seat. It may have been older than the trailer."

"Do you remember the license plate number?" Cat asked.

Dent scratched his head again. "Nope, wrote it down, just don't remember it. He still had two days left on his rental. I was surprised he didn't ask for a refund before he left. Not a real friendly sort."

"Why's that?" Cat asked.

"When he paid, he'd drop the cash on the desk and leave. I tried to strike up a conversation, but he never wanted to talk. Came in one day, wanted to borrow the phone book. I told him he could look at it but couldn't take it out of the office. He got real agitated. Could hear him muttering as he flipped pages."

"Any idea what he was looking for?" Kevin asked.

"Nope, but I think he tore out some of the pages. Was out the door before I could stop him. I decided to let it go. Nasty lookin' person."

"Where's the phone book?" Cat asked.

"Over there on the table in front of the window."

Cat moved to examine the phone book while Kevin continued to question Dent for information on the suspect, his truck, and trailer, entering the details in the small notebook he carried in his pocket.

Kevin glanced over his shoulder at Cat. She flipped the pages of the phone book with a pen. He turned to step toward her when an idea occurred to him. He stopped and turned back to Dent. "I'm surprised you didn't see his picture on TV. The news channels have shown it several times."

"Couldn't, TV's on the fritz. Matter of fact, it happened yesterday."

"Were you here when he left?" Kevin wasn't sure what prompted him to ask the question.

"Nope, I'd gone to town to pick up groceries. When I came back, he was gone."

"Anything unusual happen?"

"Well ..." Dent said and rubbed his belly with one hand and scratched his head with the other. "I found the door unlocked when I got back. I was sure I'd locked it before leaving, then reckoned I didn't remember it right."

Cat walked to stand next to Kevin. Considering the man's state of intoxication, it was a remarkable performance.

"Your front door?" Kevin asked and stepped to examine it.

"Yeah."

Though he observed several scratches around the old lock, the door's dilapidated condition made it impossible to determine whether they occurred the day before or a year ago. "Anything else?"

"There *was* something. I think some of the money was missing from the till. Maybe I miscounted. If someone's going to steal money, they'd take it all, right?"

Kevin pulled the information piece by piece and prayed he didn't miss something because he didn't ask the right question.

"Several pages are missing in the V section. I'd have to check against another phone book, though, I'm certain the missing pages include vet clinics. Has anyone handled this phone book since JD?" she asked.

Once again, Dent paused as he went through the belly rub, head scratch routine. "No ... no, don't think so."

"Kevin, we need to take the phone book. Do you have any evidence bags in the car?"

"Yeah, a container in the trunk, with bags, receipt forms, and rubber gloves," and handed her the car keys.

"You ever been arrested?" Cat asked.

"Huh? Why the hell do you want to know that? Besides, it's none of your damn business."

"We need your prints, and it would be a lot easier if a set were on file," Cat said.

"No, I ain't ever been arrested. Told you I run a clean shop," he said as he eyed Kevin, who had pulled his phone from a pocket.

"I'll get my crime scene unit out here to get his prints," Kevin said.

Dent's voice squeaked in protest. "Wait, just a damn minute, you can take the phone book, but I ain't givin' you my fingerprints. I didn't do nothin' wrong."

"I need your fingerprints because you handled the phone book. Yours have to be eliminated."

When Cat returned, Dent was still complaining. As she filled out the receipt form for him to sign, Kevin continued to reassure him. It took a few minutes before he calmed down and realized it was to his advantage to cooperate.

While Cat bagged the phone book, Kevin asked, "How many other trailer spaces are rented?"

"Seven, all full-time."

"Give me their names and slot numbers. I want to talk to each of them before we leave. Where did JD park?"

Dent wrote the information on a notepad, tore off the sheet, and handed it to Kevin.

Back in the car, Cat grinned at Kevin. "He sure bowed up over the prints. For a few minutes, I didn't think you'd win that battle."

"Yeah, I did too. It's a longshot we'll get anything. Still, it's worth a try." He punched a number on his phone. When Roger answered, he passed on the details of what they had discovered, and that the PTC was on the move, possibly to another park.

Kevin drove to the space that JD had rented. It was surrounded by trees and shrubs. Cat moved along the tree line, scanning the ground while Kevin searched the area where the trailer would have been parked. Nothing but oil-soaked dirt.

Suggesting they split the list, Cat headed to the first trailer armed with a sketch. Everyone was home, and that's where their luck ran out.

When they met in the roadway, Kevin said, "Nothing new. One said he never saw him. The other two recognized the sketch. None of them ever talked to him. Their description of JD, his truck, and trailer match what Dent described. What did you find?"

"The same except for the trailer next to his. She said his truck was parked in front of the trailer most of the day. Mrs. ..." Cat paused to check her list for the name. "Calhoun said she was a light sleeper and heard his truck drive in and out during the night or early hours of the morning. She figured he worked nights somewhere and slept during the day."

"I still have one more." Kevin nodded to a trailer parked on the opposite side of the lot.

Cat followed him and waited as he stepped on small steps attached to the side of the trailer and pounded on the door.

It swung open, and a man, dressed in dirty jeans and a t-shirt, leaned out. Though he eyed Cat with interest, his tone was surly as he said, "Whatever you're sellin', I ain't buyin'." The stink of marijuana drifted out the doorway.

Kevin said, "I'm Police Chief Hunter ..."

His hand still on the handle, the man stepped back to pull the door shut. Kevin jumped to grab the handle before it closed and jerked it open. The door slammed against the side of the trailer as he rushed inside.

Cat heard a crash as she followed.

Inside, the two men grappled. A fist struck the side of Kevin's face, and his head rocked back. He swung and clipped the man on the chin, knocking him to the floor. Kevin rolled him onto his stomach and pulled the man's arms behind his back. "I've got handcuffs in the glove box."

Cat rushed out, grabbed the cuffs, and raced back inside.

While Kevin cuffed the man, she surveyed the interior of the trailer. The air reeked of marijuana from a butt that burned in an ashtray. Drug paraphernalia, pills, bags of weed, and cocaine were piled on a small table.

"Judging by what's here, he's a dealer," Cat said.

Kevin stood and put a foot on the man's back to keep him from rolling over while he recited the Miranda rights. The prisoner spewed obscenities that covered most of Kevin's words.

When he finished, Kevin said, "I'll step outside to call the sheriff's department and request a deputy to haul him to jail."

She pulled the prisoner's wallet from a back pocket and removed the driver's license. "All your protests won't keep you out of jail, so I suggest you shut up," she said, which only set off another round of curses.

Cat heard voices and stepped to the open door. Kevin stood in front of the trailer steps with two of his officers. She recognized them from the Lewis crime scene.

"Fingerprint the owner. He's waiting in the office. Also, check the TV, file cabinet, and till for prints. When you're done, I want pictures of the inside of this trailer and the drugs on the table."

When he stepped inside, she handed him the wallet along with the driver's license. "His name is Milton Bates."

Cat rolled him over. "I'm FBI Special Agent Morgan. I have some questions about JD."

"I ain't answerin' any of your damn questions."

"Mr. Bates, I'll explain it this way. If your answers help, it might make a difference in how many years you spend in jail."

"I know my rights. I want a lawyer." He turned his head away from her.

"Okay, have it your way. Chief Hunter, how soon will the deputy sheriff get here to take him to jail?"

Kevin glanced at his watch. "It'll be another fifteen to twenty minutes. The dispatcher said he was a few miles away."

Cat moved to the table. "Based on the amount of drugs on this table, Bates can be charged with distribution. When your officer gets back with the camera, have him take a picture of your face. You have a red mark on your cheek from his fist. That's an assault on a peace officer and resisting arrest." She tapped Bates' leg with her foot. "Ka-ching, jail time is adding up."

The man's face turned toward her, his gaze livid with hostility.

"But ... he doesn't want to talk to us, so he's on his own." Cat sauntered around the small living room of the trailer. At the end of the couch was a built-in table.

"Well, look what I found." She reached behind a stack of magazines and picked up a semi-automatic pistol. Cat unloaded it and laid the gun and magazine on the table next to the pile of drugs.

"We can add a weapons charge. Does this state prohibit a felon from having a weapon, Chief Hunter?"

"Sure does. Another charge, more jail time."

"I wonder if he has been convicted of a felony?" She looked down at the man, "Are you a felon, Mr. Bates? I hope so."

"I ain't sayin' nothin'. I want a lawyer."

If Kevin had not understood the urgency behind the pressure tactics Cat used, he'd have been amused.

"Possession and distribution of drugs, assault on a peace officer, resisting arrest, weapons charge, the list is growing." She dropped to one knee beside the prisoner, her voice as grim as the expression on her face.

"Before I'm done investigating your activities, I expect to add a murder charge, maybe even more than one to the list. JD is wanted for multiple homicides. It's a federal offense. If I find you were involved, you will spend the rest of your life in prison, that is, if you are not on death row."

Panic flashed across Bates' face, and he screamed in protest. "Wait, wait! All I did was sell him some dope. I didn't kill nobody."

"Are you telling me you want to waive your rights to an attorney and answer my questions."

"Yes! Son-of-a-bitch, yes! I don't know nothin' about any murders."

"Start with his name."

"JD … never told me his last name, though it might be Hicks. I was inside his trailer once and saw an old magazine addressed to Thelma Hicks. He said his momma had died."

"What was the address?"

"Somewhere in Texas, it's all I remember?"

"Did he ever mention living in Texas?"

"No, though his truck had expired Texas plates. I told him he needed new ones. He didn't like that I noticed them, said to shut up, it wasn't any of my business."

"What kind of truck did he drive?"

"A black Ford, early 90's. Looks like a piece of junk, but JD said the engine was good."

"Did you talk to him often?"

"Nah. He stayed by himself and made it clear he didn't want anybody comin' around. Most of the time, he was high on dope, liked weed and PCP. Said it really gave him a good rush."

"Did he mention he was leaving or where he planned to go?"

"I came home yesterday, and he was gone. Never said nothin' to me. Just up and left."

Cat stood. "What else do you remember?"

"That's it, never had any long talks with the guy. Wait, there is somethin' else. He's got a strange necklace under his shirt. He bent over one day, and it fell out. It was a creepy piece of metal. I asked what it was. Said I didn't need to know and stuffed it back inside his shirt."

Cat pulled out her small notebook and drew the symbol of the horned god. Holding it in front of Bates' face, "Is this what you saw?"

"Yeah, that's it."

Voices sounded through the open door. A deputy sheriff followed by a Clinton officer with a camera in his hand entered.

As it was crowded in the trailer, Cat stepped outside. She keyed in Nicki's phone number. When she answered, Cat relayed the new information on the PTC and asked her to run a search on JD or Thelma Hicks. Nicki said she'd call as soon as she had any information.

A few minutes later, the deputy hauled the prisoner out the door and put him in his squad car. Kevin followed, swinging his handcuffs.

"We traded out cuffs," he said as lights flashed inside the trailer.

The deputy walked up. "Chief, once your officer is finished, I'll collect the evidence. I'd appreciate a copy of the photos for my case file."

"I'll send you a set. If it would help, I can have my officers bag the evidence for you."

The deputy's face lit up with a smile. "I'd appreciate it. I can get the prisoner to jail."

"I'm done. Anything else you need, Chief?" his officer asked as he stood on the steps of the trailer.

"When Jeremy is finished inside the office, the two of you bag the evidence inside the trailer, then drop it off at the sheriff's office on your way into town. Send a set of the photos to the deputy."

"What was the deal on the TV and file cabinet?" Cat asked as they walked away from the trailer.

"Remember Dent said the TV went out the day the PTC left. I bet JD broke into the office, took his registration card, and stole the money. He probably sabotaged the TV so Dent wouldn't spot the sketch on the news."

"Makes sense."

Before he drove off, he called Roger and asked the status of their search.

"We just crossed our last site off the list. If he does show up at any of the parks, we should get a call," Roger said.

"Stop by the office and issue a BOLO for JD Hicks, along with a description of the trailer and truck that I gave you earlier," Kevin said.

As they left the park, Cat said, "I sense he's still here, just found a new place to hide."

"I think you're right. Damn good work on getting Bates to talk. You got the last name, and it puts us one step closer to stopping him before he kidnaps another woman." Kevin didn't mention he was terrified Cat was the next target.

Twenty-eight

"I contacted Nicki and gave her the latest information. As I talked, I could hear the clicks of the keyboard. The woman is phenomenal when it comes to tracing an individual on the computer."

"I was amazed at the information she uncovered on Bingham and how quickly she found it. I'd been searching for weeks."

"She's good, probably the best the Bureau's got, at least according to Scott. He doesn't believe there is anyone in the FBI who can come close to her ability."

"What have we got left on the list?" Kevin asked.

"There are two, and both are on the way back into town. We need to check them just to make sure he hasn't set up shop at one of them."

At each location, the owner denied any knowledge of the killer, and a sketch was left in case he showed up.

Kevin gazed at the setting sun as he drove toward town. "There's nothing else we can accomplish today. Do you like Chinese? There's one on the way into town."

Cat laughed. "Are there any good places to eat you don't know?"

"Well, what can I say? It's a beat cop thing. In patrol, the first order of business at the start of the shift was to decide where to eat. You soon learn where the best restaurants are located. So, Chinese tonight?"

"Yes. I was hooked when I was in college. My roommate was Asian.

She introduced me to dishes that were not typically mainstream Chinese food."

Located on a hill overlooking Clinton, the restaurant was pagoda style with a covered patio on one side. As they walked in, she eyed the patio. If it was warmer, it would be nice to sit outside, enjoy the evening air and not worry about women dying, corrupt politicians, and dreams where she fell into a lake filled with blood.

Inside, the waitress showed them to a table, handed them a menu, and took their drink orders. Both decided on hot tea.

The menu was written in English and Chinese. "I haven't seen a menu with the Chinese translation since I left college. The roommate I mentioned had a cousin who owned a restaurant. It was a local hangout for the Asian community. Maylin always claimed a menu with both Chinese and English was your clue to an authentic restaurant. Chinese for their primary clientele, and English for anyone else who wandered in."

Making their selection only took a couple of minutes, and both were ready to order when the young waitress set a teapot and dainty cups on the table.

They sat next to a window overlooking a rock garden. In the center was a fountain, and water cascaded over several large bowls. Plants added color and contrast to grayish-white rocks. Lights illuminated a path that curved through the garden. Small benches were positioned along the side of the walkway.

The setting sun painted the sky in tints of red and gold. Slashes of hazy white clouds crisscrossed as if a giant hand had swiped a brush across the sky.

With her chin propped on her hand, she gazed at the beauty as it unfolded. Cat sighed as the tension and anxiety faded away. "I love watching a sunset. The colors evoke a sense of peace. It's one of the few times I wish I could paint. What a joy it would be to capture those glorious hues on canvas. Unfortunately, I can't even draw a decent stick person."

Kevin watched her, not the view out the window. Those cat-like eyes seemed to take on the glow reflected in the glass. Her hair tumbled around her face and over her shirt collar. Today, she had left it loose, not clipped back from her face as she usually did. The colors of the sunset gleamed in the soft strands.

Images of lying next to her in bed flooded his mind. Even though heat hit deep in his groin, he recognized his attraction went beyond lust. This woman moved him, made him want a lifetime of feelings, moments, and memories. A sensation he had never experienced even in the disastrous mess with his former fiancée. He forced himself to sit back and relax in the chair. *I'm in so much trouble here.*

Lost in the contemplation of the sunset, Cat suddenly realized Kevin had not said a word. She turned her head. The look in his eyes caused her to catch her breath as her heart raced. A feeling akin to panic and exhilaration flooded her senses. If a gaze could impale, the penetrating gleam in his eyes pinned her to her chair. Though his body seemed relaxed, she could sense his intense control.

The moment was broken when the waitress walked up. Cat took a deep breath as she stared at the plate in front of her. Her thoughts were chaotic and jumbled. *Wow, where do we go with this? There is so much I don't know.* Now was as good a time as any to find out.

She picked up her fork. "Hmm ... any serious relationships?" Glancing up, Cat hastily added, "If you don't mind my asking."

His eyes twinkled with mirth. "Other than casual dates, only one. I was engaged in college. Didn't last long," he said and took a bite of egg roll covered with hot mustard.

"What happened?"

He gasped and quickly sipped his tea. "Love the stuff, but it is potent," he said and motioned to the mustard in a small bowl. "When I altered my career path, the arguments started. She didn't want a cop for a husband. Since then, I've seen what the job can do to a marriage. It's tough. She was probably right to cut and run."

Detecting the slight edge of bitterness in his voice, she said, "A difficult situation for both of you. It was better, though, to find out before rather than after. Have you ever regretted your decision?"

"No. It's one regret I don't have. I like the work and the challenge it represents. Okay, same back to you. Any men I need to be worried about?"

Cat chuckled. "No, no one. There never seemed to be the right time or person. Plus, the Bureau moves us around and makes it more difficult."

"Something to consider," he replied. "How much does your exceptional talents, for lack a better word, affect your decision?"

Cat hesitated, then said, "I don't believe I could keep my abilities or mystical links, as I view them, a secret in a close relationship." She chuckled, then said, "It's hard enough to hide what I do from my coworkers; to come up with explanations on how I found a body or some detail."

A burst of merriment erupted. Kevin said, "Oh yeah, the raccoons."

Laughing, Cat said, "That one didn't go over as well as it has on other occasions."

"How is this going to work with your new team? I sensed some unusual dynamics with Ryan and Nicki."

Gesturing with her fork, she said, "Kevin Hunter, sometimes you are downright scary. Not much gets by you, does it?"

"No. So, what's the deal?"

"Hmm …I'm not certain. Oh, by the way, Ryan knows."

"Knows what?"

"The owls and ghosts. We had an interesting conversation when I discovered Lindy Denton's body."

"Did you really. Now that doesn't surprise me. Ryan struck me as an individual with a curious perception. Does he have a secret as well?"

"Damn, there you go again. Yes, there is something, but I can't say."

"I understand," Kevin said, respecting her decision.

"There has been an undercurrent of odd gossip in the bureau about

Scott Fleming and his new team. Even my old boss alluded to it before I left Houston."

Kevin scooped up the last bite of noodles and pondered Cat's comments as he chewed.

"Know what I think?" he said and pushed his plate aside. "Your whole team probably has some type of special ability."

Stunned at his acuity, Cat leaned back in the chair. "Uh …I have my suspicions, but other than Ryan and myself, well, I just don't know."

When the waitress picked up the plates, Kevin said, "I hate to ruin what has been a delightful evening, but I have to ask. Any idea where we go from here on finding our killer?"

Cat filled their cups with the last of the tea. "No, I don't. We have a statewide alert out, maybe someone will spot him. I am hoping Nicki will be able to locate a vehicle registration or some other detail."

She sipped, then sighed as she stared out the window at the glow of the lights in the garden. "He's going to strike again. I know it with absolute certainty, but don't ask me how I know. It is just a sense of terror that is constantly at the back of my thoughts."

Kevin gazed at her troubled face. He felt the same certainty and terror she had described. Only it was for the woman who sat across from him.

He picked up the tab as soon as the waitress laid it on the table.

"Hey, I think it's my turn," Cat protested.

Kevin's only response was a grin she labeled as the male, 'got one up on you,' and pulled his wallet from his back pocket.

As they walked out the door, and Kevin draped his arm across her shoulders, a different tension began to build. While the contact was casual, the jolt caused a momentary lock on her breathing as it raced through her body.

When they reached the car, Kevin turned her toward him. Leaning into her, he lightly kissed her. Cat melted into him, wanting more. Her arms circled his neck, and she pulled him closer. Kevin deepened the kiss. His hands stroked her back. Cat groaned as a flood of desire swept over her.

"Come home with me," he whispered into her ear. "What's happening between us is not going away. I'm not sure where it's headed, but I want to go down this road with you. We can swing by the hotel to pick up whatever you need for tonight and tomorrow. I'm not letting you leave. I want to wake up with you curled in my arms."

Cat gazed into his eyes, the desire that simmered in his gaze fueled the fire that raged in her body. Before she could respond, his phone rang.

Kevin stepped back and pulled it from his pocket. "It's dispatch."

As he answered, Cat had a premonition; the plans for the rest of the night had changed.

"Let's go! I have an officer down."

Twenty-nine

The minute his tires touched the roadway, he punched it. His tone grim, he explained, "One of my officers, Jason Bentley, was in a car accident and is badly injured. I'll drop you at the hotel. I have to get to the hospital."

"No. I'll go with you."

Kevin's phone rang again. After he finished the conversation, he said, "Jason's supervisor, Chuck Mason, is at the scene. Jason's squad car was broadsided in an intersection. The other driver ran the red light. He's intoxicated, blew almost twice the legal limit on a portable breathalyzer."

Angry, he pounded the steering wheel. "A damn drunk and one of my officers is hanging onto his life by a thin thread."

The emergency entrance was a scene of hectic turmoil. The rear doors of an ambulance backed up to the sliding glass doors were still open. Squad cars lined the driveway.

When Kevin entered, the cluster of officers stepped to the side to clear a path. Cat recognized Lieutenant Grayson as he approached. His face grim, he nodded to her, then turned to Kevin.

"Tim, what's the situation?" Kevin asked.

"He's in critical shape, head, and chest injuries, plus his hip and arm are broken. The doctor I spoke to didn't hold out much hope they could save him."

"Have you sent a unit to his home?"

"Yes. The family should be here shortly."

Kevin surveyed the crowd. "We need to move everyone out of this area, so we don't clog up the entrance." He expected more would arrive as there were already several in casual attire. Word of the downed officer had quickly spread.

Tim turned to the crowd and directed them to the waiting room. Kevin sent a quick glance at Cat, who had moved to a chair in the corner of the room.

She leaned back, her gaze flicked over the waiting officers. A few she recognized. *What the hell am I doing here? I can't help. It might be better if I headed back to the hotel.* She even pulled her phone to call a cab but then hesitated. Maybe she couldn't help, but Kevin would know she was here and slid the phone back into her pocket.

At the sound of a commotion, Kevin turned. The officer's family had arrived.

A woman followed by two boys stopped in front of him. Even from a distance, Cat could see the anguish on her face. The boys, who appeared to be high school age, moved to each side and wrapped an arm around her. Scared, their eyes never left Kevin's face. After talking to them for a few minutes, he escorted them into a room across the hallway.

A nurse set up a coffee machine in the waiting room, and as the minutes turned into hours, the pot was refilled countless times.

Sipping her coffee, Cat watched Kevin move from officer to officer, stopping to make a comment and then circling back to the officer's family. His actions clearly revealed his concern for the men and women under his command. They were not employees but his extended family. It was equally evident his officers held him in high esteem. The only time he sat was when he talked to the officer's wife. He'd duck his head toward her and hold her hand. Occasionally he'd slip an arm over the shoulder of one of the boys.

If Kevin had not already earned her respect, he had it that night. Then the revelation washed over her. Stunned—*how did I miss it? It's love. I'm in love with this man. Holy Hell! Now, what do I do?*

Her dilemma occupied her thoughts. She didn't realize a doctor had arrived until the low murmur of voices stopped. The family rose as he approached. On each side, a son gripped their mother's hand.

Everyone could hear the doctor's voice. "He made it through surgery. We've stopped the bleeding in the brain and have mobilized his lungs. Both were punctured. He's stable. I can't tell you yet that he is out of danger. As soon as he's moved to intensive care, you'll be able to see him."

The officer's wife let go of the tears that had been held back during the long hours. As she collapsed against one of her boys, they lowered her into a chair.

It was time for Cat to leave. Kevin had stopped the doctor in the hallway. She waited until their conversation ended before she tapped him on the shoulder. When he turned, she said, "I'm going to call a cab and head to the hotel." She wondered if her newfound emotion was visible.

"No. I'll have one of the officers take you. I can't leave yet." He laid a hand on her shoulder. "Thank you for staying."

"I didn't do anything except sit in a chair."

"No, you did a lot more. It helped to glance over and know you were still here."

Cat felt a rush of awkwardness. "I'll talk to you tomorrow. No, I guess it will be later today," she said as she looked at her watch.

Kevin called to one of the officers. Her last sight of him as she headed out the door was holding the arm of the officer's wife as they moved down the hallway.

Inside her room, she dropped her briefcase and backpack in a chair. The shower helped ease some of the tension. Pulling on a large t-shirt, she collapsed in bed. Despite her fatigue, sleep eluded her. The events of the day and thoughts of Kevin circled endlessly in her mind. Fear weighed on her. At first, she believed it was due to the officer fighting for his life. Then the fear morphed into terror, sending fissions of icy chills. She curled under the covers for warmth. It was the PTC, not the officer who was the source of her premonition. He was on the hunt, and all she could do was wait.

Exhaustion finally pushed her into a deep sleep. When the dream started, her body twisted and turned. Flying, she swooped over a small strip shopping center. A man dragged a woman across the parking lot, then tossed her in the front seat of a truck. She soared over the countryside, following the vehicle as it wound along remote county roads. Turning into a driveway, it passed a dilapidated old house with a nearby barn. Behind the barn was a trailer. When he pulled the limp body from the truck, she screeched in agony. At the sound, his head snapped up, and he stared at her as she circled. When blood rained down, coating her wings, and she began to fall to the ground, he smiled.

Her eyes flew open, and Cat bolted upright, a cry of anguish torn from her. "NO!"

Dear God, how much time do I have? Can I find her before he kills her?

When she tapped the speed dial, her hand trembled. "He's got another woman."

Thirty

Dressed in tactical pants and shirt, she strapped the tie-down holster to her thigh. Pulling a gun in an ankle holster from her backpack, she secured the adhesive strips to hold it in place on her leg. Once the pants were bloused over the top of the boots, the small pistol was invisible. With her coat, backpack, and briefcase, she raced out the door. Traffic was light, and she was at the PD within minutes. When she parked, she was surprised to see Kevin's car.

Walking into his office, she asked, "How'd you get here before me?"

"I didn't go home. Instead, I crashed on the couch in the breakroom. If Jason took a turn for the worse, I wanted to be close to the hospital. I keep extra clothes in my locker. After you called, I made a quick call to the hospital and then hit the shower."

"How's he doing?"

"There has been a slight improvement. The doc upgraded his condition from critical to serious. Tell me what happened."

She dropped her briefcase and backpack on the floor in front of the desk and said, "I haven't told you about my dreams. Sometimes, I get bits and pieces of odd details that are connected to an investigation."

Agitated, she paced. "This time … oh, god." She drew a deep breath and continued. "This time, I saw a man drag a woman to a truck. He drove out of town and ended up behind an old barn near a run-down house. He hauled the woman inside a trailer parked behind the barn. It was Hicks."

She stopped in front of his desk. His face somber, Kevin stared downward while fingertips lightly tapped the surface. Her heart sank. He didn't believe her.

He glanced up and asked, "Can you find the abduction location and the farmhouse?" At the look of astonishment on her face, he said. "What! You didn't think I would believe you?"

"No, I really didn't. Who in their right mind would believe such a wild, crazy story?"

"I've learned not to doubt you. Now—can you find the place?"

"I can try. The first was a strip mall. There was a restaurant with a drive-thru. It was located along the freeway. I would need to examine an aerial to be sure."

He casually asked as he typed on the keyboard. "Why the aerial map?"

When Cat did not immediately answer, Kevin glanced up at a face pale and drawn. Though he hated to pressure her, Cat's abilities had so far been the key to the investigation. "Okay, what's going on? You need to tell me how you saw all this."

She sighed. "Kevin, this is even crazier. I flew overhead."

"Considering your link to the owls, I don't find it surprising. Look at it this way, it's not any crazier than what you have already told me. Let's just say crazy may be normal in this situation. Here's the map."

Cat walked behind the desk and looked at the screen. Kevin scrolled along the freeway as she scanned the aerial images.

"There!" She pointed to a long L-shaped building. On one end was a drive-thru.

Kevin manipulated the images until he could identify the location. He picked up the phone and called the dispatcher. "Tess, Chief Hunter. Have we had any calls that a woman is missing?" He listened for a minute and then said, "Send an officer to the Cup & Bagel Shop. I want the owner of any vehicle in the parking lot located."

As he hung up the phone, he reached to turn up the volume on the police radio on his desk. He turned to Cat. "No reports of any missing persons. The farmhouse, what do you remember?"

While Cat explained what she had seen, Kevin followed her instructions on the computer map until the road reached a small lake south of Clinton. She lost the truck's path from that point.

"Uh ... the owls. Any chance they'll lead you to her?" he asked.

"I don't know. God, how I wished I did. I looked for them when I left the hotel." Her voice cracked, and she gulped back the tears. "This is all new. I don't know what to expect."

"We've got a chance to find her. It's almost daylight, and I don't believe he'll kill her until tonight. At least we know the area he is in. It's a starting point to set up a search."

Cat nodded her head in agreement. Needing a few minutes to get her emotions under control, she said, "I'll get the map from the conference room." When the dispatcher's voice came over the radio, she stopped. A unit was sent to a missing person's call. The image of the woman from her dream flashed through her mind.

Kevin's phone rang. "Chief Hunter." He listened for several seconds, then said, "Tess, send a message to the officers dispatched to the restaurant and the Swartz residence to call me. I want to keep as much traffic off the radio as possible," and disconnected.

His eyes bleak, he stared at Cat. "Jenny Swartz didn't make it home from work this morning. She is a night clerk at a hotel near the Cup & Bagel. Her sister has been trying to call her on her cell phone for the last hour. This is probably our victim."

Cat's fear ratcheted another notch as she raced down the hallway to get the map.

With it spread across the desk, they were bent over, marking the grid search lines when the phone rang again. This time it was the officer dispatched to the Cup & Bagel. Kevin told him to check every vehicle on the lot. If one was registered to Jenny Swartz, call him.

The next came from the officer on the way to the Swartz residence.

He was told to obtain a recent photo of Jenny, and a clothing description, then get it to the station.

As he hung up, she said, "This is a large area to search."

Kevin studied the map for several seconds. "Yeah, it will take more manpower than I can provide. I'll contact the state patrol and the sheriff's department for additional officers."

Another call; they'd found Jenny's Swartz's car. The remote hope she was wrong vanished.

Kevin contacted the dispatcher and told her to send a detective to the crime scene and have the officer contact him.

It was Ed that called. Kevin explained the missing woman was likely the killer's latest victim.

His next call was to Tim Grayson, telling him to report to the station. While they waited for the details of the investigation to reach them, they continued to section the map. The sense of urgency overwhelmed her. They had to find Jenny before nightfall.

When Jessie walked in, Cat darted a look of surprise at Kevin. It was early, even for his dedicated assistant.

"After your phone call, I called her."

"He said another woman is missing. What do you need?" Jessie asked.

"Two more county maps and coffee as a starter," Kevin replied.

The next to arrive was Grayson. Kevin filled him in on the details and then added, "Tim, I want you to control the search from the command center. Have your team on standby. Decide where to park the van. Also, contact the state patrol, we need their helicopter and whatever personnel they can provide. Same with the sheriff's department. They know the county better than we do."

"I'll get my men enroute and then get the rest set up," he said and headed out of the office.

Another call, it was from Ed. As he hung up, Kevin said, "A syringe was found next to her car. An officer is on the way to the M.E.'s office to have it tested. It shouldn't take long to confirm its ketamine."

Jessie entered with two cups of coffee, and a stack of maps tucked under her arm.

"Jessie, we'll need briefing packets set up. A photo of the missing woman should be here shortly," Kevin said.

Cat's phone rang as she took the cup Jessie handed her.

"Nicki, you're up early. I'm putting you on the speakerphone. I'm in Kevin's office. The PTC grabbed another woman."

Nicki said, "I haven't been to bed. I figured I'd wake you. Do you have any leads?"

"Yeah, we do and are putting together a search team. He abducted her early this morning. If we are right in our assessment, he won't kill her until tonight."

"You won't believe what I found."

Kevin interjected, "At this point, I wouldn't disbelieve anything the two of you told me."

"JD Hicks is definitely the PTC. I found a JD and Thelma Hicks in Mineral Wells, Texas. It's a small-town west of Ft. Worth. I am sending you a file that contains dates of birth, social security numbers, pictures, and other details. JD's been arrested several times for petty theft, assault, and minor drug possession. His mother was on welfare. A little over a year ago, they dropped off the radar, nothing. Her mail was returned as undeliverable to the known address."

Cat could hear the clicks of the keyboard as Nicki paused, then said, "Remember your inquiry to the Weatherford PD?"

Cat said, "Yes. I asked them to search for any unusual deaths over the last five years."

"I'm in the middle of this research and up pops an email from a detective with Weatherford PD. It contained a file in response to your request. A year ago, a Jane Doe was found in the city landfill. She died from blunt force trauma to the head and face though her arms had been sliced open. With the facial disfiguration and nothing on file for the fingerprints, she was never identified. I'll bet my pension this is mom."

"Were you able to get any pictures from the autopsy?" Kevin asked.

"Yes, they're in the file I'm sending you."

"Are the cuts similar to our victims?" he asked.

"In my opinion, yes. The Jane Doe isn't the only body. A month later, another body, Ezra Meeks, was found at the same landfill. Like the other victim, his face had been beaten. Meeks was identified by his fingerprints. He'd been arrested several times and lived in Mineral Wells. I traced a connection between JD and Ezra."

Nicki paused, more clicks, and then continued, "I spoke to the Mineral Wells police chief. He went to school with Hicks and claimed JD was always a bit off bubble. He said JD and Ezra had been running together for the last several years and that Ezra, in his words, was also one strange duck. Practiced Satanism and had all kinds of satanic metal symbols and drawings on the walls of his house. The chief said he suspected Ezra dealt drugs though he'd never been able to prove it until after he was killed. A large quantity of marijuana, cocaine, and PCP were found in his house."

A low chuckle came over the phone.

"This is going to boost Ryan's ego. The police chief said Hicks had been hospitalized for several years at a state mental hospital. He also worked for a couple of years at a local meatpacking plant. He confirmed that little over a year ago, JD and his mother disappeared. They just hooked onto the trailer and left town. The chief never saw either one of them again and had nothing to tie JD to Meek's murder. And ... mom had red hair. Want to bet, she's the trigger that set him off. JD kills her and then likely kills Ezra."

While Nicki talked, Cat booted her computer. A beep signaled an incoming email.

"Good work, Nicki. I don't suppose you came up with the truck's license plate number?"

Nicki laughed. "Of course, I did. It's in the packet I sent along with the additional details on Hick's background I got from the police chief. This one, though, is on you. It was a damn good hunch you had. While

I would have eventually found the information, it would have taken a lot longer if you hadn't asked for the search. Their records are not computerized. Keep me posted on the search," and hung up.

Cat opened the file attached to the email and hit the print key. Picking up the papers from the tray, she sifted through them. "Jeez, the woman is a miracle worker. There is even a set of fingerprints from when Hicks was arrested."

An officer knocked on Kevin's door. He had the clothing description and picture of Jenny Swartz. Kevin thanked him and told him to give the documents to Jessie.

Cat studied Nicki's file. "It says here Thelma worked for several years at a vet clinic. She was suspected of stealing drugs and was fired. JD dropped out of school and became friends with Ezra. They were caught killing chickens for one of Ezra's rituals. Hmm … meatpacking plant, state hospital, access to drugs, yeah, Ryan hit this one out of the ballpark."

Cat pulled the vehicle and trailer registration and the copy of JD's driver's license and gave them to Jessie to copy and place in the packets. Then she went back over the documents, absorbing each detail of JD Hick's life. Her instincts said they could be the difference between living and dying for Jenny Swartz.

Cat and Kevin carried the briefing packets and the master map to the conference room. Lt. Grayson and his SWAT team were already inside, along with several Clinton officers. Cat spotted Ed and Roger seated against the wall.

Overhead a whir of blades sounded as the helicopter landed on the parking lot. The pilots walked in, followed by the sheriff deputies and state troopers. Cat had a sign-in board. As the officer filled in their information to include cell phone numbers, she assigned each a grid number, then added their name to the grid on the master map taped to the wall. Kevin passed out the packets. When everyone was settled, Kevin introduced Cat and then gave a quick rundown of their suspect.

"We are searching for a killer who has been tied to multiple murders across three states. His name is JD Hicks. His picture, vehicle registration, and information on the trailer he is towing are in your packet. Hicks uses drugs to subdue his victims before killing them in a satanic ritual. His last known location was the Almost Heaven RV park on Noel Rd."

Kevin stopped for a minute to allow everyone to review the material. He picked back up with the missing woman.

"This morning, around four a.m., Hicks abducted a woman from the parking lot at the Cup & Bagel on I-20. Her picture and clothing description are in the packet. We've received information Hicks may be hiding in a section of the county south of Clinton. Your maps are divided into grids. Check every road in your grid for a deserted, run-down farmhouse at some distance from the roadway. A barn will be close to the farmhouse. Hick's trailer will be parked behind the barn."

He motioned toward Lieutenant Tim Grayson, who stood near the front of the room. "The command unit will be located at the Fill and Go on Morgan Rd. Tim will control the search. Grab a portable radio on your way out. Use channel nine. Once you have cleared your grid, contact the dispatcher for a new assignment. If you spot Hicks or his vehicle, call Tim or me. Our phone numbers are on the front of the packet. We want to avoid a hostage situation. Any questions?"

Not a hand was raised. "One last item. We expect Jenny Swartz will be killed once it is dark. That's only a few hours to find her."

Grayson removed the map. It would be mounted in the SWAT van. When the room was empty, Cat grabbed her equipment, followed by Kevin.

Jessie stopped them in the hallway to say the M.E.'s office had called. The syringe found at the Cup and Bagel contained ketamine.

Outside, she turned to walk to her car. Kevin grabbed her arm. "I thought we were going together."

"Separately, we can cover twice as much ground. Kevin, I have a terrifying feeling deep in my gut that we won't find her in time."

"No! You don't understand. You can't be out there by yourself."

Anger started to build as Cat stared at Kevin's face. "I'm an officer just like you, and there's no reason I need a babysitter."

"Yes, you do. You're his next target."

"What!"

"Ryan alluded to a reason that he hadn't left. I believe Hicks has fixated on you. I've have had this strange sense of danger, and it's directed at you."

Cat felt a tingle of trepidation as she recalled Ryan's comments, then brushed it away. It wasn't logical that she could be a target. "No, I don't believe it. He's never seen me. Besides, it doesn't matter. I am armed and able to protect myself. I'm going to search for him along with everyone else."

"That's the problem. Everyone will be spread out. If you need help, it'll take time for someone to reach you."

"I have the radio and my phone, so it's not like I will be out of contact with anyone. We're wasting time."

Kevin watched her walk to her car and drive out of the parking lot. An intense, eerie dread created a chill deep in his bones. The terror wasn't for Jenny Swartz, but for Cat Morgan. When he reached to open his door, he heard the screech of the owls. In the clear blue morning sky, they circled then flew away. Even as the sense of foreboding flowed through him, he wondered—*why three birds, instead of two.*

Thirty-one

The silence was creepy, no catfights, dogs barking, not even the sound of a car. A chill raced over him, and he snuggled deeper under the covers. Why was the damn room so cold? Good thing he'd left his clothes on when he went to bed. Then it dawned on him, there wasn't even the hum of the furnace. Damn, he must be out of propane. The bottle would have to be refilled. He'd better check the fuel in the portable generator since he didn't want to lose power to the trailer. Well, he had lots of time today to take care of the problems.

JD chuckled to himself as he thought about how he had outwitted the cops. *Keep on searching those RV parks. You'll never find me.* Once he grabbed the female cop, he'd be gone.

His thoughts drifted to the woman. JD had never felt a burning desire for one of his offerings. They served a purpose, and then he got rid of them. This one was different. Day and night, her image filled his mind, along with the overwhelming obsession to control her. She'd see the force of his power when the old one, his master, answered and would learn to fear him. The thought sent a rush of ecstasy through him. It won't be long, and she'll be on the floor.

When a groan split the stillness, he tossed the blankets aside and erupted out of bed. Rushing into the small living room, he gazed at the naked woman on the floor.

Deciding it was easier to inject the drug than sitting inside hoping to dope their drinks, he'd cruised the parking lots. Discouraged, he was ready to head home when this one walked out of a coffee shop. Her hair flashed like a bright red halo under the parking lot lights.

Before he went to bed, he had prepared her body for the sacrifice. Now, her face contorted as she groaned and tried to move her arms and legs. Syringes, filled with ketamine, were on the table along with his knives. He grabbed one and jabbed it into her arm. Within seconds, the only motion was the slight rise and fall of her chest.

Tossing the needle in the trash, he lit a joint and sat in his mother's chair. As he rocked, he gazed at the woman and pulled the smoke deep into his lungs. The rush from the weed warmed him, and the creak of wood was soothing. Back and forth, as he took another drag and thought about his plans for the cop and her boyfriend.

Once he was done with this one, he'd go after the agent. Tomorrow night she'd be on the floor. And before he left town, he'd take care of the police chief. His laughter echoed in the silent room. Yes, he had a foolproof plan to kill him. Time to leave as he threw the butt in the ashtray.

Outside, he disconnected the propane bottle and dropped it in the bed of the truck. After pouring the last of the gas in the generator, he tossed the can alongside the bottle.

The screech of an owl broke the silence. Looking up, he saw three birds circling overhead. They drifted down and landed on the barn roof, their golden eyes stared at him. A ripple of fear flowed through him. He considered grabbing his shotgun and getting rid of them. No, not a good idea. What if someone heard the shot. They might decide to check it out. Besides, they're just birds, no reason to be afraid of them as he got into the truck. He didn't notice the birds take flight and follow.

∽ ∾

It didn't take long for Cat to reach the first grid. She slowly drove as she scanned the terrain for the farmhouse, occasionally diverting onto weed-infested driveways. Each time an officer reported in to get a new assignment, she'd pull to the side of the road. On a copy of the master map, she drew an X over the section that had been searched.

The hours passed, the sun sank lower in the sky. Cat estimated they had another two to three hours of light before the search would have to be called off. The sections left to search slowly decreased, as the number with a large X increased.

Even the helicopter pilots had been unsuccessful and had returned to the airport for fuel. From the conversation between Grayson and one of the pilots, it was doubtful they could return before dark. With each grid that was searched and eliminated, a new fear began to build. Had she misinterpreted the dream? Did she send a search team in the wrong direction?

Up ahead was the convenience store they contacted yesterday, and she needed to fill the tank. She stopped next to a pump, slid her credit card through the reader, and flipped the handle to start the flow of gas. Locking the car door, she walked inside.

The same clerk from the previous day stood behind the counter with a phone to his ear. His eyebrows raised in amazement, and his mouth dropped open when she entered. Then he stammered and stuttered as he told whoever was on the other end to wait a minute.

"How did you know?" he asked.

"What?"

"The man you were looking for. How did you know he was here? I just called the police chief to tell him the man came in and bought propane. He's on the phone. He was here, son-of-a-bitch, he was in this store and bought propane." The excitement and fear pushed the pitch of his voice until it squeaked.

"Chief Hunter's on the phone?"

"Yeah, that's what I am trying to tell you," he said and waved it in the air.

Cat grabbed it from his hand. "Kevin, I'm at the store. Where are you?"

"Twenty miles south of you."

"I'll get the information and call back as soon as I'm in the car."

"Wait until I get there, don't follow him."

Cat hit the disconnect button. *Yeah, right. As if I'm going to quietly wait here until help arrives* and handed the phone to the clerk.

"How long has he been gone, and which way did he go?"

"Five minutes or so before you pulled in. He turned west."

Her phone rang. She glanced at the screen, it was Kevin. She ignored it.

"I got the license plate number." He held up a slip of paper. Pride added to the mix of emotions in his voice.

Grabbing the paper, she ran for the door. Cat pulled the nozzle from the car and left it hanging. As she drove onto the highway, her foot stomped the gas pedal to the floor. Tires squealed, leaving a long stretch of rubber on the asphalt.

Kevin called her on the portable radio. She keyed the mike. "I'm west on Gooseneck Road. The PTC left a few minutes before I got to the store. He can't be far ahead of me." She relayed the plate number. As she raced along the road, she listened to Grayson redirect officers toward her. The net would close until the killer had no place to run.

The gap was closing too fast, and she reduced speed. She wanted him in sight, yet not close enough, he'd realize he was being followed. She had no way to know the killer had already spotted her.

He'd seen the car gain on him, then slow down. It piqued his interest, and he slowly reduced his speed.

Let's find out who's back there. It didn't take long to recognize the car. *I'll be damned, the agent is behind me.* Excitement surged through him; his hands trembled on the wheel. Erratic thoughts tumbled in his mind. Did she know this was his vehicle, what was she doing out here, how did she find out, had she told anyone? The questions buzzed like bees in his head. This was his chance. A plan—he needed one fast—grab her and hide the car.

While JD wasn't smart, he had the instinctive cunning of a predator. When he moved the trailer to the farmhouse, he'd spent hours driving the surrounding roads in case he had to make a fast exit. He couldn't take a chance on getting lost on a backroad in the middle of nowhere, especially with a trailer in tow. A right turn at the next crossroad would lead to a series of curves, and he'd be out of sight for several minutes.

Mounted on the front of his truck was a heavy metal push bar. Ice and snow storms would occasionally hit West Texas. Drivers would lose control and end up in a bar ditch. He could pick up a few bucks by pushing them back on the roadway. If he could find the right place, he'd ram her car.

As soon as he rounded the second curve, he spotted what he needed—a narrow dirt driveway lined with trees. He quickly braked and backed into the driveway. The trees would block her view as she came around the curve. She'd never see him until it was too late.

He turned right, and she lost sight of him as the trees along the road obstructed her view. As she approached the intersection, she searched for a road sign with a name or number to alert the command center of her change in direction. When she turned, the only one she spotted was a warning sign for a series of curves.

Cat caught a quick glimpse of the truck as it rounded the curve. Slowing her speed, she entered the first bend. *Damn, still no road sign.* Even if she didn't know what road she was on, Cat had to tell dispatch she had turned north. As she approached the second curve, she reached for the police radio tucked in the console tray. Rounding the bend, her peripheral vision picked up movement. Cat's head turned, but it was too late to react as the truck rammed the side of her car, pushing her across the road. The radio flew out of her hand. Her head slammed against the door window.

She woke up on her back in the bed of a truck as it bounced over a bumpy road. Tape covered her mouth, making it difficult to breathe, and sharp stabs of pain ripped through her head. Terror clawed its way through her body and locked around her brain. It threatened to choke the breath from her lungs as a dark cloud swirled around the edge of her mind. As the bile rose, she fought it back down. *I can't get sick or pass out.*

Focusing on her body, she pushed past the nausea and fear. The side of her face felt wet, and she assumed it was blood. She didn't feel drugged, so her only injury seemed to be the blow to the head. Her hands and feet were tied.

There was no way to know how long she'd been unconscious. The position of the sun was considerably lower in the sky than she remembered. It would soon be dark.

The truck hit another pothole, and her head bounced on the floor, setting off another round of pain. At least, she could lift her feet and brace them against the side of the bed to stop the battering of her body into the old tires and propane bottle next to her.

Holy hell, he didn't find it! A surge of elation shot through her. While the holster on her thigh was empty, the backup gun was still on her ankle.

The truck slowed. Over the edge of the bed, the roof of a house was visible, decrepit, and filled with gaping holes. It was the roof in her dream. Terror ratcheted another notch, and she shivered, cold to the bone.

Then, owls swooped into view as they dived, coming closer and closer to the truck. Their calls filled the air with sound. A sense of warmth flooded her body, pushing away the numbing chill. Even though she knew they couldn't help her, for a few seconds, the terror was gone. The birds swept over the bed of the truck as it came to a stop before circling and disappearing from her view.

What replaced them was JD Hicks. He laid his arms on the edge of the bed and gazed down at her. Narrow lips pulled back over dirty, yellow teeth in a parody of a smile. "Looky, here, just looky here at what I've got. What a gift for the old one, though I might keep you for a while before I offer you to him. I already have a gift inside all set for tonight. You get to watch."

When she stared into his eyes, desolation swept over her. Cat found the place of darkness that destroyed every sense.

Thirty-two

When Grayson lost radio contact with Cat, a soul-shattering foreboding pervaded Kevin's body. Calls to her cell phone rolled to her voice mail. Every instinct screamed Hicks had her.

Pulling to the side of the road, he called Grayson on his phone. "Tim, she's not answering her cell phone. Something's happened. Move the van to the convenience store on Gooseneck Road and reassign the search team to the grids in that area."

The store would be centrally located to their search and cut down on the response time if he needed the SWAT team. "I'm a couple of miles from the store and will follow the route she took. Any chance we'll get the helicopter back up?" Kevin was amazed his voice didn't reflect his emotional turmoil.

"It's doubtful. I just got a call from one of the pilots. When they tried to refuel, they found a problem in the fuel line."

"Damn, that's going to make the search even more difficult," Kevin said. He didn't think the fear could get any more intense, and Grayson's words just proved him wrong.

Pulling back on the highway, a bizarre tug pulled at his thoughts as danger repeatedly echoed in his head. An eerie sensation, as if someone was near and whispering a message of urgency in his ear. Shaking his head to clear his thoughts, he slowed once he had passed the store and focused on examining the roadway for any clues. He listened to Grayson, and the search teams exchange updates. Each time the radio pinged, he felt a surge of hope, then a crushing disappointment as another report was negative. *How could a car and driver just disappear?*

Reaching an intersection, he stopped. *Hell, which way do I go?* Straight would take him into the grids they had already searched. Cat likely turned, but which direction? Going right would take him back to town, left would be farther into the countryside. Logic said, left. Hicks would be as far away from town as possible. The tug hit again, this time, stronger and accompanied by an uncontrollable urge to turn to the right. The sense of anxiety and urgency grew.

Not understanding why, he followed the inexplicable premonition and entered a series of curves. If not for his slow speed, he would have missed it. The weeds along the side of the bar ditch had been flattened. He stopped, got out of his car, and walked along the edge of the road. The fading sunlight flashed off an object in the bar ditch. He leaned down and saw it was a piece of a mirror.

Turning back to examine the road, he spotted the skid marks. The line of travel indicated a vehicle had pulled out of a driveway and crossed the road. Small pieces of metal and glass littered the blacktop. It had been several years since he had done any accident reconstruction, but a vehicle had hit something.

Faint tire tracks were visible on the dirt driveway, but it was impossible to determine when they had been made. Riddled with potholes and trash, he couldn't take a chance on driving over it and end up with a flat tire. He'd walk a short distance. If he didn't spot anything, he'd continue his search of the main road.

When he spotted deeper car tracks in the grass and weeds, he picked up his pace. Someone had recently driven down the lane. Ahead was a curve, and he angled, following the tree line to get a glimpse around the bend before he charged forward. An old windmill creaked in the breeze and stood next to a dilapidated three-sided shed. Inside, the rear end of a vehicle was visible. *Dear god, that's Cat's car.*

Gun in hand, he burst out of the trees to reach the side of the building. At the corner, he peered inside. The car had been struck on the right side. Moving alongside it, he saw Cat's coat on the back seat. As his gaze shifted to the front, his chest clamped until he could barely breathe. Blood streaked the driver's window and door. For a moment, paralyzing fear streamed through his body, until logic took over. If she wasn't here, she had to be alive.

Then he saw the keys in the ignition. He slipped his gun into his holster as he stepped to the driver's side. Opening the door, he grabbed them and walked to the back of the vehicle. He didn't realize he had stopped breathing until the trunk popped open. All it contained was Cat's rifle case and equipment. Kevin gasped as his lungs sucked in air.

He radioed Grayson he'd found Cat's car and its location. It would take several minutes before any officers arrived. Since there was no reason to stay with the vehicle, he started back to the main road. Their cries faint and distant, he heard the owls before he saw them. The closer they got, the louder the calls. Kevin searched the sky, but it was getting dark, and he couldn't see them.

When he finally spotted them, three great-horned owls flew in formation as they approached. Suddenly, they plunged downward, circled and dived around his head, their screeches abrupt and disjointed. A sense of panic and fear shot into his mind. *My god, am I feeling their desperation?*

They flew down the dirt road, only to turn and circle around him. At first, he'd watched in amazement. Then the illogical tug struck again, pulling him forward. *I'll be damned! They want me to follow them.* The birds flew ahead of him as he ran to his car. Confused and uncertain, since this was as crazy as anything Kevin had ever done, there was the hope they would lead him to Cat. These were her birds.

❦

Hicks dropped the tailgate. Cat's head hit the metal flooring as he jerked her out of the truck bed. Throwing her over his shoulder, he hauled her into the trailer. Her head hanging down increased the excruciating agony from her head wound, and the tape across her mouth made it difficult to breathe. *I can't pass out.* She closed her eyes to stop the dizziness and forced herself to concentrate on her one hope—she still had her gun.

He tossed her on the couch. Patting her on the cheek, he said, "I'll be back in a few minutes, and then … we're going to get to know each other." Chuckling, he walked out the door.

On her back, she opened her eyes and stared at the fly-specked ceiling. Once the spinning in her head stopped, she swung her legs to get her feet on the floor. She squirmed and pushed until she was upright.

When she looked down, horror, older and more rudimentary than any human emotion, engulfed her. A movie director could not have staged a more grotesque scene. Taped trash bags formed a large square with a ragged sheet in the center. On top, was the naked body of Jenny Swartz. Long red hair was spread above her head and along the sides of her face. The strands gleamed like streaks of blood against her pale skin.

The girl was still breathing, but thank god she was unconscious. Otherwise, the terror of what awaited her would drive her insane.

She reminded herself, sanity and ingenuity were all she had to cling too if they were both going to survive. Pulling her gaze away from the young woman, she surveyed her surroundings.

A short hallway with a door on one side led to the bedroom where the corner of a bed was visible. If she had to guess, the door was for the bathroom. The kitchen was on one side with a window over the sink. On the opposite wall was another window and a table with two chairs. Another jolt of panic hit at the sight of several knives and syringes. She thrust the fear to the back of her mind and continued her visual search of the trailer.

Beside the table was the door to the outside. The couch butted up to the end of the kitchen counter and curved in an L-shape on the other end of the trailer. In the corner was a cabinet with a TV and next to it was a rocker. Dirty dishes covered the kitchen counter, and trash littered the floor. A heavy odor of burnt marijuana hung in the air.

There must be something she could use to get her hands free and get to her gun before he stripped off her clothes or drugged her. And, just how the hell did he miss it? She considered it a small miracle.

Her eyes moved back to the table, and the knives strewed across the surface. Could she reach one? Probably not. What about the kitchen. Yes! A small butcher block with knives was beside the sink.

She quickly glanced at the door. She had to try. Maybe the loud thumps of whatever he was doing would keep him occupied.

She slid down the couch until she reached the end next to the kitchen counter. The tricky part was to stand. If she overbalanced, she'd topple on top of Jenny. Slowly, Cat pushed up, letting her thighs do the work; the same technique she used for a squat at the gym. She braced against the side of the couch until she felt steady. There was just enough of a gap between her feet to let her scoot sideways. She grabbed the edge of the counter with her hands, and the grip helped her slide over the floor until she stood with her back to the knife block.

To reach them was near impossible. On her toes, Cat pushed her butt tight against the counter, leaned backward, and extended her arms as far as she could reach. Her fingertips touched the wooden block. Moving her hands upward to grasp a knife handle, she groaned at the excruciating pain in her shoulders. When she started to pull it out, the block tipped. She stopped and pushed back. *Damn, I can't let it fall over. He might see it and know a knife is gone.*

Her fingers numb from the freezing room and the tape wrapped around her wrists, she flexed them as best she could before reaching for the handle again. Slowly, she pulled. This time, the block stayed in place, and the knife slid out. Once she had a solid grip on the handle, she let her arms drop. The instant relief from the intense pain sent waves of dizziness swirling in her head.

Several loud bangs and the hum of a motor broke the silence. No wonder the room is so cold as she remembered the explanation from the owner of the first RV park she and Kevin had contacted. He had no heat because he was out of propane.

With warm air flowing into the room, she sensed she had run out of time. Reversing the process, she slid, and when her legs pressed against the couch, she dropped.

The door opened, and Hicks strolled inside. Despite the lingering chill in the room, sweat ran down her back. As he made his way over to her, Cat pushed the knife between the cushions. He gazed at her with a look of triumph on his face.

"Didn't think it would be so easy to grab you. I've been following you for days. Had it all planned out. You sure saved me a lot of trouble drivin' after me the way you did. Oh, we're gonna have a fun time tonight—you and me."

He knelt beside Jenny, his stained fingers stroked her body, then moved to her face. Strands of hair across her forehead were pushed to the side.

Cat's stomach heaved at the grisly sight of Hicks' hands on the young girl.

"Time for her to have another injection." He looked up at Cat. "Not gonna shoot you full of dope. Not yet, anyway. I want you to watch since you'll be next."

His laughter caused icy chills to overlay the sweat on her body. JD Hicks was a dirty, scrawny, characterless person until you looked into his eyes. Whoever said the eyes were the pathway to the soul was right. His were dark, bottomless pits, nothing lived there, no soul, no humanity. She didn't believe her fear could spike any higher, yet it shot up the scale as those empty eyes focused on her. Whatever existed inside Hicks wasn't human.

Thirty-three

JD stood, picked up a syringe from the table, and knelt again beside Jenny. He jammed the needle into her arm. "Yeah, that should be enough to make sure she stays nice and quiet until it's time. Won't be long now."

Humming, he walked to the refrigerator and grabbed a bottle of beer. Popping the cap, he sat in a chair by the table and periodically took a gulp. His lifeless eyes fixated on her face. When he set the bottle down and picked up a large butcher knife, her fear skyrocketed.

He twirled it in his hand, then his fingers stroked the sides and edge of the blade. "I worked in a meat plant and learned why it's important to keep knives sharp. It's the difference between a smooth cut and one that hacks away at the meat."

The macabre vision of the knife slicing into human flesh made Cat's gut heave again, and she repeatedly swallowed to stop the bile from rising in her throat.

Hicks laughed and laid the knife back on the table. He pulled a small plastic bag out of his pocket. It was filled with homemade cigarettes, and several were wrapped in foil. Removing one, he waved it in the air. "Good stuff, laced with angel dust. The foil keeps it fresh."

Cat had thought she had reached the limit of the horror she faced. When she heard angel dust, she knew she was wrong. It was the street name for PCP and the most dangerous drug an officer could encounter. Users hallucinate and became violent while losing all sensation of pain. Combined with marijuana, it would intensify his instability.

Hicks moved to the counter to pick up the lighter. Cat shifted her body to catch his attention, afraid he would spot the missing knife. When he looked at her instead of the knife block, she mentally sighed in relief. *Okay, another small miracle. Small miracles can add up to a large one.*

As he drew the smoke deep into his lungs, he settled into the rocking chair. The creak of the wood was all that broke the silence as he gazed at her with his emotionless stare.

He motioned with the joint. "Want a hit? It'll really make you enjoy what's coming."

In the small trailer, it only took a few seconds for the smoke to fill the room. The smell was sickening, and she began to take shallow breaths.

"When I saw you on TV, I knew you'd be my perfect sacrifice. It's why I didn't leave when you came up with my picture. How'd you get it? Guess it don't matter now. We'll soon be gone." He rocked, smoked, and stared at her. The woman on the floor was forgotten as he exulted in the joy of seeing the agent under his control.

"I'm gonna kill your cop boyfriend before I leave town. He had no right to touch you. You belong to the old one, and that bastard has to pay for defiling you. For your blood to wash you clean, I'll have to cut deep."

The joint down to his fingertips, JD sucked one more draw, then tossed it in a bowl on the table beside him. Sweat beaded on his forehead and rolled down his face. The PCP was already ramping up his system.

"Yeah, I got that all planned out too, how I'm gonna kill him. It'll be easy, then we're out of here. Got a spot already picked out in another town." Rising from the rocking chair, he stepped over the body on the floor. He reached down and yanked the tape from her mouth.

A moan of pain escaped before Cat could control it.

He smiled in response, then stared at something above her head. "Don't tell me what to do."

Cat twisted her head to look above her. *Who is he talking too?*

"What difference does it make if she can talk, she ain't going anywhere. No, I'm not ready to kill her."

In disbelief, she listened to the one-sided argument.

When Hicks stepped to the window over the table, she pulled the knife from the cushions, turned the blade toward her back, and shoved it upright between the cushions. Up and down, her hands moved. *Damn, it's too dull, this will take forever. I guess it's not necessary for this one to be sharp.*

"Shut up. I know what I'm doing," JD said.

Whose voice is he hearing? Is it something I can use?

He turned to stare at Cat with those cold, empty eyes. "Not long now. My master will come. Then you'll see my power." Another burst of maniacal laughter echoed in the room.

Instinctively, Cat knew she couldn't show the terror ripping through her. Predators sensed fear and used it to help kill their prey. Her hands continued to move against the knife.

He unwrapped another joint and lit it before turning back to the window to stare out.

"JD, who are you talking too?"

Shocked, his head twisted to look at her. "How the hell do you know my name?"

"Oh, I know more than just your name. You're JD Hicks from Mineral Wells, Texas. Did you really believe I wouldn't find out? You can't escape. Officers are searching for you."

He grunted, then said, "You think you're so damn smart, but you're the one tied up on the couch. They won't find me. This place is well hidden. It's why I picked it." He took another deep drag.

An appalling sensation he might be right dampened Cat's lingering hope. He turned his gaze back to the window. Her hands, slippery with blood from nicks on her fingers, moved faster against the knife.

"Besides, I'll be gone before the sun comes up. You up for a road trip?" A raspy crackle of glee erupted.

The hazy smoke that filled the room had begun to affect her senses—blurred vision and a return of the nausea. Hell, this isn't good. How could she get him to open the door?

"JD, you don't look so good. Matter of fact, you look downright sickly with all that sweat running down your face and into your eyes. I bet you're about ready to keel over. Oh, yeah, I'd enjoy seeing you lying on the floor, passed out from the heat."

JD wiped his sleeve across his face as he grinned. "I can make sure it's real cold in here, bitch. Once you're naked, you'll be singing a different tune, whining that you're cold, but then once I put you under, you won't feel anything." He flung open the door, and the flow of cold air brought instant relief from the putrid smoke.

He stared out the open doorway for several minutes while he finished smoking his weed. Cat kept her mouth shut, not wanting to disrupt whatever was going on his head. She needed that door open for as long as possible.

"Time for the candles." Tossing the butt outside, he swung the door shut. It didn't close, leaving a small gap that allowed more of the smoke to dissipate.

He tilted his head as if listening, then said, "I told you before, she ain't going anywhere. So shut up. I know what I'm doing."

"JD, you still haven't told me who you are talking to."

"None of your damn business." He picked up a large box with several thick candles. One by one, he lit and set them around Jenny's body.

The candlelight cast an obscene glow over Jenny's skin. Horrified, Cat realized he was ready to start his bloodletting ceremony. *I can't stop him.* The tape was beginning to split, yet not enough that she could tear it.

"Where's your mother, Thelma? How come she's not with you?"

JD screamed. "Shut up! I don't want to talk about her. They were right. I shouldn't have taken the tape off."

Moving back to the window, he leaned against the side to stare at the black night. Reaching inside his shirt, he pulled out an amulet. Fingers stroked the metal, and he began to mutter.

This isn't a good sign. "Who was right?" When she didn't get a reaction, she tried again. "JD! What's hanging from your neck?"

His head swiveled toward her, a blank look on his face.

"Did Ezra give it to you?"

"Ezra, do you know him?" His voice calm and detached.

"Yes, he lived in Mineral Wells near you. Tell me about him."

"He showed me the way to the old one. He always wanted ..." His words trailed off as he stared at the body on the floor.

"What did he want? How did you meet Ezra?" She was desperate to keep his focus on her and not let him fixate on the comatose young woman.

His eyes shifted back to her. "Ezra was my best friend. He helped me."

"How did he help you?"

"Police were chasing me, and he hid me from them." His eyes shifted from her face to the woman on the floor.

"JD! Why were they chasing you?"

"Uh ...I broke into a store."

"Where is Ezra now? Does he still live in Mineral Wells?"

"He's dead."

"How did he die?" She felt a slight give in the tape. *How much longer do I have before he starts his gruesome ritual?*

He looked at the window. "He's coming," he said and picked up a knife from the table.

With both hands, he held it above his head and cried out. "It is you I serve. I worship at your altar of blood and offer this sacrifice."

Cat shouted. "JD!" hoping to break through his drug-induced stupor. "JD, tell me how Ezra died."

Hicks lowered the knife. "He tried to stop me from contacting the old one. He had to die, but he didn't."

"What do you mean he didn't?"

His fingers caressed the blade. "He's still with me. I hear him every day. They both tell me things."

He turned back to the window. "The master comes. He's in the sky." His calm voice was more chilling than his rants.

Cat had to keep him talking. "JD, who tells you things?"

"Ezra and Mother. She whines a lot. I can hear her now, telling me to kill you. I can, I have your gun." He laid the knife on the table and pulled Cat's pistol from his jacket pocket.

"No, I don't care what you say, it's not time for her to die. She belongs to my master and will be my perfect sacrifice."

Head tilted, he listened to sounds only he could hear.

"How many times do I have to tell you she's not dangerous. No, I'm not goin' dope her. I want her to watch and know my power."

JD stared at the wall over Cat's head.

"He waits." He stuck the pistol back in his pocket and picked up the knife. "It's time. He will protect me. He always protects me. I tried to tell you. You didn't listen. Now you're dead. Both of you are dead."

He stepped to the side of Jenny and gazed down at her. "When he accepts this sacrifice, his power will be mine. We will be one. You'll see I'm right."

JD knelt beside Jenny. With raised arms, he held the knife over the girl and chanted, "I call to you, the old one. You are my master. I worship at your altar. Bring forth your power and make it mine. Accept this blood offering from your servant and seal your power within me. Master, heed my call."

Nothing Cat had ever heard was as unnerving as Hick's words. Desperate, she increased the pressure against the knife, unconcerned her movements might be seen. She could feel the tape weaken, yet she couldn't stop him. Helpless, she watched as he leaned over Jenny and lowered the knife.

Thirty-four

Over his career, he had been afraid many times, but nothing had prepared him for the paralyzing terror that overwhelmed him. Kevin's only chance to find Cat and Jenny before Hicks killed them was gone—the owl had disappeared.

As he had raced to his car, two of the owls flew away. Briefly, he wondered why? But the third still buzzed around him, almost as if it was herding him until he reached his car. Then, it had led him along narrow county roads. Now, it was gone.

He stopped, stepped out of the car, and searched the terrain. Hell, nothing. The only illumination came from his headlights and the edge of the moon that was visible above the horizon. The moon! Hicks trigger for his deadly ritual. He was out of time.

A screech broke the silence. The owl circled above him. Instant relief flooded his mind and body. When the bird turned and flew back in the opposite direction, he shouted in frustration. "Hell, what did I miss?"

Back in the car, he turned, and then stared in amazement. The damn bird stayed right in front of his headlight, forcing him to repeatedly tap the brakes to keep from plastering it all over the asphalt. *I guess you're making sure I don't lose you this time.*

When the bird veered to the right and left the roadway, he stopped and saw what he had missed in the darkness—a narrow dirt driveway lined with trees. No wonder he hadn't seen it.

He quickly exited, grabbing his flashlight. Swinging the beam along the road, he could see multiple tire tracks had flattened the weeds. The owl dived again. This time, wings brushed Kevin's head.

The baffling tug pulled at his thoughts, and an image of a farmhouse flashed in his mind. It fit Cat's description. The vision shifted, and he was looking down at a barn with a truck and trailer parked behind it. Lights were on inside the trailer. *How the hell am I able to see this?* The images vanished, but Kevin knew he had found Cat. He had also found the other two owls. Their frenzied calls echoed in the night air.

Kevin raced to his car. Turning onto the dirt road, he switched on the parking lights. It should be enough illumination to stay in the middle of the road. As he drove, he called Tim's cell phone. He didn't want his conversation on the police radio.

Earlier, Kevin had called off the search due to darkness. He told Tim to keep the team at the convenience store; he was following a lead. When asked what lead, Kevin almost choked. He couldn't tell Tim the truth; instead he fobbed him off, saying he'd explain later.

When Tim answered, he said, "Send the team to the coordinates I'm texting. I've found Hicks. Wait on the highway until I call you. No sirens." Kevin didn't want the killer to know the cops had arrived. He hit the send button, then switched the phone to mute.

When the trees gave way to a large field, he stopped. In the spreading moonlight, he could discern the outline of a large house with a barn behind it. The scene matched the image he had just seen.

With the flashlight stuck in his back pocket, he grabbed his rifle from the trunk. At the end of the barn, he peered around the corner. Parked in front of him was a run-down trailer, just as he'd seen in the bizarre vision a few minutes earlier. The sound of chants came from inside. Light spilled through the window and the trailer door that was ajar.

He sprinted to the end of the trailer, then crept along the side. When he reached the window, he leaned forward to peek into the room. The view was an image from hell. Cat was on the couch, tape wrapped around her ankles. Her hands behind her back. Dried blood streaked the side of her face.

His back to the window, Hicks knelt on the floor and chanted, calling to the old one. Upraised arms held a large knife over a nude woman lying on trash bags in the middle of the floor. Candles partially circled her body. The butt of a gun was visible in the pocket of Hick's coat.

Kevin laid the rifle and flashlight down on the ground and drew his gun. His options were limited. He couldn't shoot through the window. Cat was in the line of fire. That left trying to get the door open and get inside before Hicks could grab the weapon, or go around to the window on the other side of the trailer. Kevin ducked under the window to move closer to the door.

Loud thumps echoed. Someone was pounding on the side of the trailer. Kevin spun to look back through the window.

The chanting stopped, and Hicks stared at the window over the sink. Jumping up, he dropped the knife next to Jenny's body and stumbled to the kitchen. Leaning over the sink, he banged on the window with his fist.

Thunderstruck, Kevin realized the thumps were the owl's bodies striking the trailer. Repeatedly, they flew at the kitchen window. With Hick's attention on the birds, this was his chance. He jerked open the door and jumped up the steps.

Hicks turned and grabbed the gun in his pocket.

But Cat was already on the move. Bent over, she'd pulled a pistol from under her pants leg. Swinging the gun upward, her shot rang out, a deafening sound in the small trailer.

Hicks crumpled. Blood spewed from a hole in his chest.

"Are you okay?" Kevin asked as he shoved the gun away from Hick's hand with his foot and holstered his weapon.

"Yeah, a few cuts on my arms and a ding to the head, that's all. God, am I glad to see you."

She dropped the backup pistol on the couch, reached behind her, grabbed a knife, and cut the tape around her ankles. Wobbling as she stood, she grabbed the edge of the counter to steady her.

"I'm a bit shaky. Kevin, the candles."

Hick's body hitting the floor had knocked one over. Kevin quickly extinguished the flame flickering at the edge of the sheet under Jenny.

While Kevin blew out the rest, she dropped to one knee beside Hicks. Her voice, cold and hard, matched the fierce expression on her face. "You bastard! I said I'd take you down—I did. You won't get a chance to cut another woman because that's your blood running across the floor. You're the offering tonight, and I hope you rot in hell along with your master."

As she spoke, his soulless gaze never left her face. His voice faint and raspy, Hicks said, "Momma told me to kill you." His hand moved across his chest. Raising it, he stared at the dripping blood. "Guess she was right." It fell. His eyes never changed. In death, they were as lifeless as when he lived.

Cat gave him one last glance, taking a moment to relish the thought he'd never kill again, before turning her attention to the living. Moving to kneel beside Jenny, she felt the woman's pulse. Kevin laid a blanket over her that he'd grabbed from the bed. Cat tucked it around her body. At the moment, it was all she could do—that's when the reaction set in, and she started to shake.

Kevin reached down, pulled her up, and wrapped his arms around her. "She's alive because of you."

Cat laid her head on his shoulder. She was cold, so very, very cold. The warmth of his body seeped through her. As the trembling diminished, so did the terror that seemed to have taken root inside her. She was safe, and so was Jenny. Another woman had not died. There would be time to process everything that had happened later; for now, there was still work left to do.

She pulled back, kissed Kevin on the cheek, and said, "Time to call for backup."

Kevin laughed. "First, let me look at the cut on your head and your arms."

The wound on her temple still oozed blood. It might take a couple of stitches. He pulled the remaining tape from her wrists and examined the nicks that covered her hands. They weren't deep, and most had stopped bleeding.

"We'll have to wait until the paramedics arrive to have them cleaned. I wouldn't want to use anything in this trailer."

Kevin called Tim and told him Hicks was dead, and Cat and Jenny were alive. The Lieutenant said they were about five minutes out. His next call was to the sheriff's department to request an ambulance and their homicide detectives. This section of the county was the sheriff's jurisdiction, and his office would be responsible for the investigation.

Leaving Cat to watch over Jenny, he headed outside and retrieved his rifle and flashlight. As he walked toward his car, he searched the sky for the owls, but they had disappeared. Driving to the main road, he assessed the events of the night. If he had to tell the tale to anyone, they'd consider he had gone mad. It's possible he had. He pondered that idea for a few seconds and decided no. The owls and their actions were real but would be a story only Cat would hear.

The flash of red lights broke his thoughts. Leaving a squad car to wait for the arrival of the county officers and ambulance, Kevin led the rest down the dirt road to the old farmhouse.

Tim entered the trailer. Cat still knelt on the floor next to Jenny. They briefly spoke before he headed back outside.

"Goddamn, Kevin, that's a sight that will take a long time to forget. Do you want our crime scene unit?"

"No, let's leave it to the county personnel."

Another group of cars drove in. The sheriff's department had arrived. Captain Dale Hartson approached. Since several of his officers had been assigned to the search team, he was already familiar with the hunt for the killer.

Kevin explained the events that had transpired. Together, they entered the trailer, and he introduced Dale to Cat.

Hartson nodded to her and stepped over to look at Hicks.

"Are your hands still bleeding?" Kevin asked.

She held them up. "They're okay. I'm worried about Jenny. Her breathing is shallow, and her skin feels clammy. Hicks injected her again just before you got here. How soon will the ambulance arrive?"

Dale squatted beside Jenny. "It should be here any minute. Kevin filled me in on what happened. I would appreciate it if you would give one of my men a verbal statement before you leave. The written report can wait until tomorrow."

"Dale, one of my officers had Agent Morgan's car towed to the pound. My crime scene personnel will process it for evidence. I'll send their report to you."

"Thanks. I expect I'll be here most of the night." He looked at the dead man on the floor. "In my thirty-two years as a law enforcement officer, I've never seen anything to equal what I see here."

The wail of a siren signaled the arrival of the ambulance. A few minutes later, a stretcher waited outside the door. The paramedics decided it would be faster to carry Jenny to the gurney than to move it in and out of the trailer.

Cat refused their help. She didn't want any delay in getting Jenny to the hospital.

As they stepped outside, Kevin slipped off his jacket and draped it around Cat's shoulders. Its warmth began to dissipate the lingering chills. Dale called two of the officers who waited by their cars and introduced the detectives.

After providing a statement, Cat handed over the backup gun and informed the detective the gun in the trailer was also hers. As they talked, another officer approached with Cat's briefcase and backpack. They'd been found in Hick's truck. Finally, their involvement in the investigation was over, and they could leave.

Cat walked alongside Kevin as they headed to his car. He had slung her backpack over his shoulder and carried her briefcase. His free arm slid around her shoulders. Her steps were still shaky.

She looked up at the night sky and drew a deep breath. The moon was full and rode high overhead. Its light flowed over the countryside. She had survived. A killer was off the street, and the life of his victim saved. It was why she wore the badge. This one, though, had been too close, and she was sure she would feel the residual effects for many months to come. She glanced at the man who held her close to his body as they walked. Once again, her feelings for him had to take a backseat.

"I'd like to stop by the auto pound and retrieve my rifle."

"Not necessary. It will be waiting for you at the station. I told the officer who had your car towed to remove all your gear, including the rifle in the trunk."

"How did you know it was still there?"

"Hicks left the keys in the ignition. When I found your car, I unlocked the trunk to make sure he hadn't ..." He shot a mocking glance at her. "... stuffed you inside. If you recall, I did mention not to go chasing after him by yourself."

"Hmm ... no, I don't remember."

"It's because you disconnected the call."

"Hmm," Cat murmured again. Hoping to change the subject, she said, "I want to stop at the hospital and check on Jenny."

"That's where we're headed. You're going to have those cuts on your arms and head examined," Kevin responded.

He'd left his car parked on the side of the road to allow room for the incoming vehicles. They stopped when they saw who waited. Three owls perched on the roof. The gleam of six golden eyes shone like bright beacons in the night.

"Three! There's never been three at one time. How odd," Cat said.

In a soft tone, he said, "I haven't had a chance to tell you what they did tonight. I'd just found your car when they showed up. I've never seen birds act the way they did. The closest I can come to describing their frenzied actions is a bird trying to protect their chick. They made it clear, I was to follow them. Once I did, one stayed with me, and the other two disappeared. They flew back here to watch over you." He went on to explain how he had been led to the farmhouse and the distraction they caused by flying into the window.

"The owls? That's what banged against the side of the trailer?"

"Yep."

"He had my gun in his pocket. That distraction gave me a few extra seconds to cut the tape and grab my pistol. If he hadn't moved to the window, I don't know if I could have reached it before he fired." The what-ifs played havoc with her thoughts.

Cat slowly stepped toward the car. The owls sat motionless. Their gaze never wavered as they watched her approach. She had never attempted to touch them. They'd never let her get that close to them.

As she reached the side of the car, she lifted her hand. Kevin's jacket, forgotten, slid to the ground as she ran her fingers over the folded wing of the nearest bird. The owl's only movement was the slight swivel of its head to caress the side of her arm with its beak. The other two birds stepped closer. They softly clacked. In turn, she stroked each head and their wings while they tapped her arms. Beaks, so powerful they could rip their prey to shreds, were as gentle as a wispy breeze.

"We crossed into unfamiliar territory with this case. You let me fly and see through your eyes. You saved her life and mine. Because of you, he can't kill again. Thank you," she whispered.

Bewildered, Kevin said, "I had these images in my mind, the farmhouse and trailer parked behind the barn. And ... I saw everything from overhead. I'll be damned, that's what happened. It was all through their eyes." Three heads swiveled to stare at Kevin, and once again, he felt the strange tug. This time, he sensed gratitude.

The birds stepped back, away from Cat's hands. One by one, they spread their great wings and lifted off. They circled, then flew upward, their silhouette a dark shadow against the moon. They were gone.

Cat turned back to Kevin and wiped the tears that flowed down her cheeks. "Time to go."

In the car, her body relaxed, but like a broken record, the horrific events replayed again and again in her mind. It helped to talk it out with Kevin on the way into town. She covered everything from the point of her last transmission. As Kevin listened, a flood of fear again raced through him as he realized how close Cat had come to being killed.

When she finished, Kevin did the same. All he left out was the panic and fear he would not find her in time. "There is one curious coincidence if it is that. I'm not sure."

Her interest piqued, she asked, "What?"

"The window. There was one over the couch. Instead, they flew at the one in the kitchen. It made a difference."

"Damn, you're right," she exclaimed. "If the owls had struck the one behind me, that's where Hicks would have looked. He would have immediately seen me pull my hands from my back. I would never have reached my gun in time."

"Until he moved to the kitchen window, I didn't have a shot; you were in the way. It also gave me a chance to get inside."

For a few seconds, the only sound was the car engine. Cat sighed. "Wow! Was it intentional or just a coincidence? I don't know."

"I have a feeling it's one piece of this puzzle we'll never know. One point we do need to agree on, and that's our story. The owls don't need to be part of it."

"I agree. Can you imagine the field day the media would have if they found out? I can see the headline, 'Mysterious owls hunt down a serial killer.' Oh, my god, how bad would that be?"

Kevin laughed. "Exactly. I do have one question. Since I have this connection thing going with the owls, can I expect to see a ghost next?"

Cat's laughter erupted.

Thirty-five

Their first stop was the hospital. They learned Jenny would make a full recovery with no memory of the disturbing events in the trailer. Cat's arms and the cut on her head were treated. The head wound required a couple of stitches. Her tetanus shot was current though she had to endure the needle for an antibiotic injection. The sight of the syringe was enough to trigger a flashback of the fear she had experienced inside the trailer.

While Cat was being treated, Kevin left to check on the status of his officer. When he walked into the treatment cubicle, his face lit up with a broad smile. "Great news. Jason has been taken off the critical list. He's going to make it even though he has a long recovery ahead of him."

As they left the hospital, Kevin said, "I know tonight's not the right time to pick up where we left off at the restaurant last night. God, was that really last night? It seems like I have lived a lifetime in the last twenty-four hours."

He glanced at her. Cat's head leaned back, her face drawn from exhaustion.

"Since I'm not sure what's going to happen now that the case is wrapped up, I want you to know that I'd like more than just a night or two. I'm not sure if we can work it out or if you are even interested."

As Cat started to speak, he cut her off. "No, don't answer, just think about it. We've got time."

Cat felt an immense relief at his words. Yes, they did have time, thanks to three owls. Unbelievably tired, her reserves were depleted. Now was not the time for emotions or decisions.

At the hotel, he carried the backpack and briefcase to her room. Setting the items inside the door, he pulled her into his arms in a tight embrace. His voice whispered in her ear. "I believed I'd lost you tonight. Are you sure you're going to be all right? I don't mind staying."

"I'll be okay. I need time to process what happened," Cat said.

"We'll talk tomorrow. Call me when you are ready. I'll send an officer to bring you to the station. I would, but I have to be at the PD for an early meeting." He pulled back and held her face with both hands. He lightly ran his thumbs over her lips before he bent and gave her a soft kiss.

Even though she was exhausted, her immediate need was a shower. Despite the doctor's warning about getting the stitches wet, she had to wash her hair. She reeked of marijuana smoke. Her bloodstained clothes were stuffed in the plastic bag the hotel provided. She pulled on her oversized t-shirt, wrapped a towel around her wet head, and crawled beneath the sheets.

Cat expected to be consumed with thoughts of her near-fatal encounter with a killer. Instead, it was all Kevin. He was the love she didn't think she would ever find. Yet how could they possibly make it work? She was afraid the quandary would haunt her, even in her dreams. Finally, sheer exhaustion shut down her brain.

❧

Hallelujah! No dreams—her first thought as the incessant ring of the hotel phone pulled her from a deep slumber. The agenda for the day preoccupied her mind as she dressed. Most of the items were paperwork, though she did need to find out about the damage to her car. God, what a welcome relief to return to mundane tasks.

Contacting Scott was the first priority. The call lasted longer than she expected as he questioned her in detail about the investigation and its deadly conclusion. He ended with a well-done comment and then told her to return to Washington, ASAP. Another case had hit his desk.

Well, hell! The euphoria plummeted, and distress rippled over her. Wanting to spend time with Kevin, she wasn't ready to leave. And this was why she had been afraid of getting involved with him. How could any relationship stand up to the demands of their careers? Maybe this is the best way. We cut it off now before anyone is hurt. *Who am I kidding?* The agony of leaving had already found a home and living with the pain was a reality she had to accept.

The phone rang as she argued with herself. It was the desk clerk. An officer waited in the lobby. She grabbed her gear and headed out the door. The smell of food hit as she walked down the hallway and suddenly realized she was ravenous. She greeted the young man who waited for her, saying she had to make a pass by the buffet where she picked up her usual—a sandwich filled with scrambled eggs and a cup of coffee.

Jessie's face lit up with a huge smile when she came through the door. Before Cat could make a comment, Jessie grabbed her and held her tight. Stepping back, she studied Cat's face. "Are you okay? My god, what little I heard of what happened yesterday scared the hell out of me."

Cat had managed not to spill her coffee during the energetic hug and said, "I'm doing fine."

"You may be sorry you came in. The news media has been like a pack of jackals, and the Chief is on a tear. Go on in, he's off the phone. What a horrible night!" she said as she plunked back down in her chair.

"It was, still a killer is off the street," Cat said.

Kevin was on his computer when she entered and sat in the chair in front of his desk. The smile on his face when he looked at her made her insides quiver. *Oh, god, this is going to hurt.*

"Jessie says it's been hectic around here."

He stood and stepped around the desk to examine her head and hands. "Requests for interviews about Hicks hasn't stopped. I agreed to a press conference this afternoon, so hopefully, the requests for individual interviews will taper off. It's up to you whether you want to be there or not. How are you feeling?"

The light touch of his fingers pushing her hair to one side to look at the wound set off a flood of yearning and desire. Tears clogged her throat. "I'm doing good, and I'll pass on the interviews. Kevin, I've … uh … I've been recalled to Washington. I talked to Scott this morning and need to finish up here and leave as soon as I can."

Stunned, Kevin stared at her, silent as he absorbed what she had said. "Hmm, uh," he stammered. He moved to the door and closed it. Stepping behind her chair, his hands gripped her shoulders. Cat reached up and put her hands over his.

"I thought we'd have a few days," he finally said. He cleared his throat. "Okay, this is not how I planned to tell you and certainly not my first choice of locations. I had this romantic evening all planned so I could tell you I love you."

For a few seconds, the only sounds were muted voices and the ring of telephones outside Kevin's office.

Whatever doubts or reservations she had, the only answer was one of honesty. She twisted in the chair to look up at his face. "Oh, Kevin, I love you too. I never believed I'd find anyone who could accept me along with my owls and ghosts. But I did. Love, though, isn't always enough. We've discussed the demands of our profession. I don't know how to solve that, or if it can even be fixed, and—I have to leave. Time has run out."

Cat stood and walked into his arms. Tears filled her eyes. She had no choice. She had to walk away.

Kevin clung to her; his arms wrapped so tight they squeezed the breath from her lungs. When he let go and stepped back, she felt she had fallen into another bottomless pit, this one filled with pain and agony.

"For now, then, this is the way it will be. What can I do to help you?"

Cat took a deep breath, grateful once again for his understanding.

They headed to the sheriff's office to retrieve her weapons and take care of the written statements. Kevin had already arranged for a rental, and it was waiting in the parking lot when they got back. She loaded her rifle and other gear in the trunk. As the time to leave drew near, her misery intensified until it was a lead weight in her gut. How could she go, yet how could she stay—an endless litany in her head.

She stopped by the desk of each detective to say goodbye. It was astounding how fast friendships developed. Each wished her well and hoped to work with her again.

Tears rolled down Jessie's cheeks when she hugged Cat. "You stay in touch with us and have a safe trip back." All Cat could do was squeeze Jessie's hand and nod her head before she turned away. If she said anything, she didn't believe she could stop the flood of tears that threatened to erupt.

Kevin walked out to the car with her. Cat planned on stopping at the hotel, load up her suitcases, and start the long drive back. This would be their goodbye.

She leaned against the car door and looked at him. Straight and tall in his uniform, the sun at his back created a faint halo around him. It was an image she would carry with her.

He reached for her hand and ran his fingertips over the back, sending tingles down her spine. "Are you planning on spending the night at your parents?"

"No, I don't want them to see my injuries. It would only create more distress and worry. I'll drive straight to Washington."

"There's nothing more I can say other than I love you." He leaned over and lightly brushed her lips with his before turning to head inside the building.

"I love you too … with all my heart," she whispered.

At the hotel, it didn't take long to pack. As Cat did a final check to be sure nothing had been forgotten, she spotted the bag with the clothes she'd worn the day before. She planned to wash them when she got back to her apartment. Picking it up, a faint odor of marijuana wafted in the air. Suddenly, she realized they would always be a memory, a reminder of what happened. Then, another idea occurred to her.

Her gear loaded, she headed to the hotel where it all started; where she had found Janet Lewis. Parking at the back, she grabbed the bag of clothes. The metal dumpster still sat in the corner of the parking lot. As she studied it, the memories of her time in Clinton ran through her mind. With a heave, she tossed the bag inside. The irony had not escaped her. It ended where it began.

Epilogue

Two weeks later

Cat stretched to ease the tension in her shoulders from the long hours spent in front of the computer. Adrian Dillard and Blake Kenner, the newest member of the team, were in Indiana tracking the ringleaders of a pornography ring. She had spent the last two weeks tracing the source of the pictures and videos for sale on the internet, along with the buyers.

This wasn't the typical case for the Trackers, but the Indianapolis police chief contacted Scott and asked for his unit's assistance when several women had disappeared. So far, all but one had been found.

Research wasn't her particular forte, and she had wondered why she'd been assigned to the case instead of Nicki. Cat suspected the in-house activities were Scott's way of letting her decompress.

Her return had been difficult, and it started the first day back. Scott called her into his office to discuss the Hicks investigation. She had been astonished to discover he wasn't satisfied with her reports. The conversation was still fresh in her mind.

"How are you doing?" he asked as she settled into the chair.

Her file folder from the Hicks investigation was in her lap. Cat wasn't sure what to expect but was prepared for any question, just not that one. It caught her off guard. She suspected his query dealt with more than her physical injuries. "I'm okay. It helps to stay busy."

He nodded his head as if to agree with her assessment. Scott tapped his pen on his desk while he gazed at her.

Cat had noticed whenever he was deep in thought the pen would set up a rhythmic beat. On a couple of their phone calls, she had heard the tapping in the background. This time, it caused an inexplicable sense of uneasiness.

"Cat, I've read your reports. I don't understand how Hunter found you."

"I'm not sure what you are asking. The reports detail the events as they occurred."

"I'm sure they include the pertinent facts, but I am good, very good at reading between the lines, and in this case, there are glaring holes."

Scott paused and stared at Cat's reports spread on the desk in front of him. Tap, tap, tap. The uneasiness morphed into a knot of tension in her chest.

His eyes flicked up, his keen gaze sharp and intuitive. "I researched your previous cases and know you withheld information, just as I am aware your reports on the Hicks investigation are incomplete. There are missing details. I also know why. It would mean the end of your FBI career."

Stunned, she'd felt the blood drain from her face. This was a conversation she never expected to have with a supervisor. "Uh …"

Scott interrupted. "Let me finish before you try to deny…shall I say…your talents. I understand your reticence and, in most instances, would agree with it…but not here."

Tap, tap, tap, the sound pulsed in her head. His gaze relentless, he said, "Let's put it this way. What you say … stays in this room. It will not be repeated without your permission."

Could she take a chance? Ryan's comments on working as a team flashed in her mind, followed by the memory of the conversations with Kevin. If she hadn't been honest with him and told him about the owls, she and Jenny Swartz would be dead. Maybe it was time for the truth, and if there was fallout, so be it.

Cat had leaned back in the chair, taken a deep breath and began the long explanation—the owls, her ability to communicate with the dead, the conversations she had with Janet Lewis and Susan Benson, the dreams, seeing Jenny kidnapped, Kevin's interaction with the owls and the images he saw through their eyes. All she withheld was what happened with Ryan. His secrets were his to divulge.

Occasionally, Scott would interrupt to ask a question. Surprised at the level of Kevin's involvement with the owls, he questioned her in detail regarding his actions. When she finished, it dawned on her that not once had she detected disbelief. There was a sense Scott already knew her abilities.

Cat left his office relieved. At least with Scott and her team members, she could tell the truth. She knew Ryan's power, and it was only a matter of time before she learned the secrets of the rest of the team.

The ache in her back brought her back to the present. *How does Nicki do this day after day?* She shifted in the chair, tired of being in front of the computer. Her thoughts turned to Kevin. Dealing with the roller coaster of emotions from the Hicks case had been easier than handling the aftereffect of her feelings for Kevin. When she drove out of town, her anguish deepened as the outline of Clinton receded in her rearview mirror. Two weeks later, her mood hadn't improved.

It didn't help the team still worked with him. The investigation of Bingham's activities had been ongoing as Nicki and Ryan had continued their research. Every day she'd heard reports of their progress. Earlier this week, they uncovered evidence of voter fraud. This, combined with the illegal kickbacks for construction contracts, would ensure Clinton would need a new mayor. Which was why she couldn't entirely blame the computer for her tension. Nicki and Ryan were in Clinton for Bingham's arrest.

Cat wanted to be there. Nicki had promised to call as soon as the man was in jail and give her an update. She was the only one in the office who knew Cat was in love with Kevin. The woman seemed to have an uncanny ability to read the innermost thoughts of people she met. Downright scary at times. *Hmm ... is that is her ability?*

A couple of days after she returned, Nicki had pulled her into the restroom. The topic of discussion was Cat's feelings for Kevin, and what she planned to do about it. Cat went over the reasons why it wouldn't work.

Nicki had looked at her and in her forthright manner, said, "You're nuts if you let a man like him get away. He's perfect for you" and walked out. Her comments stuck in Cat's mind. She wondered whether she'd taken hills and made mountains out of them to keep him at arm's length.

The ring of the phone broke into her thoughts. "Special Agent Morgan."

"Cat, it's Nicki. It's a done deal. The man is behind bars. I wish you could have seen it. When Kevin told Bingham he was under arrest, he went crazy. He was stupid enough to take a swing at Kevin. The tussle lasted about ten seconds. Kevin jerked his arm behind his back, pushed him over the desk, then slapped on the handcuffs."

Nicki's laughter bordered on diabolical before she said, "When Kevin read his rights, Bingham's face got so red I thought the man would keel over from a heart attack. He sure had a lot of descriptive names for your guy. Kevin never lost his cool and never responded to Bingham's provocation."

"Are you at the station?" Cat asked.

"Yeah, we're finishing up the paperwork for the indictment. We'll be here for another few hours. Why?"

"I'd like to talk to Kevin if he is there. I ...uh ... but I don't want to disturb him if he is involved in anything."

There was a hesitation before Nicki responded. "I'm not sure where he is. I know Kevin turned off his cell phone before he headed to Bingham's office. Said he didn't want any interruptions. As soon as I see him, I'll tell him you called."

"Okay. Tell him I said congratulations."

"Will do. I have to go. I'll call you tomorrow."

Cat hung up the phone. That was odd, but she couldn't pin down why.

The rest of the afternoon and into the evening, she worked on the research. She didn't have a reason to rush home. Before she left, she sent several reports to Adrian that included information on the eight men who were running the ring, and several more buyers she had located.

It was dark when she pulled out of the garage. Debating whether to stop for takeout, she decided it wasn't worth the effort. She'd make a sandwich and call it a night.

Cat parked in her designated spot and grabbed her backpack and briefcase from the backseat. Her apartment was off an inset of the garden in front of the complex. She could reach it by going through an inner hallway or across the garden. The night air, while cold, was not uncomfortable. The walk would do her good. Lights twinkled along the edge of the sidewalk. They reminded her of the garden outside the window on the last evening she and Kevin had dinner. With a deep sigh over the memory, she locked her car door.

Her head tilted down; Cat slowly followed the pathway. She caught a movement out of the corner of her eye. Instinctively, she moved into a self-defensive stance when she saw a man in the shadows.

Then, *I must be dreaming.* She had been thinking of him, and her mind conjured him up. But it wasn't a dream. Kevin walked towards her.

She didn't think she reacted. Backpack and briefcase hit the ground as she ran toward him. Opening his arms, he wrapped them tightly around her as she collided with his chest.

"I don't care whether you believe this relationship will work or not because we'll make it work. I can't let you go. I love you too much," Kevin said.

The words were music to her ears. She looked up, her throat tight with unshed tears, and could only nod yes as his lips closed over hers.

The uncertainty and doubt vanished as if they never existed. They would make it work.

It wasn't until later, much later, as they lay together in bed, sated, and tired that she understood why the conversation with Nicki had been weird.

"I left as soon as I read him his rights. I let Roger and Ed have the joy of taking him to jail," Kevin said.

Cat snuggled her head against his arm as her fingers lightly trailed down his chest. "No wonder the conversation with Nicki was so odd."

"She knew I was on a plane headed to Washington. I'm sure she didn't want to spoil my surprise. And … I have another."

Her thoughts elsewhere, she said, "Another what?" Her fingers crept lower down his body.

He grabbed her hand and said, "Another surprise."

"Well, I don't think you can top this one," Cat said.

"Oh, yeah. Want to bet?"

Cat propped her head on her hand and stared down at Kevin's face, which had a smirky grin.

"Okay, I'll bite. What is it?"

"Tomorrow, I have an interview with your boss for that last opening in your unit."

A squeal of joy erupted from Cat. "This is one bet I'm damn glad I lost. Looks like Clinton will not only need a new mayor, but also a new police chief," as Kevin's lips covered hers.

Thank you for reading *SENTINELS of the NIGHT*. I have included the *Story Behind the Fiction* as well as an excerpt from my second Tracker novel, *GOING GONE!*

The Story Behind the Fiction

When I decided to write a novel, selecting the genre, suspense/thriller, was an easy decision. As a retired police officer, I'd write about what I know, cops and crime. Still, I wanted my characters to have something that was extraordinary and unique. As an avid fiction reader, I gravitate toward characters with an extra edge, a special ability to overcome adversity and danger.

I also enjoy reading the myths and legends of Native American Indians, along with Scottish and Irish folklore. It's amazing how many stories have the same elements that span time and miles, even continents. It was in those magical stories that I found the paranormal gifts for my characters.

During my research for *Sentinels of the Night*, I came across a woman, Alice C. Fletcher. (1838-1923) She was an American ethnologist, anthropologist, and social scientist who studied and documented American Indian culture. This was a woman who was ahead of her time in a man's world, and one I would have liked to have known.

She lived with the Indian tribes and translated the chants and songs used in their ceremonies. In 1904, she published the translation for the Hako, a Pawnee ceremony. It was in her translations I found the inspiration for Cat Morgan's unusual abilities. I used an excerpt from a translated chant at the start of *Sentinels of the Night*.

Owls are revered in many cultures. They are believed to be the guardians of the night and the messengers of death. Their appearance, especially in the daylight hours, means someone has died. Their screech is considered to signal a violent death, even murder. Dying is crossing over the owl's bridge.

More information about Alice C. Fletcher's extraordinary life can be found at the following:

https://en.wikipedia.org/wiki/Alice_Cunningham_Fletcher

https://www.amazon.com/Hako-Unity-Pawnee-Calumet-Ceremony/dp/0803268890

https://www.nebraskapress.unl.edu/nebraska/9780803268890/

Turn the page for an exciting sneak peek at
Anita Dickason's
next heart-pounding Tracker thriller

GOING GONE!

Kerry Branson, ex-homicide detective turned private investigator, inadvertently rescues a six-year-old boy on a fog-laden backroad in the Piney Woods of East Texas.

When she discovers Tristan is the kidnapped son of a U.S. Senator, her call to the FBI is just the start, not the end of her problems. Dodging ruthless kidnappers who know her every move, she's forced into an uneasy alliance with the agent assigned to the case, FBI Tracker Ryan Barr.

Protecting Tristan soon puts Kerry and Ryan in the middle of a plot that strikes at the heart of the government—the White House. The horrific plan has drug cartels and terrorist groups lined up to cash in.

There's no backing down when they find their lives are on the line.

One

Texas

His heart raced, and lungs heaved as he gulped in air. Huddled under low-hanging branches, rocks and pine needles jabbed his bare feet. Tristan's body trembled, but not from the cold, damp air seeping through the thin material of his pajamas. He was afraid, so very, very afraid. A dirt-encrusted hand swiped at the tears trickling down his face, leaving muddy streaks across his cheeks.

He'd escaped, but where was he? What happened? He knew he'd gone to sleep in his bed. Tristan remembered how his momma tucked the blankets around him, then kissed him on the forehead. But when he woke, he was in a room he'd never seen and on a bed that stunk. His head and stomach hurt. A strange man with an angry face stood beside the bed and peered down at him.

Hoping this was just a bad dream, Tristan had whispered, "Who are you?" As a deep, harsh voice told him to shut up, he leaned over the edge of the bed and threw up. That's when he knew it wasn't a dream. The stuff hit the floor and splattered the man's pants and shoes.

Shouting, he grabbed Tristan by the arms and shook him, then tossed him back on the bed. No one had ever done that to him. Scared, he had scooted backward until his back was against the wall. Still yelling, and using words Tristan wasn't supposed to know, the man stomped out of the room and slammed the door shut.

Tristan didn't move until the footsteps faded away, then he slid off the bed and crept across the room. Gripping the doorknob with both hands, he slowly turned it to keep it from squeaking, just like he did at home. He peeked out before stepping into the hallway.

Tiptoeing on the wood floor, he passed the living room where two men sat, their backs to the door as they watched TV. Another doorway led to the kitchen. The room was empty though a smell of coffee made his stomach rumble, and he had to breathe through his mouth to keep from getting sick again.

When he reached the back door, he eased it open. If he could get outside, he'd find someone to help him. That's what his momma said — find people, then run and scream to get their attention. When he slipped through the doorway, there were no people, no houses, no lights, only trees covered by a gray mist.

The awful voice shouted, "He's gone."

He ran, weaving around the trunks and bushes as he headed deep into the woods. When his feet slipped, he belly-flopped on the ground. Sobbing, he'd picked himself up. The slam of a door had him scurrying under the nearest tree to hide.

Footsteps crunched the pine cones that covered the ground. Tristan pushed back, pressing against the trunk until the bark dug into his back. Arms hugged his chest as he tried to stop shaking. If he made any noise, they'd hear him, and he didn't want to go back into the room with that man.

The footsteps came closer. A beam of light flashed over the ground. Pulling his knees tight to his chest, he wrapped his arms around his legs, tucked his head under his arms, and squished his eyes shut. Tears clogged his throat. *Momma, where are you?*

The harsh voice sounded over his head. "I don't see him over here. I'll circle the other way. The damn brat can't get far."

When the noisy steps faded away, Tristan scrambled from under the tree and ran. Pajama bottoms flapped around his bare ankles. Ahead was a break in the woods, and he raced toward the opening.

A shout echoed not far behind him. "He's running toward the

road."

It was the man from the bedroom. Terror pushed him. His legs pumped, but he couldn't go any faster, and it hurt to breathe. He had to find another place to hide, but where? It was getting dark, and the mist made it hard to see. Behind him, footsteps kept getting louder.

Ahead was a fence, a road—then—lights. There was a car. Could he get there before it passed? Dropping, he crawled under the barbed wire and felt a hand scrape the sole of his foot.

I hope you enjoyed this excerpt. *Going Gone* is available at all online retail outlets in paperback, hardback, and eBook.

For more information, please visit my website:

anitadickason.com

Best Wishes

Anita Dickason

About the Author

Anita Dickason is a retired police officer with a total of twenty-seven years of law enforcement experience, twenty-two with the Dallas Police Department. She served as a patrol officer, undercover narcotics officer, advanced accident investigator, tactical officer, and the first female sniper on the Dallas SWAT team.

She uses her extensive law enforcement knowledge and experience to create her plots and characters. Anita continues to reside in Texas.